called

THE STORY OF A MOUNTAIN MIDWIFE

PHYLLIS STUMP

CALLED: The Story of a Mountain Midwife

copyright ©2010 by Phyllis Stump

ISBN-13: 978-1-930154-24-7

All rights reserved. Except for brief quotations embodied in critical articles and reviews, no part of this book's contents may be reproduced or transmitted in any form or by any means without written permission of the publisher.

Front and back cover photos copyright ©2010 by K. Scott Whitaker
Title page photo copyright ©2009 by Robert Stump

Proudly printed in the United States of America

design & production by Whitline Ink Incorporated
Web: www.whitlineink.com
ph: 336-367-6914   e-mail: info@whitlineink.com

thank you...

THIS BOOK is dedicated to members of the Hawks and Puckett families who have so generously shared their memories of Aunt Orlene. I especially wish to express sincere appreciation to "Miss" Wavy Worrell (now deceased) who served as the inspiration for the person of Orlene Puckett; also to my husband, Bob, for helping "polish" the finished manuscript; and to my two granddaughters, who proclaimed after watching me perform at the Cherry Orchard Theatre, "Marmee, you are one wonderful actress!"

note: The following dialect is representative of the speech patterns of those who have lived in this area.

September 28, 1939

THE GOVER'MENT MEN GIVE me thirty days to move out from my house after they took my land, but I made up my mind I'd be out and livin' somewheres else 'fore the deadline was up. I beat it by two days. This morning they moved me from my cabin to the farmhouse that belongs to my niece Tavia Puckett, even though I'm near to being one hundred years old. At least that's what they tell me. I don't for the life of me know exactly when I was born 'cause, accordin' to my mama, early on there was a fire at the farmhouse and all the records relatin' to the family was destroyed. Over the years, the memories of Mama and Daddy gradually faded from actual facts into what one or the other might recall with the help of the other.

Others argue that I'm almost 102, while some from my ma's family won't bend one year tryin' to prove that I ain't even ninety-five. As for me, I've lost track as the years have moved on and they've moved mighty fast. Too fast for me to git myself all worked up as to who is right and who is wrong over when and where I was borned. Details have a way of fadin' into the distance when a body has been around as long as I've been on this earth.

The fire feels warm on my face and Tavia has wrapped me up good and tight with the old quilt that I can recall stitchin' together with my ma when I was young, maybe nine or ten years old. My bones, misshapen and rusty with age, feel as cold as death. Nothin' brings warmth to the depths of my physical bein' these days. My movements are as slow as molasses pourin' out of the grinder that the mule used to turn as he walked round and round, slow and steady when sorgum makin' time come in the fall. There ain't hardly no strength left in my feet to push the old rockin' chair that belonged to Grandmama Puckett, but I keep workin' at it. The motion helps me believe that I am still capable of havin' a purpose to my life.

My niece Tavia speaks to me, much as if she was hollerin' to a body off in the woods somewhere. I am old, I tell her, but not deaf, somethin' she should know for herself since she has lived right near to my cabin, not more'n a half mile away for more years than I can count.

"Aunt Orlene, don't ye want me to be a fixin' yer bed so ye can get yerself a good night's sleep? I know ye must be plumb wore out with the move from yer cabin. We've put yer old bedstead over in the corner yonder and I'll be a movin' to the upstairs whar the boys uset to sleep. Hit ain't no inconvenience fer me to be goin' up and down the stairs and we done figured you was better off bein' down here closer to the kitchen and the fireplace."

"If hit ain't no bother, Tavia, I'd just as soon sleep here in the rockin' chair clos'et by the fire. Hit'll make the gittin' up and down easier on these old bones. I'll already be half way to a standin' position as compared to startin' from a flat out, layin' down position and besides, hit'll be more comfortin' to me than layin' thar thinkin' this is how hit'll be when I'm a restin' in my coffin."

I start to laugh at my own foolishness, but Tavia scolds me as if I was a child. "Aunt Orlene, don't you be a talkin' like that. You have a lot of good years yet to live. Why, except fer yer poor eyesight, people say you are as strong and sharp in yer mind as ye were when you was just ninety. No one in these parts can believe ye are near to a hundred years old or more, as a few in the family like to claim. I'm countin' on ye spendin' a few years here in the house with me so I can larn some of the wisdom you've stored up all the years. And I'll write down yer recipes, like fer yer sweet potato cobbler and all the medicines you've made from the plants and trees that grow in these parts."

She tucks the quilt around me, then adds a few more logs to the fire as she talks, but she has not given up on tryin' to entice me into the bed that I have slept on every night since John and me moved up to the top of Groundhog Mountain from our little shack down in The Holler near to fifty years ago.

"You'll rest a heap better in yer own bed, Aunt Orlene. And after such a hard day, there'll be no trouble at all droppin' into a good night's sleep. I'll put some extra quilts on the bed and you'll be as snug as a bug in a rug." I smile as she almost sings the sayin' that has passed down from mother to child over too many generations to count.

"No, child. I've made up my mind. Bein' here in front of this good fire warms me deep down to the inside of my old bones." It's not the whole truth of the matter, but I hope it will put a stop to Tavia thinkin' that she is my mama in my old age. "Just make sure the chamber pot is near by in case I need hit 'fore mornin'."

With that, I close my eyes and pretend to sleep, waitin' for a hard earned rest from the day's upheaval of the life I believed would end on

{ September 28, 1939 }

my own terms, but other forces have intervened. So-called progress has brought an end to the life that I can only call memories. I am a displaced person, removed from my home, forced to depend on another person for shelter and food. I wonder if my niece Tavia, in spite of her kinship and kindly ways, views me as just another old woman who has lived too long and is now unwanted and unwelcome.

Such thoughts bring a chill to my heart and in no time at all it settles over me and works deep into my bones. I look into the fire, certain that the last logs have too quickly turned into embers. Though it blazes mightily away, the coldness has overtaken me and I cannot feel its warmth, even as I continue to stare into the flames. Sleep will not come. Instead I am visited by the many ghosts of my own past hoverin' over me like the mountains I now love and honor, in spite of their hardness and forebodin'. Comin' to live on the crest of the Blue Ridge Mountains was not my choice. I did John Puckett's biddin', followin' my husband's lead, as had all the women of my generation. But the journey up the mountain had led me to myself, the person that God wanted me to be. In spite of the trials and tribulations that had come, there was no doubt in my mind that I was where God intended me to be, even if the place was not of my own choosing, even if the cabin that I had called home for so many years would in a few days no longer exist.

Well, I think, as I jerk myself out of my trough of self pity, Git over it, Orlene. You'll probably be gone before they tear it down and you won't know a thing about it. Whether it's a cabin, a tree, a rockin' chair, or a human bein', nothin' lasts forever, includin' you. You've had your time on this earth. When the good Lord decides He wants to bring you on home, He'll make the call, not you.

I nod off into sleep just as the thought comes to me that I am soundin' more and more like my mama, always bringin' the Lord into her teachin' and admonitions. As for the part about not knowin' when they took down my cabin, I was not convinced. I was sure that even in heaven we keep up with what is transpirin' down here on earth. Otherwise, with its angelic choirs and a hundred percent perfection, the place called heaven might turn out to be just a trifle borin'.

September 29, 1939

THE SMELL OF STRONG COFFEE is tinglin' my nostrils and Tavia is fussin' over me like a mother hen. "Did you sleep good in that ole rockin' chair, Aunt Orlene? I put some fresh logs on the fire and I'll be rustlin' us up some breakfast in no time. How about fresh eggs and hot biscuits with honey? Does that sound good? I know hit's hard fer ye to bite into bacon or ham since ye done lost most of yer teeth. I'll make sure to cook soft food fer ye so ye can git hit down real easy, ye know."

"Ye don't need to coddle me, Tavia. Hit's no secret that I have only two teeth left in my head, but I'm mighty thankful that the good Lord see'd fit that thar'd be one on the top and one on the bottom that meets don't ye know, so's I kin have me a ham biscuit onct in a while. Don't go babyin' me so any more than hit's called fer. I've been doin' fer myself all these years since John died. Nothin's changed except fer the fact that the gover'ment is a buildin' a road up here on top of the ridge and they done took land from most ever'body in these parts, includin' cuttin' my farm right down the middle. I'm sorry that the kinfolk done see'd fit to move me into yer place, but hit warn't my doin'. I was prayin' that the Lord would take me on home 'fore they started clearin' the land and that would be the end of hit, but no, He's goin' to keep me around a while jest to be aggravatin' me, hit seems."

"Aunt Orlene, don't be givin' yerself sech a pity party! I never heerd ye sound so contrary in my whole life. Hit ain't Orlene Puckett that done waked up in my farmhouse this mornin'. Hit's some stranger I ain't acquainted with."

"Maybe so. I'm headin' to the outhouse. Maybe a good pissin' will get hit all out of my system."

"Aunt Orlene! Ye are in a bad way this mornin', talkin' in sech a common way. Cup of coffee and some breakfast will sweeten that disposition, I'm a hopin'. And ye don't have to go to the outhouse. The chamber pot will make hit easier. Ye're free to use hit here in the house."

"Well, hit won't make hit easier fer ye. I ain't aimin' to make hit harder fer ye, Tavia. As long as I can git up and move about, I'll do fer myself. And I'll help you with the cookin' and the other chores as long as I'm able. I don't want to be beholden to no person if I can hep hit."

{ *September 29, 1939* }

I push myself up, wrap the quilt around me and head out the door. Even the outhouse seems like a haven of sorts for the time bein'. A body needs to be alone onct in a while, I'm thinkin'. I know Tavia has good intentions and wants to make my last days as easy as possible, but a body can take just so much motherin'—after a time, the air has a smotherin' feelin' like you can hardly breathe.

When I come back in, Tavia is standin' at the door handin' me a plate heaped with grits, eggs and hot biscuits. "If ye want to set thar in the chair 'fore the fireplace, hit'll be jest fine with me. I'll pull up a chair and set beside ye if ye want conversation; if not, that's fine with me. You can take all yer meals in that ole rockin' chair so's ye can keep close to the fire and not have to move about and disturb them tired bones of yers."

"Tavia, I'm old. We both know as much, but I ain't ready to jest lay down and die, at least not today. I'll be happy to set here with ye a spell as long as hit don't keep ye from doin' whatever chores has to be done. I can help some, ye know. Clean up the dishes, put things in their place onct I know whar hit all belongs. Course my eyesight is mighty poor. Seems hit always has been so, but things appear mostly dim and fuzzy these days. I cain't hardly make out yer face, but I don't need to see so good to tell ye that yer biscuits are mighty good. Bestest I've tasted in a long time and the rest of hit goes down right fine."

"Well, as fer seein' my face, Aunt Orlene, I kin say ye ain't missing much. The wrinkles keep on comin' which makes breakin' the one mirrer I had in the house not a sign of bad luck as fer as I'm concerned." Both of us start laughin' at the same time.

"Hit's good to hear ye laugh, Aunt Orlene. Ever'body in these here parts, family or not, says ye have the heartiest and purest laugh on the face of the earth. Onct ye git started, hit takes ever'one along with hit. Makes a body feel as if the day is worth livin', no matter what comes our way."

"Well, hit's either laugh or cry, I always say, at least when hit comes to the troubles that keep on testin' our spirits. I try to make the best of whatever comes along. Most of the things that upset us and cause us worry, when we look back from a distance seem not to be worth a hill o' beans, as Mama uset to tell us when we was growin' up. I'll confess to ye, Tavia, that the older I git, the harder hit is to recall the things that happened in the past. Sometimes the days of my childhood seem as clear to me as this day settin' here aside of ye, eatin' my breakfast and talkin', woman-to-woman like. Then comes the times when I'm tryin' to recall a certain day or special time and I cain't fer the life of me bring hit clear to my mind. Hit saddens my heart, Tavia, that I never got my education, never larned to read and write, other than a bit here and thar. Of course, I did larn about numbers, so I could do a little addin' and substractin', even larnin' my multiplication tables up to ten. That was my daddy's doin' so I could help with keepin' up the accounts fer the farm, but writin' a sentence or knowin' how to spell words jest seemed foreign to me. Mama blamed hit on my bad eyes, but I confess to ye that I owe hit to a stubborn streak. But that's a story fer another day."

"Aunt Orlene, you done hit on somethin' I've been thinkin' about and some of the kinfolk has put hit to me to talk to ye about. Have ye had enough to eat now? Thar's plenty more biscuits on the stove and the coffee's still hot. Ye're probably wantin' to take a wash in the basin, so I'll heat up some water fer ye. Then ye kin bundle up in front of the fire and take a rest. But here's what I want to put to ye, Aunt Orlene. Ye jest think about what I'm askin' ye since ye brought hit up and we kin talk about hit later."

"Tavia, ye're wanderin' around like a scared rabbit and ain't makin' a bit of sense. Yes, I'll be glad to freshen myself up if ye'll heat up a bit of water and I thank ye mighty kindly fer the good breakfast. Hit'll be fine to set 'fore yer fire and maybe take a catnap or two, but don't be treatin' me like I'm a piece of china waitin' to be broken into bits and pieces. If the Lord ain't finished with me yet, then I ain't finished with myself. If the opportunity done come my way, I feel right sure I could still find my way to go out and catch another baby or two. I'm tellin' ye this so's ye'll let up a bit and not be so nervous about havin' me around, child."

"I ain't no child, Aunt Orlene. I'm gittin' up in years like the rest of us, though I still have a long ways to go to catch up with you."

"Well, git on with hit then. Hit seems both of us ain't got no time to lose. What kind of bee do ye and the rest of the kinfolk have in yer bonnet that has to do with yer aunt Orlene?"

"Here hit is, Aunt Orlene, straight out. We've been talkin' about yer life and all the babies ye done borned up here along these mountains, goin' out and about mornin', noon, and night to the families that settled these parts. We got to thinkin' that while ye're stayin' here with me fer whatever time ye have left, and we're all a hopin' ye still have many more years to go, that ye could tell me yer stories. Stories about growin' up and marryin' Uncle John, havin' yer babies, and comin' up the mountain to become a granny woman fer the past fifty years or so. There's some

{ *September 29, 1939* }

records to be sure, but most of what any of us know is scattered about in bits and pieces. We could set here by the fire of the evenin' and I could ask questions that people have wrote down, some have already put one or two in my hands, and ye could give me the answers. I would take notes and write out what ye recall and tell me. Maybe we could git hit put in somethin' like a book and make copies to give out when the Pucketts and the Hawkses have their get-togethers at the churches onct a year. What do ye think, Aunt Orlene? Hit would be like a history of yer life so's people could read hit and know what ye lived through, yer gittin' married and livin' through the Civil War and all that come after."

"What I think, child, is that ye done wore me out with yer talkin'. I cain't believe people don't have nothin' better to do than set around speculatin' about what life was like fer some old wore-out mountain granny woman. Seems like thar's more excitin' things goin' on in the world, like the gover'ment spendin' the citizens' hard earned money on a road on top of the mountains wanderin' to who knows where. Even if I could recall one tenth of what my life was like, and I ain't sure that I can, who in the world would care about readin' somethin' that would be mostly borin' to them that ain't had the same upbringin'? I cain't imagine sech a thing, Tavia. Sounds plumb foolish to me."

"Don't be makin' no quick decision, Aunt Orlene. Promise me you'll take time to think hit over a bit, maybe as a way of passin' the time in the evenin' when we've had our supper and are jest settin' in front of the fire havin' a nice, quiet conversation. I've known you all my life, Aunt Orlene and I've heerd stories about yer doin's, but who's to know what's the truth and what' been made up and spread around. Ye're the only one that kin set things straight and I'm willing to do my part to bring out the truth about the real Orlene Puckett. Jest a reminder, time's a wastin'. Neither one of us is goin' to live forever. I've said my bit for now. Let's have you a warm sponge bath and git you settled down in front of the fire. I'll be bringin' some fresh logs in after I clean up the kitchen."

I pushed myself up from the chair and headed fer the washstand in the corner. "So, Tavia Hawks, ye're a thinkin' we ain't goin' to live forever. That so? Mama always told us that a body larns somethin' new ever day. While I'm a takin' a little nap, maybe I'll dream up the answer to yer question."

After we had our supper that night, and I can relate to whoever is a reading that my niece Tavia makes the bestest venison stew that ever I put into my mouth, even if I can't chew on the meat. I was expectin'

Tavia to start in on the story of 'Orlene Puckett's life' bit, but no, she pulled my nightshirt over my head after takin' my black dress that I had wore more years that I care to count off over my feet, while I was in the process of gettin' into my old rocker. A whisk here and a grab there and in less than a minute she had changed me into my nightdress. Though I scolded myself for not thinkin' of such on my own, I realized that a body would need at least three arms to handle the chore and I was mighty pleased that Tavia was smart and capable enough to take on the care of her old aunt Orlene. Of course, I was still pretendin' to those who would listen that I could still fend for myself, but the actions of my poor old body belied the words that came forth from my mouth. Starin' into the flames of the fire, I saw my mama as clear as day pointin' her finger at me while shakin' her head. "Miss Independent, Miss Too Independent," she intoned in her "what I know from the Bible" tone. "Someday, my dear little girl, that independent streak of yers will cause you a heap of trouble."

I saw myself standin' in front of her, my head almost on my chin while I stared at my toes, unable to look at her steady blue-gray eyes that stung me with her obvious disappointment. Just at the second my tears were ready to spill over into a sudden downpour, she put her arms around me and pulled me close. I smelled the freshness of her newly ironed apron, mixed with the special talcum powder that Papa managed to give her every year on her birthday even when times was hard and we knew there was not a cent in the house.

How long ago had that been? I wondered as I continued to stare into Tavia's fire, willin' more figures from my past to emerge from the flames and call forth other memories of my childhood, but no one else appeared. I settled into a fitful sleep, perhaps because I forgot to check to see if Tavia had placed the chamber pot near my chair. Her voice startled me as a dream began to overtake me. "Now Aunt Orlene, don't fall into that fire if ye have to use the chamber pot. The family will not forgive me if somethin' happens to you while ye're a stayin' here." She reached over me and pulled the quilt up around my shoulders.

"Are ye comfortable? Are you sure ye don't want to sleep in yer own bed that we brung over from the cabin? I could sleep down here so's I'd be closer to ye at night, but I don't want to take over yer bed that ye've slept in fer so many nights. Hit wouldn't seem right."

Though I loved my niece and appreciated her kindness to me, Tavia had one failin'. Once she opened her mouth to say somethin', she was

{ September 29, 1939 }

wound up like a top, goin' round and round all over the place without ever seemin' to come to a stop.

"I'm mighty comfortable, Tavia. Settin' in my chair and sleepin' by the fire brings me a heap of good feelin's. My bones don't feel near as cold as they did yesterday, or this mornin' even." I was about to add that gazin' into the fire was callin' forth remembrances from my long ago past, but I caught myself just in time. Orlene Puckett, I thought, hold yer tongue. It's late, the sun's gone behind the mountain and it's time to get some rest, although that don't seem so important considerin' that I'm headed for my permanent rest in the not so distant future. Then I scolded myself for the self-pity I could feel taking a deep hold of somethin' way down inside of me.

"Hit's yer soul," my mama's voice said to me. "I was walkin' in yer shoes not so many years ago, my dear child, so I understand what ye're thinkin' and feelin', but hit ain't so bad; dyin' ain't so bad. In fact, hit's a wonderful thing to be free from pain, hurt, disappointment, and the meanness that human bein's have a way of spreadin' around. Take heart, Aulene, take heart." My mama was the only one who ever said my name without that hard "r" sound because she was the one who did the spellin' on the birth certificate. There was no doubt in my mind that it was Mama talkin' to me that night.

She was, however, not finished. "When ye git here, we're goin' to have so much to talk about—things we never got around to when ye was growin' up, or when ye was married and havin' yer babies and later on when ye was so busy goin' hither and yon up and down these hills birthin' babies fer the women of these here parts. I'm waitin' fer ye, Aulene, yer mama's waitin' fer ye. We're goin' to have a wonderful time 'cause God has a special surprise when ye git here. You'll see. You'll see."

As I waited for sleep to come, I was relieved that Tavia had forgot the business of askin' questions about my life and writin' down my answers. If she had, I would have missed the visit from Mama and the powerful message she had prepared fer me. For the first time since they had come to tell me I would have to leave my cabin, I felt at peace with myself and the world. I'm convinced of the truth of my mama's admonition to accept life on its own terms because only God Almighty knows how it's all goin' to turn out. He knows. I'll just have to be patient to find out. I smiled as sleep overtook me, recallin' how impatience had plagued me for most of the days I had spent on this earth. Still, I was certain I had not been the only victim of that affliction.

September 30, 1939

THE NEXT DAY SEEMED NO different from the routine of the first two that I spent with my niece, but when the supper dishes was put away, Tavia came and sat down beside me holdin' a big pencil and a writing tablet. "Hit's still early, Aunt Orlene, and ye rested right well last night. I thought we could set here and talk a bit, recollectin' yer growin' up years, the events that stand out in yer mind about when ye was young."

"They's a many a place and a many a person I can't call to mind, Tavia. I don't hardly know where to start. They's things that ain't clear to me even to this day, like the whole business of when I was borned. One person says this, another tells me another story. To this day, when people ask me how old I am, I tell the truth. I ain't sure, I say, somewheres between ninety and a hundred. One feller asked me right out, 'Well, how old do you feel, Aunt Orlene?' Hit was a day when my feet was all swolled up and ever bone in my body felt like hit had been broke in two and stuffed back under my skin. 'Today, mister, I'm a feeling about as old as that Methuselah man in the Bible,' I told him, and he commenced to laughin' so hard I thought his heart was goin' to give out. By the way Tavia, I hope ye kin spell right good 'cause I never did git the hang of hit that one day that I went to school with the boys. Hit ain't no exact science as fer as I can tell."

"That's a good place to start. People are always tellin' that story about the schoolmarm that give ye such a bad time that ye come home a bawlin' so hard, yer mama didn't make yc go back."

"No, hit's not a good place to start, but I'll finish the story fer ye since ye brought hit up and then we'll back up. I'll try to give ye a story or two from when I was a young'un, stories that Mama would tell about me and the other children when folks come together at a church meetin' or a barn raisin' or jest socializin' at a square dance or a weddin'."

"However ye want to go about hit. Hit's yer show, Aunt Orlene. I'm listenin' as hard as I kin and writin' down what ye say. If ye git ahead of me, do ye mind if I stop ye and ask if I missed somethin'?"

"No, but as slow as I'm doin' anything these days, I would think hit ain't goin' to be no trouble to be keepin' up with me, but one thing's fer sure. We ain't goin' to be settin' up nights tellin' about ever little thing that comes up. Ye keep track o' the time, Tavia. I figure I should be in my chair by the fire no later than two hours after we've had our supper. Since hit takes a bit to git me into my night dress and ready to sleep, I'm allowin' one hour or so fer this story tellin' to take place if that suits you and I hope hit does. That's about as much as I'm up fer these days. I git tired real easy and I have to conserve my strength in case somebody comes fer me to catch a baby."

"Hit ain't goin' to happen, Aunt Orlene. I reckon ye done borned yer last child, Maxwell Hawks, this past year. The folks up here know yer plumb wore out and besides, they's a doctor set up down thar in Mt. Airy. He's doin' a right smart business, they say. Besides, I ain't goin' to let ye head out anywheres on yer own, even if a body brings a wagon or one of them automobiles. At this time of yer life ye should set back, rest a bit, and take yer ease. Now let's go on with that story about yer first day of school."

"That day come about because my mama put hit to Papa to let me go to school and get an education, which was not a common occurrence in my time, Tavia. The boys in families could go to school if thar was no work on the farm to be done on a particular day and if the family had a way of payin' the schoolmaster or the schoolmarm. They could pay with money, which most people did not have, or they could pay with goods, sech as food or household furnishin's. Papa worked hard and turned out a good set of crops, but money was hardly ever seen in them days. A penny to a child was a fortune that could be took to the tradin' post and traded fer a piece of hard candy. That might happen onct or twice't in a year's time.

"At any rate, us children had gone up to the loft at bedtime. Mama and Papa was settin' by the fire, jest the way we are a doin' tonight, and through the openin' I could hear Mama say to my daddy, 'Mr. Hawks,' which is how she always addressed him, 'I think we best be sendin' Aulene down to the schoolhouse to larn some readin' and writin', maybe a bit of cipherin' as well because she seems to have a good head for numbers.' Did I ever tell ye when my mama and daddy come to be married?"

"I don't recall that I've ever heerd tell that part of yer story."

"Mama related to me that they was married down in Surry County, the onliest place whar thar was a magistrate in them days, on October 31, 1836. Well, that led me to a askin' her how come they was a married on All Saints' Day. She come back with somethin' to the effect that she didn't rightly know but, and these was her exact words, 'Hit was the scardiest day of my life!'

"I wanted to ask another question or two but if Mama didn't want to talk about somethin', she'd set her mouth in a prim line and ye'd know jest by lookin' that thar warn't no used to go no farthener than that. Now whar was I? "

"You was about to tell about that first day of school and you was listenin' to yer mama sayin' to yer daddy that she was a wantin' to send you to school."

"As I was a tellin' ye, sometimes a family would send the boys fer a day or two when the rains come or the crops didn't need no tendin', but girls mainly stayed home to help with the household chores, cookin', sewin', makin' soap, preservin' vegetables and preserves. Education fer a girl was looked on as wasted money 'cause womenfolk had no use fer readin' and writin'. Takin' care of our husbands and babies was the main thing we was supposed to do with our lives.

"Then I heerd Papa answer back, 'Is that so? How come ye to this reasonin'?'

"'Well,' Mama told him, 'in case ye ain't noticed, the child is as plain as a pound cake. She's goin' to have herself a hard time getting' a husband.'

"Listenin' to 'em a talkin' I warn't even thinkin' about gittin' me a husband at my age, but goin' off to school seemed to be a grand adventure in them days. I couldn't hardly wait fer the openin' of the schoolhouse door come September. Then one day Papa come up from the tradin' post, carryin' a parcel wrapped in brown paper. He handed hit to me and when I opened hit, thar was a piece of yeller cloth, jest enough, he told me, fer my mama to make me a dress fer my first day of school. I had bright yeller hair with some natural curl to hit and Mama was always catchin' me a brushin' at hit when I was supposed to be doin' my chores. Hit was, accordin' to Mama, my one redeemin' feature. I recall one day when she caught me lookin' at myself in a little mirrer that Papa had give her fer Christmas:

"What are you doin', child?" she asked me, although I knowed she could figure hit out fer herself.

"Brushin' my hair, Mama. Ain't hit purty and shiny?" I whispered meekly.

"That ain't nothin' but vanity, Aulene." She pointed her finger at me and fixed her steely blue-grey eyes on mine.

"What does that mean, Mama? I ain't never heerd you use that word afore." I was doin' my bestest to turnin' her mind away from givin' me a tongue lashin', which was far worser than the switchin's my papa could lay on us.

"Hit means that ye think too highly of yer outward appearance than you do of the rightness of yer soul, and the Lord don't take too kindly to sech," she answered in her preacher's-voice kind of way.

"Oh, Mama," I implored her, almost beggin' my way into submission, "you are the purtiest and the smartest mama in these parts. Papa is always callin' you his comely little bride. I am fer certain that I'll never be as purty or as smart as ye nor do I reckon," I continued as tears begun to run down my cheeks, "that I'll ever be a body's comely little bride." I ended with a giant sob risin' up in my throat, causin' me to start hiccuppin' into Mama's clean apron as she gathered me up into her arms.

"One thing fer ye to recall, child, afore you consume yerself with feelin' sorry fer yerself, is that the ugly ducklin' did finally turn into a beautiful swan."

I looked up at her with all kinds of questions bubblin' inside of me. "Is that a story you read onct upon a time when you was a girl like me?"

"I never had the chanct to read the story, but my mama told hit to me when I was about yer age."

"Will you tell hit to me now?" I asked her. I wanted to hear how a ducklin', which I had never thought of as anything but soft and cuddly, could first be ugly and then turn into something beautiful.

"We have chores to do, Aulene. And I need to start workin' on that dress of yers if yer goin' to wear hit to the first day of school. Maybe tonight after we've had supper, I will tell hit fer yer brothers to enjoy as well. Ye ain't the only child in this family, ye know."

"But boys don't like stories that ain't scary and full of fightin' and bein' lost in the woods," I reminded her. Hit was not in me to give up so easy.

"A story is a story," she pronounced in her no nonsense way. "Ever' story can teach us some truth about life that we need to recognize and take with us. That's why people who can tell a good story and hold yer attention is special."

"And you are one of them people, Mama. People love to hear yer stories and listen to the old songs that you sing so purty. You can read and know the scriptures by heart. When I grow up I want to be as smart as you, Mama. Hit don't matter if I ain't purty, but I think bein' smart can make a heap of difference in a person's life. But how come you to know so much about so many things, Mama, when ye ain't had the chanct to go to school at all?" I wanted to know.

"We know what we know, child. That's the onliest way I can answer yer question. Life has a way of teachin' us a lesson ever' day that we stay on this earth. The thing that puzzles me the mostest and fer which I ain't ne'er figured out the solution is this: What is that that gits us in the deepest trouble? What we think we know but don't really 'cause we never use hit or what we don't know cause we never took the time to larn hit?" As she said the words, a troubled look came to her face. Then she looked down at me and started to laugh. "I think I done messed with both of our minds with that one, Aulene. I cain't fer the life of me understand what I'm talkin' about and I can see by the look on yer sweet little face that ye don't neither. That's enough philosophizin' fer one day."

She hugged me one more time and turned to the stove to tend to the pot of soup she'd put on that morning, but I had not completed my day's assignment. "What's that big word ye jest spit out, Mama? That *philo- philosof...*" I could not git my tongue untangled as I struggled to repeat the word that sounded so mysterious. Mama patted me on the back as her soft musical laughter pealed forth fillin' the rooms of our four-room farm house.

"Aulene, honey," she said, "I'm not sure the world is ready fer a child sech as you, but I'm glad you come my way 'cause as long as ye're about, we'll have a thing or two to talk about."

It had been a long while since I'd thought of the times I'd been in awe of my mama's down-to-earth knowledge and her patient, carin' ways of instillin' that wisdom born of plain livin' into her children. The silence that came over us after memory had filled Tavia's cabin was broken only by the sound of my niece's pencil as it scratched out the recallin' of that tellin' moment in my life.

"I think I've done wore myself out with sech story tellin', and I'm fer certain that yer fingers air plumb cramped from writin' so many words. I don't see how ye managed to keep up with me, Tavia. A cup of sassafras tea would go down mighty smooth after so much hard work. I'm about as tuckered out as I'd a been iffen I'd headed down the mountain fer the catchin' of one of my babies. After I've had my tea, I'll be in need of a little rest afore bed, I reckon."

In spite of the hard trip back into sech a far off time, I felt days, if not years, younger than I had only three days before when I had arrived at Tavia's cabin in a fallin' apart farm wagon driven by one of John's greatnephews, which one I could not say. By this time, they was so many Puckett men here about, nephews, cousins, in-laws, I could not tell one from the other. At times it seemed to me that every one of 'em looked like John Puckett to me and it warn't uncommon for me to address which ever one happened to be talking to me as "John." It did not escape my notice that the other kinfolk would look at one another and shake their heads as if to say, "What do you expect? She's old. Her mind ain't what hit uset to be. Her memory seems to be failin'. Sometimes I think she makes up a good bit of whatever she happens to be tellin'."

And I would think you're not the only one. I have the right to correct the happenstances of my life if they didn't live up to my expectations, which many of them didn't.

Tavia's voice interrupted my thoughts. "Aunt Orlene, ye never did come around to the part about how yer first day of school turned out to be yer last. That's what we was supposed to be writin' down—the facts of what happened that day would come from yer own mouth, not from rumors and gossip and bits and pieces that this person and that person keeps passin' on as the gospel truth, even though they warn't around to witness what hit was that you was a doin' on sech and sech occasion. I appreciate the good times you had with yer mama and I know she was a mighty powerful influence in yer life, but hit seems as I'm a lookin' over my notes, that we done wandered off the path from whar we was headed."

I laughed at my niece's attempt to keep the blame from fallin' on the shoulders of this old woman with her ramblin' mind that couldn't keep straight on the trail of a story. I saw myself as a child with the same failin', always leavin' the path to chase after a baby bird or look for wildflowers under dried leaves, followin' deer tracks hopin' to find a doe with her newborn baby. Of course, when I was young there was a semblance of a plan in my mind. I knew what I wanted and that I could find my way back when necessary. Mama or Papa or one of my brothers was never so far away that I couldn't holler to let 'em know in what direction I had traveled or if I was in need of rescuin', though that was a last resort as far as I was concerned.

"So be hit, Tavia. I'm ready fer a bite to eat 'fore ye help me git myself ready for my night's rest. Hit don't have to be nothin' fancy, a piece of cold cornbread and a cup of buttermilk will do jest fine. But first, if ye'll help me up from this chair, I'll make a trip to the outhouse."

"Aunt Orlene, that ain't necessary. I don't mind one bit emptyin' the chamber pot. Been doin' hit my whole life. Hit ain't safe fer ye to be trekin' back and forth that far back into the woods."

"Been doin' hit all my life same as ye, Tavia. I feel a need to stretch these old bones if I can. When my mama was gittin' up in age, she was always sayin' that when a body stopped movin', the end was a comin'. She walked up the hill and back ever' day that I can recall up to the day she died. I recall real clear how hit was when we was called in fer our last time together, she looked around and smiled jest as proud as could be. 'Well, at least I got to take my walk today,' she said. 'I saw a hummin' bird, the first I see'd this season and a mountain laurel openin' hits first flowers. I took hit to be a good sign with the fields as green as emeralds and the sky the color of blue birds. Hit's a fine day to be goin' through heaven's gate, I said to myself, a mighty fine day.'"

"Mama looked straight at me. 'Stop yer snivelin', Aulene. I ain't havin' no tearful farewells. Hit ain't the Christian way if ye believe that Jesus is a waitin' fer ye and life goes on forever. I ain't ever goin' to leave any of you 'cause I'll be watchin' from way up yonder, higher than any mountains ye can imagine.' She lifted her hand as if to wave goodbye, closed her eyes, and took her last breath. Hit was so peaceful like, not a one of us could break the spell with cryin' or moanin'. Each child and grandchild come up one at a time and kissed her on the cheek, told her they loved her, and filed out heads held high and backs straight, jest as she taught us to do whenever we went out into the world, as she called hit. I was proud of my mama. I hope she was proud of her children and grandchildren."

By the time I had told that story, Tavia was preparin' me to take my rest in front of the fire. "I ain't made hit to the outhouse," I protested.

"Oh, yes, ye have, and talkin' the whole time. I hope I can recall what ye told 'cause I warn't carryin' my notebook with me." We started laughin' and she continued by tellin' me that she'd try to write down what I recalled about the day Mama had died after I went to sleep. "I don't think I've ever heerd this from any of the Hawks family. Does the brothers that is still livin' tell hit the jest the same?"

"Onct in a while hit would come up at one of the reunions, but as the years passed by, we went our own ways and didn't see one another so much. Seems like I spent more time with Mama than did the boys. They was mostly workin' on the farm with Papa while me and Mama was doin' the chores in the house. To this day, I miss her, Tavia. My life would not be the same without my mama."

Tavia nodded as she tucked the old quilt around me and threw a couple of logs on the fire. As my head drooped, heavy with sleep, I caught another glimpse of Mama smilin' at me through the flames of the fire.

October 1, 1939

I AWOKE FEELIN' RESTED AND more alert than I had since the day the kinfolk and some of the gover'ment officials had arrived at my cabin to tell me they needed part of my farm for the new road. That's when I larned I would have to move as they would be tearin' down the homeplaces that was located on any of the right-of-ways, a term that one of my great-nephews, a Bowman, kept havin' to explain to me over and over.

The smell of breakfast cookin' filled the little farmhouse and I felt hungry for the first time in many days. Tavia heard me a stirrin' about and announced in a proud and perky voice, "I'm a makin' sausage gravy with biscuits fer ye, Aunt Orlene. I done crumbled up the sausage into small pieces so's ye'll be able to enjoy the taste without havin' to do a lot of chewin'. I hope ye have a appetite fer some home cookin' this mornin' and a fine mornin' hit is."

I was movin' slow, but at least I was movin', headin' to the outhouse, not so much for the necessity of it but wanting to take a breath or two of the pure mountain air and have a glimpse of birds flittin' through the trees flutterin' in all their bright colors. I loved ever' season of the year, but the colors of the fall time would fill me with wonder each and ever time I stepped out of my cabin. I felt sorrow knowin' that so many of them fine trees would be comin' down to make room for a new-fangled road that I couldn't imagine bein' put to any good purpose.

When I finally came back into the house, Tavia was a sittin' at the table with a cup of coffee in her hand. A plate of biscuits and sausage gravy seemed to be smilin' up at me as I leaned over to git a good sniff of such a feast. At least it was a feast to me after months of eatin' nothin' but grits or cornbread with a cup of day old coffee fer breakfast. I was usually too tired to make the effort to do much in the way of cookin'. Of course, several nieces and nephews took turns comin' by to check up on me each day. They'd bring food to eat, but most of it was leftovers and cold by the time it reached me. I ain't complainin', but sausage and gravy biscuits made the mornin' seem almost like Christmas, not that Christmas for the most part was different from the rest of the days of the year, but people hereabouts tried to make it special, with extra portions of ham or fresh-made apple fried pies.

"Mighty fine eatin', Tavia. I cain't recall when food has tasted so good to me. Not fer a long time. And I thank the good Lord each and ever' day fer these two teeth I got left in my head. This here breakfast is mighty tasty. I'm obliged fer takin' sech good care of yer Aunt Orlene. Hit ain't goin' to last forever, you know."

"Aunt Orlene, don't talk like that. This part of the world would not be the same without you. Do ye realize that you are famous in these here parts, Aunt Orlene? Ever'body knows you or at least knows yer name. There ain't a family around here that ain't beholden to you fer the lives of their children, grandchildren, and even great-grandchildren. Think of the families that owe their very existence to the miles ye've walked or rode with that old mule of yers, all the wagons that done pulled up 'fore yer cabin to take you up the mountain or down into The Holler to catch a baby. The names, not counting the Pucketts and the Hawks, are scattered fer miles around the Buffalo: Martins, Marshalls, Quesinberrys, Bowmans, Pruitts, Vances, Connors, Terrys; the list goes on and on. You are a treasure to the people that you've ministered to—and that ain't exaggeratin' one bit, as I'm a viewin' the matter."

"You do go on, Tavia. If I still have my wits about me this mornin', and a glorious mornin' it is, I am supposed to be relatin' to you about my first day of school and you are to write it down so's the Pucketts and the Hawkses and their kinfolk can have somethin' to brag about when I'm gone. I think we best get started after we've cleaned up this kitchen."

"Ye ain't doin' no cleanin', Orlene Puckett. Yer cleanin' up and doin' chores is over and done with. We's all come to that conclusion. As long as yer stayin' with me, I'm takin' care of ye, and jest so's you don't think I'm takin' on more'n I can handle, other nieces and nephews are on call to help out when needed. If ye feel like tellin' how that first day of school turned out to be sech a disaster, and that's the story that's been passed down fer the past ninety years or more, well, I'll git my pencil and writin' tablet jest as soon as I've cleared the table. Do you want to set here and do yer talkin' or move over to the rockin' chair whar hit's still warm from the fire? We won't need more logs till hit's evenin' time."

"I'll stay right here. I'd best be savin' my gittin' up and down fer when hit's most necessary. If ye'll freshen my coffee a bit I'll try to recollect whar we left off last evenin'—hit was last evenin', warn't hit? Read a bit of what you wrote down and I'm hopin' my memory, what's left of hit, will take over."

"To be truthful, Aunt Orlene, the last thing ye was a tellin' was about yer mama dyin'. Ye'd started on the night when she told Mr. Hawks or maybe the bestest word is *suggested* to yer papa that ye should have the chanct to git some education 'cause ye was sech a plain child. That ain't my opinion, Aunt Orlene, that's what ye done hinted at when ye related that conversation. Then thar was the bit about yer bringin' home that piece of cloth to make ye a dress to match that yeller hair of yers. After that, ye begun talkin' about yer mama and ye never come back to the first day of school."

"Here's how hit happened, Tavia. Thar I was in my new yeller dress that Mama made fer me with my hair brushed so shiny hit looked like fresh ripened wheat—Mama let me take one look at myself in her little mirrer—and I headed off to the schoolhouse with my brothers. Thar was Richard, Isaac, Andrew, and William, I believe at that point. William was younger'n me, but since I was a girl, they'd put off lettin' me go to school until I was almost nine or so, if I recollect rightly. Each one of us carried a little tin bucket with a ham biscuit and apple inside. That was our lunch. Thar was a well at the school whar the children could git a cup of water when time come to eat. Ever' one of us drunk from the same dipper. People didn't know much about germs in them days.

"When we arrived at the schoolhouse, the school marm lined us up, and one at a time, each child was asked what he had larned the last time he had come to the school. That was because, as I done told you, children didn't come to school ever' day, only when their mamas and papas could let 'em off from workin' the farm; plus they had to pay somethin', maybe no more'n five cents or so fer each child fer a day's larnin'. Some families worked out a way to pay by providin' meals or food fer the teachers that come. Onct in a while there would be a school master instead of a school marm and they would have to be paid more. Hit didn't seem fair to my mama, nor to me neither when I heerd people discussin' the wages that them teachers was paid.

"Well, I was the last one in the line because, ye see, hit was my first day, so I had no larnin' to report on. The school marm looked me square in the eye and asked me could I say my ABCs. Of course I could, my mama had me sayin' my ABCs when I was four or five years old. I knowed I could make myself proud, so I took off like a beagle a chasin' a rabbit, but the school marm stopped me right after I finished the D and announced all prim and proper like that 'that was not the way *we* pronounce our ABCs.' I looked around to see who else was a sayin'

{ *October 1, 1939* }

anything, but the other children was a workin' away at readin' and cipherin', settin' on long hard benches that filled the room. I caught the eye of one of my brothers and he was a grinnin' at me, which I thought was a good sign but hit warn't. When she told me to begin agin, and I did, hit warn't right that time either, and the other children started a gigglin' at me.

"'One more time,' she said, but by that time I had had enough. I folded my arms in front and glared at her waist. I was thinkin' that if this was what education was about, I'd had about enough. By that time, the children were laughin' out loud and the school marm, I could tell, was gittin' mighty agitated. The next thing I knowed, she walked to the wall whar a line of hickory sticks was hangin' from pegs, picked one from the middle and walked back to me, tellin' me to bend over.

"I'd been brung up to mind my elders, so's I done what I was told and the next thing I knowed three hard licks come down on my behind and I near jumped out of my skin. The children was a laughin' and hollerin' so afore I even knowed what I was a doin', I was runnin' out that schoolhouse door headin' towards the farm house. When I got thar, Mama was sweepin' the front porch. 'Aulene Puckett,' she said, lookin' me hard in the face, 'what are you doin' home from school at this time of day?' I told her, 'The teacher whupped me an whupped me hard.' I was a bawlin' at the top of my lungs. 'I ain't a goin' back to that schoolhouse. Ever.' And I didn't. My mama didn't make me 'cause she didn't take kindly to havin' no stranger beatin' up on her child. I'm mighty sure Papa was relieved not to have to put up with no educated daughter.

"But the sad thing, Tavia, is that hit cost me my chanct to git educated. My mama didn't blame me, I know fer sure. In my heart, though, I could feel the knowin' that my stubbornness and lack of patience had been my own downfall. I will confess to you, Tavia, that these are the two demons that have plagued me my whole life.

"Oh, I've heerd the talk about my bad eye, the one that turns in the wrong direction, bein' the root cause of my not bein' able to larn, and I've allowed that hit's been a hardship to bear. In the long run, hit does seem that iffen a body tries hard enough, she can overcome most any handicap if she makes up her mind to hit. I let my mama down as well as myself by givin' up too easy. Now I'd give anything, Tavia, to be able to write down my own story, to have the names and dates of the babies in a book somewheres so I could read 'em over and recollect each birthin' I witnessed in these many long years, how many I ain't exactly sure. That'd bring me comfort in these last days I'm livin'. In some ways, and I allow I'm soundin' foolish when I say the words, my life seems like a dream. How can we be sure what we done or what we ain't done when they've no record of hit to put yer hands and yer eyes on? Maybe my life is jest been made up in somebody else's mind. Hit wearies me, Tavia, to have sech thoughts goin' round and round in my head."

"Sech thoughts would weary any body, Orlene Puckett," Tavia answered. "I believe hit's time fer ye to take a bit of a rest over thar in front of the fire. I'll put on a log or two fer them tired old bones of yers. Is thar anything ye need 'fore we git ye settled down fer a bit?"

"Yes, thar is. I'm in need of headin' to the outhouse, not so much fer doin' my body's business but fer the business of upliftin' my soul. They ain't nothin' like a clear October day to bring you face to face with the Lord. They's a few things I have to say to Him 'fore I go a knockin' on His door and I figure I cain't put hit off much longer."

I stared into the fire, waiting for a face from the past to come and talk me into sleep, but the only sounds I was a hearin' was the cracklin' and splittin' of the logs, while Tavia moved about straightenin' and puttin' ever'thing to order before she slipped up the stairs into the loft where she was sleepin'. I said my prayers, poor though they was since I was never much for carryin' on long conversations with the Lord, what with the chores that begun even before I climbed out of my bed and lasted until my feet left the floor at the end of each day.

For the most part, I started with one simple request: Lord, help me make it through whatever the days hold for me and my family. The last thing that came to me as I closed my eyes went something like this: Dear Lord, we done made it through one more day. You put food on the table and nothing terrible has come our way. Thank you for takin' care of us and I'm thankin' you in advance fer a good night's rest since I'm mighty wore out from workin' in the garden and bornin' the Hawks's new young'un. I understand, Lord, that these ain't the finest words that's come yer way this day, but under the circumstances it's the best I can do. Mama always told me that you know what's in our hearts and know our needs even afore we do. I'm takin' her at her word and trustin' that in her time you give her the understandin' to teach us your truth. Amen.

October 2, 1939

I SLEPT EASY BUT WOKE WITH a sharp feelin' within me that Tavia and me had best be at the work that the family had asked us to do. "Tavia," I called, "if you'll help me use the pot and git my hands and face clean, I suppose I might take a bowl of grits right here besides the fire and git on with the story tellin'; that is, if ye can put off yer chores fer a bit this mornin'. I'm a hankerin' to be recallin' how hit was when me and the boys was a growin' up on the farm. The farm run along Stewart's Creek in a community that was named Rocksburg, although later on hit took on the name of Lambsburg. That was after me and John married and moved to the area that was called The Hollow, or The Holler as them in these parts referred to hit.

"Some days, hit seems to me, hit was all a dream, bein' a youn'un, followin' after Mama in the kitchen and out in the garden, larnin' about cookin' and sewin', workin' at my grandmama's spinnin' wheel, headin' out to the chicken house ever' mornin' all the time a thinkin' them old biddies was goin' to fly up and peck my face to bits when I put my hands in them warm, smelly nests, hoping to find enough eggs fer our breakfast with maybe a few left over to be tradin' with a neighbor fer honey or a handful of apples. Hit warn't till John and me come up here on the mountain that we had our own apple tree.

"Of course, whilst I was helpin' Mama, Papa had the boys outside larnin' the work of bein' a farmer: takin' care of the livestock, plowin', puttin' in the crops, doin' the harvestin', ever' bit of hard work you can imagine. But we never complained. No, that would not do. As Papa would tell us, 'Complainin' won't change nothin' so jest git up and git with hit,' which is what we done.

"People says hit's a hard life, workin' a farm, but to me hit was a wonderful thing livin' on the land, watchin' the seasons come and go. We worked hard, yet we had our ways of makin' life pleasurable— lookin' fer birds' nests in the spring, goin' down to the creek on a hot summer's day to fish and wade in the cold waters, watchin' the leaves turn into all the colors of a rainbow in the fall time, colors you couldn't even name. And seein' them new babies come in the spring, the calves, the little mules, the sheep, the soft chicks, and squeaky pigs. Yes, I declare hit was a mighty fine time, them growin' up days on my mama and papa's farm. We was poor but we didn't know hit, 'cause we was like ever'body else, jest makin' hit from one day to the next. We always had somethin' to eat, even iffen hit was only a cold tater or a piece of cornbread; we always had clothes on our backs. My mama never wasted nothin'; she would take one of Papa's old shirts and cut hit down fer one of the boys; scraps she would make into a quilt fer a bed.

"You know, Tavia, I done related to you that Mama was mighty smart. She could read and write a bit, she had a sweet singin' voice, and she could tell stories from way far back. She even knowed a good bit of the Bible; had memorized lines and lines of verses and was forever hurlin' them at us as a way of keepin' us in line.

"One day Isaac and Andrew was runnin' after me, tryin' to throw mud on my clean pinafore. I was a yellin' and screamin' till she caught up with us and set us down right thar on the steps of the porch. Then she commenced to preach jest about the whole Bible to us, beginnin' with the Ten Commandments in the Old Testament and movin' on to Jesus' preachin' the Sermon on the Mount afore she ended up with 1 Corinthians 13. I was plumb wore out when she come to the end.

"Did I ever tell about the time she was tryin' to teach me to write my name?"

Tavia shook her head as she continued to scribble words on the note pad. "I reckon not," she muttered. "Do you reckon we best be stoppin' fer a bit, Aunt Orlene? I don't want ye bein'too tired to take yer afternoon rest. You're a goin' at hit like a house afire. We don't need to work like thar ain't goin' to be no tomorrow, you know."

"Oh, yes we do, Tavia. None of us has any promise of tomorrow. Least be a woman that the world says is nigh on to one hunderd years old. I woke up with this feelin', child, that time is a runnin' out fer me, so if we's got work to do, thar's no wastin' time. When I cain't go on, I'll let you know."

"Hit ain't yerself I'm concerned about as far as goin' on, Aunt Orlene. Hit's me. Hit strikes me that I might not be able to keep up with you until we come to the end of the tale. Seems like a hunderd years of livin' will fill up a mighty hefty book."

"Well, iffen hit does, thar ain't nothin' to be done about hit. As hit comes to me, I'll tell hit and you write hit down. Whichever one of us gives out first, that'll be the end. As my mama used to say, maybe hit ain't what hit could be. Maybe it hit ain't what hit should be, but one thing is fer sure. Whatever hit turns out to be will be the best that we can do.

Tavia nodded, so I got back to my story. "I always loved the farm, right from the time I could walk about and foller Mama as she went about her chores. There was a plenty: cookin', sewin', cleanin' about the house, workin' in the garden, takin' care of the chickens, milkin' our cow Old Bess, pickin' sallat greens in the springtime, or walkin' to the spring fer a pail of clear, cold water. Hit was a wonder to me, Tavia, ever' bit of hit. I liked bein' out in the crisp air, watchin' the deer come to the meader behind the garden, checkin' us out hit seemed, while standin' thar, givin' us somethin' to ooh and aah about, especially in the spring when the babies with thar purty white spots would come out and stay so close aside their mamas, takin' in the world they'd come into.

"If hit was a hard life, we didn't give too much thought to the day-by-day routine. We had our play time along with the work. We'd watch fer critters in the woods and on the hillsides while Mama was findin' plants fer makin' medicines. Or we'd gather treasures sech as berries and spider webs and shiny rocks to take back to the house and ponder over. Then fall would come and we'd gather the leaves in piles and jump and roll about like we was acrobats in a circus, which we ain't never see'd but heerd of from neighbors who could read and write.

"Winter was the hardest time to git through. The snows piled up mighty high, sometimes right up to the top of the steps leadin' to the front door. The wind would howl hour after hour all through the day and night. Hit was a trial to git back and forth to the chicken house and the barn to take care of the animals, git 'em their food and water as well as take care of the milkin' and settin' the eggs fer the new chicks. I can recall goin' out to bring in logs fer the fireplace and losin' my way in a space of six foot or so. The sky would be so filled with heavy snowflakes blowin' about with the wind screamin' so loud even the bawlin' of the cow and the bayin' of the old mule was lost in the storms.

"But we made hit though day by day and at night we'd be gathered around the fire with Mama sayin' or readin' us a scripture verse or two. Papa would end with a prayer thankin' God fer all the blessin's of the day. Onct in a while, me and my brothers would open our eyes and peek out at one another as if to say, What blessin's is he talkin' about? Here we was workin' hard to put in a crop in the rocky old soil that had ruint many a plow, along with cripplin' mules and horses alike. Still we always had clothes on our backs and vittles to eat, even if they was jest grits or a piece of cornbread, a biscuit or a cold tater. That was the life we knowed fer ourselves. If thar was somewhars different or a mite better'n what we was uset to, we was ignorant of life lived any other way.

"I never went back to the schoolhouse. Mama didn't make me since she didn't take kindly to no stranger beatin' her child. But she wouldn't let me off the hook insofar as helpin' me to begin larnin' to read and write and do a bit of cipherin'. She told me that she would larn me what she knowed and when my brothers come home from school, we would sit down and go over their lessons with 'em. I was never all that good with the readin', so the writin' did not work out fer me neither. My mama and papa told me that I had a bad eye; hit wanted to go hits own way and wouldn't work with the other. Some of the neighbor children laughed at me due to my wayward eye and called me names, but Mama set me down one day when I come in a cryin' from their meanness and put hit to me real plain. 'Aulene,' she said, 'life is hard and people are not always kind. Some in anger may call you a ugly name or say bad things about you. Know this, child, no matter what names they throw yer way, you are still Aulene Hawks.'

"Like so much of what she handed down to all us children, her sayin's could be mighty hard, almost like the Bible hit seemed to me. But after a while and some thinkin' on her words, a light would seem to come on in my head and I might uncover a speck of wisdom that made some sense to me.

"Goin' back to the writin' business, in the long run I suppose hit worked out fer the best 'cause I never could git the hang of spellin', which in them days was not exactly a exact science. Did I ever tell you, Tavia, of the day Mama tried to show me how to write my name?"

"No, I don't reckon you did."

"Well, hit happened like this. I was a practicin' my letters of the alphabet and we was goin' over the sounds of the vowels and the consonants. Then Mama put me to writin' down the letters of my name. My mama spelled my name A-U-L-E-N-E and she called my name without the sound of the R in hit, though ever'one else hereabouts made hit sound like OR-lene. I asked Mama if thar was a R in thar and she commenced to laughin' at me, which I did not like one bit. And I said, 'But Mama, people says Orlene. How come?'

"She explained that hit was the way the folks talked in the foothills and mountains of Virginia and North Carolina. She went on to recite a verse about a 'rose by any other name would still be a rose,' and that jest plumb got me all confused. I asked, 'So is my name Rose now, Mama?'

"She laughed ever harder and begun a lesson about a writer named William Shakespeare and a play he wrote about two sweethearts, Romeo and Juliet, who met each other at a fancy dance, then run off and got married. It ended up with both of them dyin' because of people tryin' to help them gittin' all mixed about their comin's and goin's. By the time she finished tellin' me the story, I was sure down on the love business and made up my mind I wouldn't have nothin' to do with boys in these here parts until I was old enough to know better!

"I told her that day that life was a mystery to me and that the longer I lived, I was about ten or eleven at the time, the more complicated hit seemed to me. Mama smiled and said, 'Life is life no matter how you look at hit, Aulene Hawks.' I had no idee what she was talkin' about and I told her so. 'I can't fer the life of me understand what yer tellin' me, Mama. Hit don't make no sense to me.'

"She looked me straight in the eye and said, 'Ever' minute is life, whether ye are payin' attention or not. Whether hit is good or hit is bad; whether ye like hit or ye don't; whether ye kin control hit or not, 'cause ye cain't ye see. Cookin' breakfast is life; birthin' a baby is life; laughin' at a weddin' is life; cryin' at a funeral is life. And only the good Lord Almighty knows how hit's goin' to turn out fer each one of us livin' on His good earth. So, dear little child of mine, the bestest thing you can do is to git up each mornin' with a song on yer lips and a prayer in yer heart, since hit's fer sure that iffen you wake up with meanness in yer heart and harshness comin' from yer mouth, hit'll all go downhill from thar.'

"I thought my mama was the smartest person I'd ever knowed. She was also the purtiest and as good on the inside as she appeared on the outside. Folks that lived nearby claimed that she had the sight, the ability to see into the future. She never took advantage of her gift as far as I kin tell. A far-off look would come into her eyes and she'd be jest like she was struck dumb, speakin' nairy a word. One day she looked at me real hard and then stared out at what I could not tell, almost like she was spellbound or had departed into another world.

"I spoke up, wantin' to bring her back into the world in which I lived. 'Mama,' I was close to whisperin', 'do you know somethin'? When I grow up I want to be jest like you, exceptin' Mama, I will never be as purty or as smart as ye are. If I'm right sure of one thing about this life, that would rightly be the truth, Mama.'

"Mama looked down at me with the sweetness of one of God's

angels. She put her hands on my shoulders and pulled me so close I could hear her heart beatin' as steady as the love that she poured out to her family ever day of her life. 'Aulene Hawks," she said, "take heed to what yer mama is tellin' ye and don't ye ever forgit the words I'm about to say. The Lord has somethin' special in store fer ye. I'm as sure of that as I am of standin' here this very minute a talkin' to you. I cain't tell you when or how or where. That's up to Him, but you will be purty and smart in yer own way, a way that will be pleasin' to Him. You must be patient and willin' to listen fer His voice to lead you to His purpose. We both know that ye are willful and stubborn and at times right cantankerous, but the Lord can use even our faults to accomplish His work, if we will let Him. Don't go wantin' to be yer mama made over; jest be the person He made you to be, Aulene Hawks, to the best of yer ability to serve Him. Now run along and git yer chores done. The porch needs sweepin' and yer papa's Sunday shirt is waitin' to be ironed.'

"I ran to the porch, takin' in the sweet smell of the spring air, as I listened to the mockin'bird singin' above me in the freshly-budded-out apple tree. Life was good, I was a thinkin' till I saw in my head them old hens a waitin' fer me in the chicken house. Oh, well, I thought, sometimes you have to go through a trial to know what a triumph is. Course I wasn't sure of the meanin' of the word. Sounds like somethin' Mama would say, I told myself, and to this day I'm sure I was right."

October 3, 1939

SETTIN' BY THE FIRE IN THE early mornin's and after suppertime brought comfort to my heart. True, it was not my home and I missed my cabin up on the Renfro Ridge, but the past is the past, I kept on tellin' myself. There wasn't no use'n holdin' on to what was over and done with. Tavia was good to me and I did not want for food or warmth, though the coldness laid deep inside of me, spreadin' into the very marrow of my old bones. When I first come to Tavia's cabin, I found myself repeatin' the theme song of the old hymn, "I ain't long fer this world," until one day Tavia spoke up loud and clear.

"I've had jest about enough of yer feelin' sorry fer yerself, Orlene Puckett. Even iffen hit's the truth, moanin' and groanin ain't goin' to change how ye will come to the end of yer days. I ain't yer mama and I don't want to be babyin' you, but hit seems to me that a woman who's lived as long as you have would have better things to do with her last days. Maybe you cain't be out catchin' a baby in the middle of the night, but yer hand might be steady enough to help me slice up these here apples fer dryin' so's I can make us some pies come winter time."

"I ain't goin' to be around to be eatin' yer apple pie, Tavia. I done told you, I ain't—"

"I know, 'long fer this world.' Hit seems to me, Aunt Orlene, that yer hearin' has done gone the way of yer sight. Ye ain't heerd one word I've been sayin' to ye."

"Yes, I have. I'm slicin' up this here apple 'cause I'm plannin' to hang around jest long enough to have a bite of the first one that comes out of the oven over yonder. I promise ye, Tavia, thar'll be no more complainin', at least no more'n is necessary. My life ain't been no better nor worser than most, I reckon. Mama would tell us not to dwell on vain regrets, what we could not change, but to move on and look to the future, to what was comin' that likelier would be happier than we might imagine. I reckoned that most of the time she was referin' to heaven, puttin' her trust in the glorious afterlife, as she called hit, with her best friend Jesus. Hit seemed I was forgettin' the most important lesson Mama left to me. I'll do better from now on, Tavia, with whatever time is give to me."

"Talkin' about growin' up on the farm," Tavia said, "hit comes acrost that ye was a happy child with a good family in spite of bein' poor and endurin' hard times when crops didn't come in and sech. Was thar bad times that ye recall as causin' ye and yer family to be down on life? Seems like hit's mighty unusual fer people in them far off times to be comfortable and content each and ever day."

"The hardest time I kin recall fer all the family, mama and papa, me and my brothers, come the day that my little brother William died."

"I don't rightly recall that ye had a brother named William. How did he come to die at a young age?"

"What I kin recall is that William come in from playin' out in the woods with a cut on his arm and told Mama that a bad dog had bit him. He was about eight at the time. I was no more'n ten or eleven and my other brothers, Isaac, Andrew and Richard, was older. Mama tried to git William to describe the dog and tell whar he had been when he was bit, but he was cryin' and so upset that nothin' he told her made good sense. She sent one of the boys to git Papa, who was out plowin' a field. In the meantime, Mama washed the cut real good and poured turpentine over hit, then bandaged William's arm.

"By the time Papa come back, he had sent the boys to the nearest farm to us, warnin' them that a dog had turned bad. Later that afternoon, one of the neighbors rode up to the house and told Papa that his brother had killed a fox that mornin' in the area that come up to our woods in the back field. The fox was wanderin' back and forth and foamin' at the mouth. The neighbor shot the fox, sure hit was sick with rabies. Of course, they was no shots or medicine fer a cure in them days. No doctors lived in the vicinity of our farm. Like most families, we relied on homemade remedies and potions that had been passed down from mother to daughter; some even come from the native people that had lived on the land afore our people arrived, so our ancestors larned about their special medicines and what they was good for.

"Well, though Mama done all she knowed fer the boy, along with ever'one in the family, includin' neighbors and church people, William took the rabies. Thar was nothin' to be done for hit. He was in sech pain and agony. He could not drink water and his body twitched so, Papa finally had to tie him, arms and legs, to the bed. That jest about kilt Mama. When William began screamin' and askin' Papa to put him out of his misery, I wanted to die myself. Thar we was, his mama and papa, his brothers and me, along with two grandmamas and grandpapas, some cousins, aunts and uncles, all crowded into that tiny little room whar all the boys slept. They was prayin' and hymn singin', while the preacher was readin' scripture, hopin' that a miracle would take place.

"Finally, Papa put up his hand fer silence and asked ever' one to leave. He headed fer the corner whar his old rifle was leanin' aginst the door. My mama started cryin', beggin' him not to shoot her son, but he motioned fer my grandpapa and grandmama to take her from the room. William was real quiet. He tried to say somethin' to Papa, but no one could understand the sounds comin' from his mouth.

"The adults had herded us outside whar we was a waitin' fer the sound of the rifle shot. Me and my brothers was all holdin' on to Mama, who was whimperin' like a kitten. Minutes passed, but thar was no sound from the house. Then Papa come out on the porch and raised both hands in the air. 'Praise Jesus!' he almost sang the words. Then he walked towards Mama. 'He died real peaceful, Matilda. He smiled at me and said with words as clear as a bell, "I see Jesus, Papa. He's comin' fer me. Tell Mama not to cry."' Papa put his arms around Mama and led her back to the house to see her little boy. I did not see her cry agin, even when we buried him the next day in the little cemetery behind the Primitive Baptist church down the road from the farm.

"Hit was so long ago, I think sometimes I jest put hit out of my mind, like a body does with a bad dream. The brothers was young too, so's like most boys they had to put up a front of bein' strong and in control, like my papa done, but I saw Papa weep fer days after William died when no one was around to see. As fer Mama, somethin' changed inside of her when that young'un died and she was never quite the same to any of us. Not that she stopped bein' the fine woman that she was, or that she neglected Papa or us children in a way that could be told, but a stillness and a quiet come over her that was a presence behind her words and her actions from that day on. I cain't rightly describe hit, yet thar was times when one of us would stop and look around at each other, knowin' that in some way Mama had removed herself from us and had gone off. We called hit 'lookin' fer William.' We did not say the words out loud in front of her. I still kin hear Papa when she would git up from the table as iffen to put more food on the table and not return. 'She's lookin' fer Willliam,' he'd say, and we would nod and go about feedin' our bodies though our souls felt mighty empty. After a while she would reappear, a smile on her face, with a plate of cornbread or biscuits.

"One noon day I recall as iffen hit was yesterday. 'Had to wait a bit,'

Mama made her apology. 'I stepped out fer a bit of fresh air. The sun is a throwin' his light around and about the new leaves on the trees. Might purty, hit is.' Then she gathered up another bowl in her hand and headed back to the stove. 'I think Mama's found William,' I had said to no one in particular. Papa reached fer my hand. 'I think ye are right, Miss Aulene Hawks. Ye must have yer mama's special sight. Take care to use hit fer good and hit will serve ye well.'"

Tavia put down her pencil and wiped her eyes. I wish fer tears of my own, but awareness comes to me that they have all been used up in other times and other places. Tavia moves about preparin' the cabin fer nightfall. The fire flames leap high and draw me into their warmth. My body is not so cold at the end of this day. Thar may still be a few days left fer livin'. Hit is not so much that I am afeared of death. No, what I'm most afeard of is that after livin' amongst the glories of God's creations up here on this mountain, I'll be sorely disappointed in heaven.

When a body grows up on a farm, death is no stranger. Children's aware almost from the time they larn to say their first word or take their first step that life and death are inseparable. They are sent to the relatives or nearby neighbors when a sister or brother is due to arrive, even as they watch new calves bein' borned. They hear the news that a friend or neighbor has died and see hogs slaughtered in the fall. They mourn the deaths of the pets they make from the farm animals: A favorite chick becomes part of Sunday dinner. A stray cat wanders into the barn and gives birth to kittens; one or two may not live and are taken away fer a simple burial. Papa's work horse becomes a daughter's special friend. One day he stumbles pullin' the plow, breaks a leg and must be put down, a gentle way of avoidin' speakin' the truth. Babies come with a steady frequency to the farms hereabout, but many of them are sickly or born too soon and live only a few hours or days.

Death passes by with a gentle touch and moves on for those of us tied to the land. There is no long season of grief or mournin' except in the confines of the heart. Fires must be stoked, food cooked, animals tended, seeds sowed, and crops harvested. Each season has hits own kinship with both life and death. There is no beginnin' and no end; life is jest a circle, like the sun or the moon, each a glorious reminder of God's power. So is each life. I see the babies, my own and all the others that were mine once upon a time.

Still I have come to love this land, even with hit's harshness and inability to fergive. Will thar be dogwoods and redbuds in heaven?

{ *October 3, 1939* }

Trilliums and lady slippers? Hummin'birds and red-tailed hawks circlin' the air like square dancers at a weddin'? Newborn foals and downy chicks peckin' theirselves out of their shells? A blue-skinned babe slidin' out of his mama's wore out body?

Lord, I believe ye understand how a body fights to hold onto life. Ye put us here in the midst of this grand creation. Did ye expect that we'd let go as iffen hit had no more meanin' to us than a speck of dust? I reckon not, but we're hard pressed to see things yer way down here. Course I'm not tellin' ye what ye don't already know. How about acceptin' this as a prayer, which is the best I kin do at the end of sech a long day though it seems to me that I jest woke up. My mind has been a workin' so hard, I'm plumb wore out. Amen.

October 4, 1939

MORNIN' COME TOO SOON. I had me a good night's rest in front of the fire dreamin' of days long gone by. Seems like when ye spend time recallin' the past, the places and people don't want to leave. They foller ye to yer bed and take turns makin' appearances in strange ways throughout the night. Ye wake up and wonder what *that* was about as none of hit made a bit of sense. Dead people conversin' with the livin', the seasons all mixed up and so are ye, sometimes growed up, sometimes a child without rhyme or reason to the story that ye was a part of while ye was asleep.

Dreams tell more'n ye know, Mama uset to say to us. *Be careful who ye share yer dreams with. They mighten cause ye trouble ye can't foresee.* That was another of her teachin's I could never figure out since I was sech a private person that I had no close friends or relatives to talk to, except fer Mama and iffen the truth be told, spendin' a good bit of time with Mama was mighty wearin' on the mind as well as the behind. She'd set ye down and give ye a good talkin' to as she called hit, about whatever happened to cross her mind that day, sech as mindin' yer manners, readin' the Bible, bein' kind to the neighbors, and on one special day of my life, whar babies come from and what hit meant to be a growed woman as fer as menfolk was concerned.

"I did not want to have that conversation. No sirree, not so much as I was embarrassed myself but fer the embarrassment of my mama."

"What conversation was that, Aunt Orlene?" Tavia was standin' by the rockin' chair, a lookin' down at me. The thoughts I was thinkin' had come alive with my spoken words.

"The conversation my mama had with me the day I become a woman near to my fourteenth birthday I think hit was, although with my memory gittin' dimmer each day, I cain't be sure. I did not want to listen to any of hit and clapped my hands over my ears, but Mama slapped them away and told me straight out that she would say her piece onct and fer all and that would be the end of hit."

"I ain't repeatin' one word, so pay attention, Aulene. If ye got questions, I'll do my best to answer, when the time comes."

"How will I know when the time comes, Mama?"
"Ye'll know, I reckon."
"Yes, but when will that be and will ye be thar to answer fer me?"
"I reckon not, if yer husband has anything to say about hit."
"A husband? Am I gittin' me a husband?"
"Not right soon. Ye're too young fer one thing, and they ain't no eligible young men around these parts as far as I kin tell."
"Then why are we havin' this talk, and why are ye whisperin', Mama?"
"I don't know, child, except that ye're my oldest daughter and I ain't never done this 'fore. My mama never said a word to me about sech things. I had to larn hit the hard way."
"Was that the day ye and Papa was married, on All Saints' Day?"
Mama give me sech a look, I figured I better change the subject, and fast.

"My youngest sister was borned near to when I was ten years old and they named her Matilda after Mama. As she was a growin' up, she follered me around like a puppy, always wantin' me to play with her. When Mama was busy with the chores around the farm, she would put me in charge of tendin' to Matilda, so's I was gittin' some trainin' in the art of motherin' by the time I was of marryin' age and thinkin' of havin' my own children. Course hit didn't turn out that way, but one thing I've larned the hard way is not to count yer chickens 'fore they hatch."

I set in front of the fire, havin' a bowl of grits while Tavia swept the floor, then headed fer the table with her pencil and writin' paper. Hit warn't long 'fore the first question flew acrost the room. "Ye talk so much about yer mama. How was hit atween ye and yer papa? Was he a good daddy to ye?"

"My papa was a fine man, Tavia. Good to his wife, his children, and his neighbors. If a body in them parts needed help, Papa was the first one on the scene. Most of his time, he was with the boys out in the fields, larnin' 'em in the ways of farmin' the land and takin' care of the animals. As soon as each one larned to walk, he was follerin' along after Papa helpin' him in small ways at the beginnin', like throwin' the feed to the chickens. Then as time moved on, Papa would let him hold the reins fer the mule pullin' the wagon or the plow. Bit by bit, little by little, Papa turned each boy into a fine farmer in his own right and he was right proud of each one of his sons.

"But when he was workin' near to the house, I was a daddy's girl, even though me and Mama had a special bond that was never broke up to the day she died. When Mama scolded me fer my vanity over my hair, Papa would say, 'Shush, Mama, she's jest bein' a girl.' And Mama would come back with, 'As if ye have any notion about hit, Mr. Hawks.'

"I done related to ye how he went down to the tradin' post to buy that purty piece of cloth fer a new dress to wear on my first day of school. After that, hit was my Sunday dress till I growed out of hit, which took a while since I was a skinny bit of a child even up to my weddin' day. 'Put some meat on them bones,' the womenfolk would say. 'No man wants a skeleton fer a wife. They like a woman to be as plump and soft as a feather bed to curl up and cuddle with.' That'd git Mama huffed up. 'Hush up,' she'd tell 'em, 'the child don't need to be hearin' none of that. She ain't ready fer sech talk.'

"The women would jest laugh and talk back to my mama. 'Cain't come too soon, Matilda. Thar are girls in these parts her age already done married and with babies on the way.' She'd answer, 'That's them; this is us. I ain't sendin' my girl out into the world of men and marriage till she has a few more years on her.' 'And a bit more flesh on them bones!' one of them called out while the rest burst out in a peal of laughter. I could feel my face turnin' red. When I looked at my mama, her face was pulled tight with lines of disapproval. She nodded towards the door and I scooted out right fast as if runnin' fer my life.

"The onliest time I kin recall Papa administerin' any punishment to me come about the time I had convinced myself that I was a growed up woman and could purty well run my own life and do as I pleased. I was maybe fourteen or fifteen, aware that families considered girls my age to be ready fer marriage and doin' all kinds of manipulatin' and finagelin' in the background to make a good match not only fer their sons but fer the daughters as well. Some of the arrangin' had to do with land, puttin' two farms together with the marryin' of a son of one farmer and the daughter of his neighbor. That way there'd be more land to pass on to their children and grandchildren. The worstest thing in them days was fer a family to be left with a daughter who was without 'skills', which is how they referred to hit, and would turn into some old maid. That was a black spot on the family, ye see, that they couldn't arrange a decent marriage fer their daughter. Hit was different fer the men because a man could do fer hisself, but women was dependent on men, their fathers, then their husbands, fer their livelihood in those times. When I think back, hit almost seems like the dark ages to me."

"Ye was about to be tellin' how yer papa took his hand to ye that one time."

"Well, hit warn't his hand. Hit was a stick. Hit was a hot summer's day, hotter'n I kin ever recall since. Me and Mama was out in the garden right early pickin' beans, cucumbers, tomaters, and squash for the supper meal and fer cannin' so's we would not be out in the heat of the day. When we was finished, Mama told me I was done with the chores fer the time bein' and that I could head on down to the creek to wash my hair and cool down fer a bit. In them days takin' baths was reserved fer church goin' days and washin' hair was thought to bring on *pneumonier* so that did not take place more'n three or four times a year.

"Anyways I picked out a clean pinafore. That was the way we kept our dresses. I had three, one fer church goin', one fer ever' day, and one as a spare in case of soilin' or tearin' a hole in hit. We had pinafores, as they was called, to wear over the dresses to keep 'em clean so's not to be havin' to wash 'em all that much. I traipsed off to the creek with a cake of mama's homemade soap, not the lye kind fer washin', to git myself freshened up from the hard work and perspirin' of pullin' vegetables from the garden. Mama would not allow me to call hit sweatin' like the boys or Papa did 'cause she said hit was not ladylike.

"So thar I was settin' on the bank, danglin' my feet in the cold water and a brushin' away at my squeaky-clean hair when here come Papa walkin' up aside of me, carryin' two of them big baskets, one filled with eggs and one with vegetables that come from the garden that very mornin'. Standin' over me, he looked down at me and proclaimed, 'Yer mama done decided to do some bakin' and she wants ye to head on down to the tradin' post and do some barterin' fer some flour or cornmeal and some honey or sorgum.'

"Tavia, I declare to ye that I was in no frame of mind fer sech foolishness. Why, the tradin' post was more'n a mile's climb from the house and here hit was, the middle of the day on the hottest day of summer. Thar was no doubt in my mind that hit was sweatin' I'd be a doin' 'fore I come home in the afternoon. Without so much as a thinkin' about hit, the words come bustin' out, under my breath, I thought. 'She can damn well go do her own barterin' in this god-awful heat!'

"Well, Papa heerd me and 'fore I knowed what was happenin', he pulled out his pocket knife and cut a branch from one of the bushes a growin' on that bank. He looked at that switch and looked at me real hard. A sadness come over his face as he jerked me up by the arm and pulled my skirt up above my knees. Then he said, 'This'll hurt me a lot worse'n hit will ye.' He lit into me like thar was no holdin' back. That was the worstest switchin' of my life. All the while he was a shakin' his finger in my face and yellin' at me to never agin show sech disrespect to Mama or to him, fer that matter. But that was not the end of hit. No, then he started in on the curse words I had said and jerked me around to switch me on the other leg. I was jumpin' up and down, pleadin' fer him to stop as I promised over and over that I would be a respectful daughter in the future and never, ever would sech words pass through my lips agin. I kin vouch to ye, Tavia, that I have stayed true to my promise to my papa 'cause hit took only onct fer me to understand that misbehavin' and the consequences warn't worth the pain!

"I growed up a right smart bit that day, I reckon. I've watched people come and go in and out durin' this long life of mine. Not one soul makes hit through without sinnin' or makin' mistakes. The difference is how we handle what we do wrong. Some gits their hands smacked onct and that's enough. I ain't doin' that agin, he says to hisself. Another one does the same thing over and over with the same results: pain and misery, pain and misery. Her mama smacks her hands; she still reaches fer the pot of honey. She ain't goin' to stop no matter how many licks she gits. One body might call that persistence; another says hit's plain stubbornness. Whichever hit turns out to be, thar's one thing I know fer sure. Human bein's have a way of bringin' a bundle full of hardships down on theirselves. We don't need to go searchin' fer trouble. Hit's waitin' fer us around the next bend in the road."

Ever' night as I drifted off to sleep settin' 'fore the fire, hit seemed that the days of my youth filled both my wakin' and dreamin' moments. I saw myself growin' up clearer and clearer those days that I spent with Tavia after I moved out of my cabin. In my dreams I was young, and though never as purty as Mama, I stood tall and straight, proud of who I was and what I could do. I was almost as strong as my brothers and often times Papa would call fer me to help hitch up the mule or tend to a cow when she was a calvin'. On more'n one occasion he put a axe in my hands to cut firewood fer the winter. Iffen him and the boys found theirselves wantin' in the way of manpower to git a job done, he'd holler out my name and I'd go a runnin' to add a bit of woman power, as he called hit, to the task at hand.

Onct he had me standin' on the farm wagon stackin' the hay as the boys hitched bales up from the ground. I staggered back and forth under the weight but managed to keep up with 'em until the wagon was loaded. Papa looked up at me, my face grimy, my body sweatin', in spite of what Mama would have called hit, from the effort. "Look at yer sister, boys," he sang out. "I always wanted another son so thar'd be a even half dozen of us men to work the farm. Seems like that son's been here with us all along!" They had a good laugh at their wore-out sister who wouldn't quit even if ever bone in her body was give out.

Though I did not go back to school for a education of readin' and writin', Mama was a master teacher in the art of runnin' a household and keepin' records with her gift of cipherin'. She had no problem addin', subtractin', dividin', and multiplyin' in her head. Fractions to her was as easy as fryin' a egg. "Maybe ye'll never larn to read and write all that good," she told me, "but doin' numbers don't take nothin' but memorizin' in yer head." And she put me to workin' problems in my head ever day of my growin' up.

"If I'm goin' to bake two cakes and one calls fer a half cup of butter, how many will I need, Aulene?" Bakin' and cipherin' went hand in hand. Same with raisin' chickens or plantin' a garden.

"If a half acre of corn requires one fourth bushel of seed, how much will yer papa need to buy to plant five acres? One hen produces on average fifteen or sixteen brood eggs; iffen I want to have me sixty new hens next spring, how many hens do I need for the settin'? Yer papa needs to put new shoes on the mule. Mr. Johnson wants fifteen cents a shoe plus seventy-five cents fer the trip to do the work. How much will that cost yer papa?" By the time I was fifteen or sixteen I could answer any of sech questions in a matter of two or three minutes without havin' so much as to write one number down. In recognition of my talents, my papa made me his assistant in regards to money matters; of course, real money was a rare thing in them days. Mostly one thing was traded fer another, but still a value in terms of dollars and cents had to be placed on what was give over and what was took in hits place.

As far as runnin' a household was concerned, Mama was a stern taskmaster, no two ways about hit. She could not tolerate dirt nor disorder of any kind. Lessons in the management of food preparation, cleanin', makin' and mendin', washin' and ironin' clothes, and all else related to so called "women's work" was handed out fast and furious, in a no-nonsense sort of way. She told me onct how somethin' was done and that was that.

"Here's how ye make a venison stew," she'd begin, then go through all the motions while I stood beside her, watchin' and helpin' when she asked. A month later, she might say as we finished washin' the breakfast dishes, "A venison stew would be right good tonight as the weather's turned cool. Yer papa was give a shoulder of venison by one of the neighbors last evenin'. Hit's wrapped up in a flour sack in the spring house. Best be gittin' hit started fer hit to be ready when yer papa and the boys come in from the fields fer supper." Then she would head out to heat water fer the week's washin' while I commenced preparin' my first venison stew.

So my education continued as Mama set out to make a good wife and mother of me. I larned what she had to teach me, but by and large, hit was my mama that give me what I needed most, a sense of who I was and what I could accomplish if I set my mind to hit.

October 5, 1939

"AUNT ORLENE, YE'S MIGHTY quiet this mornin'. Are ye feelin' all right? I'm fixin' some hot biscuits. Are ye hungry?"

"How many days have I been here, Tavia? Hit seems I done lost track of time altogether. I cain't separate the minutes from the hours, or the hours from the days. Hit seems like hit's all runnin' together like the raindrops comin' down and fallin' into the creek, then hit travels on to the Ararat River and on to the ocean somewheres. Ye cain't tell one drop from t'other. That's how my life feels to me. I cain't tell one event from t'other, one day or one year, one baby that was borned to me or a baby that I borned to one of my nieces or grandnieces or another kin. Day becomes night and then back to day. Iffen I'm soundin' confused in my mind, take my word fer hit, I am. I'm old and of no uset to no person I kin think of. Why do ye think that the Lord keeps on lettin' me live?"

"Lands, Aunt Orlene, I'm a wishin' I'd jest a left ye settin' thar in that chair quiet as a mouse. I reckon I done opened a can of worms, as they say, though what they is I ain't sure. Ye've been here with me since Wednesday last; that's five days ago since today is Monday. As fer ye bein' confused and ever'thing runnin' together, I kin attest to feelin' the same thoughts as the years go by. As far as why the Lord is lettin' ye live, the only answer I kin come up with, is that He ain't finished with ye yet. That's what the Baptist preacher is always preachin'. We ain't supposed to question how God runs this world, what He does or does not do. We jest best accept our lot and move on."

"I cain't be movin' about and goin' here and thar to catch a baby at my age."

"And I reckon ye wished ye could, but thar's still work fer ye to do, Orlene Puckett."

"Ye reckon so? What would hit be?"

"Ye kin tell yer story and pass hit down to let people know what hit was to live durin' these times. Ye kin tell about what family life was like, about the war, about losin' yer babies and goin' out to help with the bornin' of other women's children. We've lived in a closed up part of this world, Aunt Orlene. People don't know what hit was like, settlin' and workin' the land, survivin' a war, havin' a child without a doctor or nurse nearby. Our history is disappearin' mighty fast. Old-timers sech as ye kin help the next generation make some sense of hit. I'm writin' down what ye're recallin' and tellin' me. What'll become of this time together who kin say, but I have to believe that good will come from hit, even if jest one Hawks or Puckett reads what ye had to say and passes hit on to another family member. The rest is up to the Lord, Aunt Orlene. Think of what yer mama was teachin' ye through the years and how hit become a part of who ye are and who ye have been to so many people in these parts. Yer life is the story of these here mountains and the generations that have lived here.

"Now 'fore we go any further, Aunt Orlene, are ye ready to have some breakfast? I hate fer my biscuits to git cold. I fixed sausage gravy to cover 'em up real good. A cup of hot coffee is a waitin' fer ye at the table. Have ye used the pot this mornin'?"

"No, I ain't. Iffen ye kin help me to my feet, I'll head to the outhouse. I think a fresh October breeze will go a long way in clearin' the cobwebs from my old brain. Get yer pencil and paper while I'm gone. I'll have me a biscuit when I come in. Don't think I'll be havin' any of that gravy. Hit smells right good, but my appetite has done left me, I reckon."

"I'll walk out with you. You need that shawl around yer shoulders. The wind's comin' up a bit."

"Ain't no need, Tavia. A few minutes enjoyin' a fine October mornin' is what this ole body is a cravin'. I'll make hit out and back on my own. Iffen I ain't back by the time the dinner bell rings, send Coy out to look fer me. I might jest take a notion to walk up the mountain a bit."

"Aunt Orlene, I don't think—"

"I said I might take a notion, Tavia. That ain't the same as actually makin' hit happen."

Onct I was outside, the fresh air lifted my spirits to the point that I eyed the top of Groundhog with a hurtful longin'. My heart was willin' but my body was tellin' me hit was no use. Wishful thinkin' could take a person only so far. I made my way back to the house with the clear understandin' that my wanderin' ways was over.

Back inside, I turned to Tavia, ready to talk some more. "I dreamed about John last night. Hit's about time I told ye about the first time I laid my eyes on that handsome young man. I come out of the meeting house that Sunday mornin' and Papa was a standin' under a big tree, talkin' to this tall, dark-haired young man. He was mighty good lookin', I promise ye. Well, I knowed who he was. John Puckett. His mama and papa was Jacob and Sarah Puckett. They had a big family, thirteen boys and two girls. One of the boys was dead, died when he was almost thirteen. Jacob Puckett owned a big parcel of land, some said over 100,000 acres on the Virginia, North Carolina border. They lived up the mountain on Renfro Ridge but would come down whar Mama and Papa lived 'cause both of 'em had family in our area. Onct in a while, they'd come to the Baptist meeting house fer services, which is how John come to be thar that day.

"Papa noticed me a comin' out the door and motioned fer me to join the two of them. 'John here wants to walk ye up to the farmhouse,' he said. I looked down at my toes, sneaked a peek at the tall young man, shrugged my shoulders and headed towards the house, John two or three steps behind me. In a minute or two, he come up alongside of me, throwin' a glance or two my way, but as I recall, he ne'er spoke one word to me as we made our way to the house. His silence was a potent indication of what was to come, iffen I'd put any thought to hit that day. When we reached the house, he looked at me with a sort of half smile, tipped his hat, and started back down the trail.

"Mama and Papa and the boys made their appearance in a short while and we settled into the Sunday routine of puttin' the meal on the table, sayin' a blessin', and passin' bowls of steamin' stewed corn, beans, mashed taters and gravy, fried chicken, cornbread, greens, and whatever else Mama would think of to round out our week's main meal. Mighty good eatin', hit was. I ne'er rose to the level of Mama's cookin' abilities, I will confess, except fer my sweet tater cobbler, which those that set at my table proclaimed 'the bestest in the world.'

"Nairy a word was said about John Puckett walkin' me from the church back to the house. But the next time him and his family showed up fer a service, the same thing happened, except this time Mama had stayed home from church and greeted us on the porch steps with the invitation fer John to join us fer Sunday dinner. I felt my face turn red as fire when he answered, 'Be pleased to join ye and the family, Ms. Hawks.' I was prayin' that he'd turn around and go on his way, leavin' us to be like we'd always been. My family was jest fine the way hit was. I warn't in any hurry to be takin' a stranger into our midst, even iffen the Pucketts had more land than Papa and all our neighbors put together.

"Durin' the meal, him and Papa and my brothers carried on a long conversation about the butcherin' of hogs come fall time. Mama's good food passed right under my nose and I could hardly eat a bite. John said nairy a word to me that I kin recall; maybe a 'please pass the taters' or 'I'll have another piece of that fried chicken, if ye don't mind, Miss Orlene.' The 'r' sound come out strong and heavy and stayed fer the rest of my life.

"Still, my mama and papa had my best interests at heart. I could've done a lot worse fer a husband than John Puckett. Either the unmarried men livin' around us was too young, too old, too poor, or had too many motherless children to tend to.

"The Sunday that John Puckett showed up in front the Primitive Baptist Church in a shiny green buggy pulled by a spirited black mare, I took note of the glance that passed atween Mama, who was conversin' with a few of her women friends and Papa, shakin' the preacher's hand while the boys follered suit. John tipped his hat toward my mama, then at me as I made my way to join the two daughters of a neighbor down the road. The look on their two faces gave off the same message: That young man is goin' to be our son-in-law! Not that John Puckett was forced upon me, ye understand. That may have been the course of action fer some families in our parts, but Mama would have none of hit.

"After John rode me up to the house in the buggy, Mama called me into the kitchen. 'Yer papa and me don't want to push ye into no early marriage. We kin have ye here at home until ye're good and ready to leave. And hit don't have to be with John Puckett. He's takin' a likin' to ye and has the blessin's of his mama and papa, but they ain't forcin' him out the door, neither. What are ye thinkin', Aulene? Could ye be happy with John Puckett, make a home fer him, and be a mother to his children? Ye kin tell yer mama the truth of how ye're feelin' in yer heart. Yer Papa will accept whatever choict ye make. And hit don't have to be this very minute. Ye kin take yer time.'

"Listenin' to Mama put the business of marryin' John Puckett in a whole new light. Maybe I had felt a few tingles and flutterin's when he walked close by me. Maybe I saw myself in a fine house built with Puckett money up the mountain halfway atween Papa's farm and the Puckett homestead. Maybe I might even have me a servant or two to do the washin' and the cookin'. But thar was the other side that I had not considered: bein' in charge of runnin' a household, dealin' with pleasin' his mama, and bearin' his children. I could hardly envision a future in a strange place, without my mama and papa and my brothers runnin' around watchin' out fer me, even if they did pester me to death. If mama's memory was clear, I was already seventeen. Most girls my age was married and takin' care of one or two babies. I fer sure didn't want to end up a old maid, but I wasn't ready to give up bein' Papa's little girl.

"I tucked my head, avoidin' Mama's questions and the intense look on her face. 'I think I'd best set my mind to thinkin' on hit, Mama. Maybe I kin love John Puckett. Maybe I do this very moment. The only thing I know fer sure right now is that I don't know my own mind nor my heart. I need some time.'

"Mama said, 'We ain't got much in the way of world goods, Aulene, but one thing yer papa and me does have is time. Ye take all the time ye need and when ye know the answer, come to yer Mama. We'll move on from thar.'

"I prayed hard about the matter, Tavia, but the Lord didn't send me no clear word that I could tell. John kept on showin' up at the church to ride me back home in his buggy. Mama and Papa invited him to Sunday dinner and he managed to say a few words ever' now and then. The boys teased me but in a gentle way that did not put me to bein' embarrassed or feelin' foolish. The womenfolk would come by the house and ask me if I was sewin' somethin' special. Papa and the neighbor men would part off and make jokes about women and their stand-off ways. I kept my tongue under control while contemplatin' my course of action. A year went by. I turned eighteen. Winter rolled by with another birthday a comin'. I looked in the mirrer and pictured myself as a plain old maid. I walked out to the hen house whar Mama was takin' care of the new chicks. She glanced at me as I leaned down to pick up one of the downy bundles of spun gold. 'I done made up my mind, Mama. If John Puckett still wants me, I'd be honored to have him as my husband.'

"But would ye believe hit? When Papa relayed the word to John and his mama and papa that I was acceptin' his offer to make me his bride, the message come back that since hit had took me so long to make up my mind, John had been rethinkin' the whole idee of marriage hisself and was havin' second thoughts about takin' Aulene Hawks to be his bride. None of that set well with my mama and papa, and fer a while hit looked as though the two families was in a real stand off. Most of the neighbors backed up my mama and papa but some of John's kinfolk who lived nearby done a lot of grumblin' and name callin' 'fore hit was over. As fer me, I was certain that John was jest bein' contrary 'cause I hadn't jumped when he made his offer to the plain and too uppity Miss Hawks. From the way he was a lookin' at hit, John and the Pucketts was doin' my family a favor by takin' me offen their hands.

"By and by peace was made atween the two families and the work of pullin' off a weddin' and helpin' two young'uns set up housekeepin' begun in earnest. Mama and the womenfolk was weavin', sewin', quiltin', and embroiderin' from sunrise to sunset. Papa and Mr. Puckett, along with all the sons and cousins from both families, headed over to a piece of land near the Ararat River at the foot of Groundhog Mountain to clear a piece of land and put up a one-room house—people would call hit a shack today—fer us to live in near some other families at the bottom of the hill. Hit had a cellar fer storin' vegetables in the winter and a bit of a porch with two steps.

"The menfolk produced a few pieces of furniture sech us a kitchen table, a rope bed, a cupboard, and three mule-ear chairs with hand-wove oak strip bottoms. My grandmama give me a rockin' chair that belonged to her mama and they was a few other hand me down pieces from the Puckett family along with some that Mama had been savin' fer me. Other kinfolk and neighbors brung us things fer settin' up our housekeepin' sech as baskets or homemade candles and soaps, whittled out spoons and bowls, whatever they could spare or made special fer ye. Hit was excitin' to watch the house take on a homey look even iffen hit was more like a dollhouse than a dwellin' fer two growned up humans. Hit was a good day's walk or a half day's ride from the farm whar I growed up, but John promised me I could visit my family whenever I wanted to go if the weather allowed fer hit and that they was always welcome to come spend time with us, though I wondered out loud whar they would stay. I remember his response clear as day:

> "They can stay with my mama and papa," John offered. "Our house is big enough since most of the children are growed and moved out on their own."
>
> "Yer mama and papa are more prosperous than Mama and Papa. They wouldn't feel right stayin' in sech a fine place; not that my mama and papa ain't as good but they don't like bein' beholden to no one."
>
> John laughed. "Is that so? Well, I reckon they's beholden to John Puckett fer takin' their oldest daughter who's knowed to be right contrary at times off their hands."
>
> "John Puckett," I sputtered, "I had no idee ye thought about me in sech a way." I turned away from him, feelin' the redness come into my face as a tear threatened to run from the corners of my eyes.

"Hold on, girl. I'm jest a funnin' ye, Orlene. I like a girl with some spirit in 'er. A bit of stubbornness or contrariness ain't necessarily a bad thing, I reckon. Hit might end of helpin' ye make hit through the hard times." He put his arms around me and I thought he was goin' to kiss me, which up to now had jest been little pecks here and thar as iffen he was workin' up the courage to git uset to the idee, but he pulled back and looked at me real hard. "I ain't big on romance and sech, Orlene. I ain't had much practice with girls. Not that I haven't had my chances, but I don't rightly know how to go about makin' up to females. My mama is a right strong woman with no nonsense ways and she's done raised my sisters to be the same way. Neither my papa nor my brothers ever stands up to a one of 'em. No sirree. As long as we stay in line, we purty much have the run of the show. I ain't complainin' and I'm expectin' hit'll be the same way with ye and me."

"Hit was the longest speech that I'd heerd from John in the two years since I'd first laid eyes on him at the Baptist Church. I also larned more about him that day than in the previous times we'd spent together gettin' ready fer our weddin'. I wasn't sure at that moment that I'd done the right thing in agreein' to wed a young man that I suspicioned might be a mama's boy. Well, I thought to myself, we'll jest have to wait and see. Still, as I looked up into his dark eyes, lightin' up that handsome face perched atop his tall, strong body, I was convinced that I could've done a lot worser than John Puckett.

"The next thing I knowed we was standin' thar in the Baptist church whar I'd accepted Jesus as my savior when I was eleven years and taken down to the creek to be baptized. A few years ago, after I done turned ninety, a few of the nieces and nephews convinced theirselves that hit never happened and I had been an infidel all my life, so they took hit upon theirselves to call in the preacher to git me right with the Lord and make sure I was headed fer heaven, since I'd led sech a sinful, misguided life. They bundled me up and the preacher dunked me into the cold water in spite of my protests that I had been saved, accordin' to my recollection and then I further declared 'once saved, always saved' and asked the preacher fer his verification. When he nodded to the affirmative, I called out to them standin' on the bank that I was forgivin' of their ignorance but hit was a mighty poor way to be treatin' their old Aunt Orlene.

"Anyways, John and me was a standin' thar, sayin' vows to be man and wife, but hit was runnin' through my head that we was jest children and what did we know of bein' husband and wife? Then I recalled what my mama said about her own weddin' day and chills run right over me. I could feel the chill bumps movin' up and down my arms and legs. When I sneaked a side look at my new husband, I couldn't fer the life of me recall who he was. Ye done married a stranger, I said to myself, and looked around, hopin' to see a familiar face lookin' back at me, but they was all strangers. I had never felt so alone in my whole life.

"Next someone was holdin' my hand and we was walkin' towards a wagon, all decorated with ribbons and shiny pieces of tin. A tall man with gray hair helped me onto the seat and a young man about my age, maybe older, set down aside of me and then we was headin' down the road. I was feelin' like I was in some kind of dream. People was a follerin' behind us, some walkin', some in buggies or wagons, some ridin' horses or mules. They was laughin' and singin' and shoutin' and I was wonderin' what the celebration was about.

"The journey took most of the day. When we arrived at a little settlement of tiny houses, thar was a jolt of recognition when we pulled up 'fore one of 'em that had a big basket of field flowers tied with a blue bow hangin' from the door. Ever'body started clappin' and yellin', while the stranger settin' aside of me jumped down, tied up the horse and helped me down. More yellin' and clappin' and laughin', then a fiddle started playin' and one by one folks begun makin' a circle fer a square dance. My head was hurtin' but nobody seemed to be payin' any attention to me. The womenfolk was puttin' big bowls and platters of food on long makeshift tables and groups of menfolk was passin' jugs about and around while talkin' loud and punchin' one another as one after the other joined in tellin' stories that produced great peals of howlin' and sniggerin'. I remember the conversation well:

> Some of the neighbors' daughters gathered around me and begun teasin' me about becomin' a woman.
>
> "I'm already a woman," I proclaimed with great dignity which set off a round of gigglin' and whispers I couldn't understand.
>
> "Thar's a lot more fer ye to larn," one of them snickered.
>
> "And the lesson won't be long in comin'," another added while the others joined in with more laughter.
>
> I was feelin' hot and dizzy when Mama come up to me and took

my hand. "Hit's time fer ye to be headin' inside."

"I don't want to," I pulled back.

"These here folks ain't leavin' as long as ye and John are out and about. Iffen ye want some peace and quiet, go out to the door and thank ever'body fer comin' to yer weddin' and fer bringin' all these fine gifts. Onct all the food and drink is run out, they'll be scurryin' on home."

"What about John?" I asked.

"What about John?" Mama's curt reply pierced right through me.

"Is he leavin', too?" I felt a quiver overtakin' my own voice.

"No, child, yer husband is not leavin'." She emphasized the word husband.

"I don't want him to stay, Mama. I want ye to stay with me, at least fer jest tonight."

"Well, I don't hardly reckon John would take too kindly to sech a thing, Aulene."

"He'll listen to ye, Mama. He's uset to mindin' strong women. He told me so."

Mama laughed, but I could hear the hesitation in her voice. "We've talked this over, child. Hit will be all right. The first time is a surprise, that's all. Ever'time after comes easier. Ye'll be fine, child. Ye're strong in yer own right and ye larn fast. Pay attention to what John does or tells ye to do. He'll be a good husband to ye."

"I don't think John knows much more'n I do, Mama."

Thar was a hint of a smile through Mama's tight lips. "Well, maybe hit'll work out jest fine, Aulene. Neither one of ye will have high expectations to live up to."

And with that, Mama slipped out of the room and left me to take my second step into womanhood. When John finally come in after the last of his friends had left, the fire that Papa built had warmed our one room into a simple coziness. I had been dozin' on the feather mattress that had been placed on our new rope bed, wearin' the fine linen shift Mama had made fer me. John blew out the candle and I heerd the rustlin' of clothin' hittin' the floor. I held my breath, but nothin' happened. John's head hit the piller next to mine and in no time hit seemed faint snorin' sounds brushed their way acrost my face. His arm reached out and drew me to him and I tensed up agin.

"Hit's all right, Orlene. We're plumb tuckered out and I've had too much corn whiskey. We're still our mama's babes with years of growin' up to do. Fer now, let's git us a good night's sleep. The growin' up part kin start tomorrow."

Maybe, I thought, I ain't the only one who's a scared of this here business of bein' married. And with that, I settled into John's arms while the sweet smell of his whiskey breath floated acrost my face. In no time at all I was wrapped up in a dream of the future that was waitin' fer us.

"Hit did not take me long, Tavia, to figure out that John Puckett was a man, in the sense that the world viewed him, not easily pleased. For my part I mostly saw him as a boy with a right smart growin' up to do since hit was right out thar in the open in his actions and his words that his mama had spoiled him and the rest of the Puckett boys fer that matter plumb rotten. In the first year or so that we was married, hit seemed that nothin' I tried to do was to his satisfaction. He'd complain or pout or go off a huntin', at least that was what he told me, with his brothers Isaiah and Churchill. They would be gone fer days and come back with hardly a critter to throw in the pot. I got to thinkin' that what they was a huntin' fer mostly was corn liquor, gamblin', and maybe sech things as I didn't want a crossin' my mind.

"Thar I was, a standin' over the hot stove, cuttin' and slicin' and mixin' up spices that I'd gathered from my plants and garden. I was hopin' to come up with a stew, along with a pan of hot biscuits and butter fresh from the churn, that would produce a compliment or a thank you of sorts, but after a bite or two, John would put down his spoon or fork, look at me and say, 'Don't taste like Mama's.' I'd promise to do better next time and set down weary with the day's work and John's endless complainin'.

"One mornin' I was ironin' one of his two Sunday shirts that his mama had made fer him, weavin' the linen on her loom and sewin' hit together to be one of her presents fer the day we was married. The irons had to be red hot so the creases would come out with nairy a wrinkle or line to be seen. John moved round and about me while I was concentratin' hard as I could on makin' that shirt look as fresh and sparklin' as iffen hit was brand new. As I was a puttin' the finishin' touches on the collar, John moved up clos't to my shoulder and proclaimed, 'Mama don't do hit that way.'

"His words did not set well with me. *Why don't ye go home and live with yer mama?!* was the thought runnin' through my head, but of course hit would not do fer a woman in them times to say the words out loud. As was usual, I promised to do better the next time and stepped out the door to gather vegetables from my garden. Bein' outside was the usual remedy I took fer dark moods that threatened to gather about me like the storm clouds hangin' over the mountains above me. Hit was durin' them times I would pray that John's brothers would ride up and kidnap him fer a day or two, givin' me time to settle my nerves and prepare fer the next battle.

"One day was mostly like the next. Hit was work in the house, work in the garden, work in the fields. Neighbors was few and far apart. We was livin' within shoutin' distance of the top of the Blue Ridge near Renfro Ridge, not far from whar John's mama and papa resided with his younger brothers and sisters. The ones that was older than John had moved out and was clearin' land fer farmin' up on the mountain and around and about the foothills. With as much land as Jacob Puckett owned, hit warn't nothin' fer each one of the boys to start off with four or five hundred acres if they wanted to work that hard. Even the two sisters was give a large parcel of land as part of a dowry, as they called hit; of course, that was somethin' that poor people had no cause to weary theirselves about. Iffen a girl come to marriage with a chest or trunk filled with fresh linens, a blanket or a quilt or two, a few pieces of handed down good dishes, and a change or two of new made undergarments, she was thought to be a right good match fer any decent young farmer.

"Fer my part, I planted the seeds fer the vegetables put on the table; milked the cow and made the cream and butter; raised the chickens and wrung their necks fer cookin' Sunday dinner; did the spinnin' and weavin' of cloth to sew my own garments—I had two ever'day dresses and one Mama made fer me to wear to church, weddin's and funerals. When harvest time and hog butcherin' come along, I worked alongside John and his brothers and neighbors, since menfolk went from farm to farm to lend a hand in return for help when others' crops come in.

"Farmers was up 'fore the sun; womenfolk cooked a hearty breakfast fer their husbands and sons so's they could tackle the work to be done without any hangin' back or complainin'. Right after cleanin' up, we was preparin' fer the next meal, puttin' vegetables on to cook, makin' pies or cakes, whippin' up dough fer bread, searin' meat over the fire to turn into a stew. While the food was cookin', we washed clothes, churned butter, made soap or candles, weaved a bottom in a chair, swept the floors, fed the chickens, gathered eggs from the hen house and brung water up from the well. Ever minute was filled with chores to be done, inside and out. Socializin', if thar was any, took place at the meetin' house on the Sundays that the preacher come around, or when thar was a weddin', a baby borned, or a funeral. When the sun went down, we set around the fire in the winter or on the porch when the weather was pleasant, mostly too tired to move. By nightfall, we was a fallin' into our beds ready fer sleep to rest our wore out bodies so's we could wake up the next mornin' and start all over again.

"Course John, in spite of the toil of tryin' to make this old rocky soil produce somethin' of value, seemed to always have a bit of energy left over that he wanted to use up. After a time, I believe we come to find a pleasure in one another, but even so many a night my eyes shut tight as soon as my head come to rest on my pillar. The next mornin' John would leave the table, sayin' that the bestest way in the world to cool down a man's ardor was to reach fer his woman and hear the sound of sawin' logs while drool run down his sweetheart's chin. He'd laugh as he pecked me on the cheek and like always, I would promise him that the next time I would do better. Onct in a while, I made good on my promise.

"Still, after four or five years come and gone, we had not had one baby. John's brothers was havin' children right and left, hit seemed. Them and John's sisters had married into many of the families that had settled the land along the North Carolina-Virginia line that followed the Blue Ridge Mountains. After a while, hit seemed that ever'one was related to ever'one else in these parts. John's mama told me one day that I should not gossip or spread talk about any of my neighbors 'since they's all related to one another.' I made the mistake of tellin' my mama that Missus So and So had told me that…and I related the story that had been passed around at a recent church social concernin' a cousin who was reported to be 'in the family way.' Mama was flabbergasted that a neighbor had told me sech, proclaimin' that family is family. 'Family don't talk about one another, especially in a way that is unkind or not known to be true.'

"I defended my source by declarin' that I'd done seen her fer myself. 'She's out and about, not even tryin' to keep herself out of the sight of people that knows her. She don't appear to be ashamed one bit.' Mama replied, 'We don't know the circumstances, Aulene. Ye cain't go around judgin' people without clear evidence. Fer all we know, she's a married woman but keepin' hit a secret fer reasons we are not privy to.'

"I tried to defend myself, but she cut me off. 'That's enough, child.

Ever' human bein' on this earth has enough to do to take care of hisself and mind his own business without interferin' in the business of his friends and neighbors. Maybe this girl needs a friend more'n anybody kin fathom, instead of havin' people whisperin' and tellin' tales behind her back. If ye cain't be her friend, at least don't make yerself to be her enemy.'

"The matter come to a close when the cousin up and disappeared, some said to head north to live with a relative and have her baby in peace and quiet. Others related that she had eloped and her husband, who had been jest a passin' through, had sent fer her after his family accepted the marriage and the child she was carryin'. Sech goin's on was not so uncommon in them days, but fer the most part they was covered up and hid from strangers and those who could not keep their minds out of other people's business. I tried hard to heed Mama's words and guard my own, but rumors, even in a community whar neighbors is spread out and a person don't see a friend or a relative fer days at a time, have a way of takin' on a life of their own. They kin do damage beyond repair to yer heart and to yer mind. Hit was a lesson that I was to larn fer myself way down the road.

"In the meantime, one day passed much like the ones that come 'fore. I was thinkin' that hit was time fer us to be startin' our own branch of the Puckett family and John would start in a teasin' me onct in a while but mostly Mama and John's mama and his sisters kept assurin' me that nature warn't to be hurried, me and John was young and healthy and had plenty of child bearin' years ahead of us. Then him and the two brothers would up and disappear fer a week or so and my faith in my husband and our future would begin to fade.

"I'd make excuses fer John and his ways; after all, Mama had always told me that no man is perfect. 'Not even yer papa,' she would say, 'but I kin testify that he comes mighty close.' When I compared John to my papa, he as good as missed the mark by at least a mile! Although ever' girl and woman declared John Puckett to be as fine lookin' a man to be found in these parts, as a farmer, he warn't always dependable. He was a daydreamin' sort, settin' out to work at one chore, say mendin' the harness fer the mule, and endin' up at the far corner of the field cuttin' down a tree. We'd probably not a made a livin' iffen his papa and his brothers had not come by on a regular basis checkin' on John and the progress he was havin' on the farm.

"Mama and Papa come to visit about onct a month bringin' whatever was comin' in on their farm. Mama made a point to dig up bushes and bulbs and roots from her yard so's I could have me flowers of my own bloomin' from spring until fall time.

"John was not a talker except when he was a drinkin' and jawin' around with the menfolk when they turned out to help with a barn raisin' or harvestin' a crop. Then the women had a chanct to do a bit of socializin' as they went about preparin' the food to feed all them hungry mouths puttin' in a full day's work. We made light of our dislikes and frustrations with our husbands' contrariness and ornery ways. Complainin' didn't change nothin'; hit jest used up energy that was needed fer gettin' the work done each day.

"We was poor compared to the way people live nowadays even though John's family was thought to be mighty prosperous next to the Hawks's kin, but they was proud and dignified in their own way. We warn't ashamed of who we was or whar we come from. We worked hard and held our heads up high. We was determined not to be beholden to no one and to make our way through this world the best we could with the Lord's help. And hit was fer sure the Lord's help I would be needin' iffen John and me was goin' to have us a baby.

Tavia stretched her arms over her head. "Aunt Orlene, I think the two of us needs to be takin' a rest hereabouts and hit's near time to be havin' some dinner. I ain't ne'er heerd ye talk so much in one spell. Why, we done spent most of this here day, with ye a recallin' them early days and me settin' here tryin' to write hit all down."

"Hit's a good idee, Tavia. A bite to eat, maybe some cornbread and a cup of buttermilk poured over hit would taste mighty good. Then I'll take a trip to the outhouse and set myself down fer a bit of a nap afore we start up agin."

But I had finished my story tellin' fer the day. I slept all through the rest of the day and the night. Bringin' back all them memories turned out to be jest about as hard a work as catchin' a baby.

October 6, 1939

"TAVIA, HOW COME I'M STILL settin' in this chair? The fire needs a tendin' and my legs don't seem to be wantin' to move. What time is hit? I'm feelin' a mite hungry."

"Land's sakes, Aunt Orlene. Ye ain't moved since ye come in from the outhouse yesterday, late in the day hit was. Ye dropped off to sleep almost as soon as ye set in yer chair and ye ain't moved since. I reckon ye are hungry and yer bones is all cramped up, not to mention that ye might have wet yerself after sech a time."

"No, I ain't reached that point in my life yet. Bring that pot close and help me a bit. I know fer sure I cain't make hit to the outhouse whatever time of the day hit is. A cup of coffee and somethin' to eat would be mighty welcome. My stomach is a feelin' as empty as a poor man's pockets."

"Well, ye ain't lost yer sense of humor, that's fer sure, or yer bossy ways either. Take care of yer needs, then I'll wash yer face and hands and git yer breakfast. I'll do a few more chores and bring in some more firewood while ye're eatin' and when ye're up to hit we'll pick up the story tellin' whar we left off yesterday."

We took care of the necessities and then I started back on my life's story again.

"The years leadin' up to the time when me and John started our married life was filled with talk and hot-headed arguments over the trouble that was heatin' up between the North and the South. Mostly people said hit had to do with somethin' about states' rights, although fer the life of me I ne'er understood the meanin' of them words. Hidden away from the light of day hit seemed to come down to the business of ownin' slaves, even iffen nobody wanted to own sech to be true . Fer farmers like my papa, havin' slaves to work the land cost money beyond their means. Growin' up, I heerd that some rich folks owned slaves and down the mountain hit was reputed that two or three families of free colored folks had set up farmin', but they was few and not hardly see'd whar we was livin' in them days.

"Even so when thar was a get-together amongst the neighbors or at the church fer whatever purpose, the talk would turn towards politics:

the gover'ment's stand on this and that, the rift that was worsenin' and takin' over the whole country, and the comin' election. The men would start yellin' and carryin' on about the rightness of this and the wrongness of that till thar was times when fights would break out amongst fathers and sons, or brothers aginst cousins. The young men would take up the cry that they warn't goin' to fight a rich man's war, which is how they thought of them that was owners of the big plantations in South Carolina, Georgia, Alabama, and Mississippi, with their big houses and hundreds of slaves workin' in the cotton and tobacco fields while the owners was gettin' richer by the minute. But the older men like my papa and grandpapa would come back with the argument that their ancestors done come from the Old World whar they was kings and no rights at all, a man had no land to call his own and they had worked this land and turned hit into a livin'; therefore, no man, not even the president of the United States, who turned out to be Abraham Lincoln, was goin' to take their rights from 'em. Property was property, whatever hit was, land or slaves; it was a man's own business. The tusslin' idees would go on fer hours at a time. Add a jug or two of corn whiskey circulatin' about with hard words bein' flung in each other's faces and hit got to be a mighty heated show 'fore hit was over, better'n any entertainment that ever come to our part of the country!

"As fer the womenfolk, we set by and listened without offerin' up so much as one little opinion. What good would've come from speakin' our minds? Nothin'. Women didn't know about sech matters, we was told. We warn't educated to the ways of the world. Men was in charge and would make the big decisions fer the rest of us, regardless of the fact that we had to live with the consequences of their actions. If a woman spoke out in a way that differed from the opinions of her husband, they was no end to the labelin' that was pinned on 'er. I kin hear the words hurlin' through my head this very day: contrary, cussedness, cantankerous, ornery, spiteful, ignorant, hard to handle, hard hearted, plus a few others that I will not repeat. I will confess, however, that I did not go without my share of criticism, if not directly from John, from his papa and his brothers and even kinfolk on the Hawks's side who was ready to go to war at the drop of a hat, or the election of Abraham Lincoln in the year 1860, one date that don't fade out of sight. Fer many a southerner, hit was the straw that broke the camel's back.

"Next spring the news made hits way up into Virginia that the South Carolina militia had fired on the fort in the Charleston harbor and had pulled out of the Union. The menfolk seemed to lose all reason when the riders brung the report into the foothills and mountains of the Blue Ridge. I kin recall men grabbin' their pistols and rifles, shootin' into the air and yellin', 'We's in the war! We's in the war!' like they was headin' to a celebration of sorts. The world turned as mad as a dog bit by a rabid fox. Then Virginia took herself out of the Union and the men headed out to join the 50th Virginia Infantry. Course, all the time, the talk was that the war would be over in six months 'cause the North had no idee what they was in for with the likes of Robert E. Lee, Jeb Stuart, Stonewall Jackson, and Jefferson Davis headin' up the leadership in the South. I think of my mama who knowed the words of many a great writer and would use 'em as lessons when the occasion warranted sech. 'What fools these mortals be,' she would say with grave severity when some acted with total disregard for the basic tenets of proper human behavior. 'Fer yer benefit, Miss Aulene Hawks, that was said by William Shakespeare in one of his plays. He understood the ways of humans better'n anyone, except fer the Lord hisself and don't ye ferget hit.' During the war and hits aftermath, the words hung over my head as heavy as clouds, even on the sunniest of days.

"But what people ferget, or won't own up to, was the fact that thar was a strong sympathy fer the Union among the settlers of the foothills and mountains of North Carolina, Virginia, and Tennesse, even up into the hills of Kentucky, West Virginia, and Maryland as hit was explained to me by my papa. That's why so many families come to be divided by the conflict. Fathers fought aginst sons and brothers aginst brothers. One of John's brothers moved up to Ohio and put on a Union uniform; fer the reason, so he explained, he couldn't fight fer the right to keep slavery on hits feet.

"I should not have been surprised in the spring of 1861 when John come into the house and announced that him and Churchill and Elijah had gone over to Floyd and signed up to fight in the infantry. He laid fifty Confederate dollars on the table as proof, but I could not take in the words that had come out of his mouth:

"What are ye sayin', John Puckett?" I asked, shiftin' my gaze from the face of my husband to the money rolled into a tight ball on the table.

"I'm tellin' you that me and the boys has signed up to go and fight the Yankees and here's the money fer doin' so. I'm a leavin' hit to ye to help ye get through the time I'll be away, although hit won't be more'n a couple of months or so, accordin' to what them that's headin' up the army is a sayin'. The Yankees ain't one bit prepared to take on us southern 'gentlemen' as they call us. They think we's all soft and not uset to hard work and hard times. They ain't ne'er tried to bring a crop out of the rocky land of our Blue Ridge Mountains. They're askin' fer a fight that'll bring 'em to their knees." He laughed as he grabbed me and pulled me so tight I couldn't breathe. I could smell the whiskey on his breath.

"Well, if ye done signed up," I wanted to know, "how come ye ain't left yet?"

"Orlene, ye're soundin' jest like a woman. They's no hard fightin' goin' on in these here parts right now. Mostly they's gatherin' the soldiers down around Stuart or up to Floyd to git 'em organized and teach 'em about marchin'. Any fool kin do that. When the time comes, we'll be headin' out. Maybe I ain't so handy at farmin', but I promise ye, Orlene, I'll be one hell of a soldier fer ye, the Pucketts, and the great state of Virginia!'"

While John was preparin' to go off and fight the enemy, I was preparin' to deliver news of my own. "John, I've been talkin' to Mama and she is sayin' we will be havin' our first baby come September. Since ye won't be leavin' to fight no way soon, maybe the war will be over 'fore hit gits here. At least promise that ye'll stay around to make sure the harvestin' is done and thar's enough wood cut to git me and the baby through the winter."

John let out a holler that could've been heerd fer miles around. "Come here, ye sweet little mama. Give yer baby's daddy a big kiss!" He grabbed me and swung me around, my feet barely touchin' the floor. "Wait till Papa and the boys hears this news. Hit's been a while since a Puckett young'un has come into this world and I'm puttin' my money on this boy bein' the biggest, the handsomest, and the smartest of them all. Orlene Puckett, I knew you had hit in ye from the first day I laid my eyes of ye and I'll be damned iffen I ain't convinced there's to be more whar this'n come from! Time fer celebratin'!" He picked me up along with a jug of moonshine and headed fer our bedstead, with me a screamin' and beggin' him to stop his foolishness in the middle of the day time when a neighbor jest might show up fer a visit.

Stop he did. He dropped me on the bed, give me a quick peck on the cheek, and headed out the door, callin' over his shoulder. "The celebratin' kin wait a bit. I'm ridin' over to Mama's to tell her and Papa that I'm goin' to be a daddy. I cain't wait to see the look on Mama's face when she realizes that her little boy John has finally growed up enough to have his own son."

"Thar ye are, Orlene Puckett," I said to myself as the door closed behind him, "playin' second fiddle to yer mother-in-law. But ye always knowed that John was his mama's boy, along with the other twelve, whether older or younger." Them boys was spoiled from the day they come into this world and me and the other daughters-in-law have had to pay the piper ever step of the way, especially since Sarah Puckett had a habit of keepin' her nose stuck in ever' child's business.

I smiled at Tavia, who was writin' fast. "Maybe hit was a bargain with the devil, but I was comforted in the knowledge that Mother Puckett took special pleasure in spoilin' the grandchildren. I knew if John did leave to go off to the war, the baby would reap the benefit of her extra attention. I decided right then I'd keep my opinions to myself jest as long as she didn't offer up advice I wasn't askin' fer.

"That summer moved mighty fast. One by one the men was signin' up to fight the Yankees, but many of 'em did not leave their homes and farms. They stayed around, spendin' the money they was paid, takin' care of their wives and children, waitin' fer the call that they was needed as the Yankees pushed south, mostly avoidin' the mountains and foothills as they deemed hit to their advantage to do their fightin' in flatlands and open areas. Talk of the war was ever present while life as we knowed hit moved on. We done the best we could to put in crops, tend to our animals, set food on the table, and bring our young'uns into the world.

"John worked extry hard during that time with the help of the older brothers and neighbors that lived nearby. He felled several good-sized trees, cuttin' 'em up into firewood fer the winter, along with clearin' two or three more acres fer plantin' a bigger garden of vegetables such as taters, sweet taters, fall squash, and pumpkins that could be stored to last through cold weather. In the evenin' he worked in the barn, mendin' harnesses and tools while buildin' a cradle fer the baby.

"Mama and Mother Puckett sewed, knitted, and crocheted purty little garments and wrappin's fer the baby. Several of my brothers' wives pieced a quilt fit fer either a boy or girl with blocks filled with toys and farm animals. I stored them one by one in the maple blanket chest that Papa had made fer my weddin'. My skin and bones figure was takin' on some additional flesh though hit warn't all baby, accordin' to Mama. John joked that my softer appearance was plumb invitin' but now that I was about to be off limits, hit warn't goin' to be of much use to him! I would turn red with his teasin' and that only egged him on with his foolishness and carryin' his tales to any man that would listen. Then somethin' would go wrong on the farm or with a neighbor, and John would turn sour and shut hisself off from me and his own kinfolk, except fer his mama and his two closest brothers, Elijah and Churchill, who was still a hangin' around, waitin' fer some real action, as they called hit, to lead them into battle.

"John Puckett stayed a mystery to me throughout our life together. On the outside, he was handsome, quick-witted, and lively—what people might call a man's man, although I was ne'er sure that he hadn't wandered off the trail a few times over the years. On the inside, he could be cold and moody, hardly saying a word fer days at a time. The leastest thing could set off his temper, though he was quick to try to make up any hurt feelins' he'd left behind. Iffen he was a drinkin', that made matters worser. A good portion of time I spent with John was like walkin' on eggs, one wrong step and they'd be broken shells scattered about the place. But his real meanness did not come to the surface until some years after the first baby was borned.

"September come upon us with a blaze of glory. The weather turned cool early that year, so the leaves was a lightin' up the sky with so many shades of color, a body couldn't think to call 'em by name. The word 'red' could not convey the color of the leaf ye was holdin' in yer hand. Hit could be crimson red, cherry red, bright red, pinkish red, sunset red, apple red, rosy red, red-striped, red checkered, red tipped. I wore myself out ever' fall tryin' to put the right shade and word with what my eyes was seein' but hit was a losin' battle. My mama loved the sound of words. She was a singer and a story teller with a special way of makin' poems and scripture and anything she was talkin' about come alive with words. She seemed to pluck words right out of the air and throw 'em upon our ears the way artists fling a bit of this and that color acrost paper and in no time a picture pops out like magic.

"Mama made the trip up from the farm early in the month with a neighbor who was bringin' a load of hay to a cousin. She wanted to be thar in case the baby was borned early. They was no doctors or hospitals in them days. The women—mamas and sisters and cousins—took care of their own when hit come time fer the baby to make hits appearance. Remedies and potions was passed down from generation to generation. Havin' a young'un was a natural thing; no coddlin' was expected nor offered. A woman did not take to the bed. She was kept a movin' as long as she could stand the pain as hit was believed that movin' about would make the birthin' easier. A woman might'n work in the field in the mornin' and drop a baby that afternoon, git a night's rest, bundle the child up to sling acrost her back, and head out to do her chores early the next mornin'. Though we viewed the process as part of nature's way, birthin' a baby was not without risks to mother and baby alike. A young or a old mother might be of a sickly nature and not strong enough to survive the long, hard labor she had to endure. Sometimes the mother died; sometimes hit was the baby. Hit was not unheard of fer a man to lose both wife and baby and be left with a houseful of young'uns to raise on his own until he could find hisself a younger woman and start all over agin.

"One mornin' in late September, I waked up with a terrible achin' in my back. I told Mama that I was feelin' bad and couldn't hardly move fer the pain. She looked me up and down, placed her hands on my middle, all the while pressin' up and down and all around. 'I think this baby will be here 'fore sunset,' she predicted.

"As fer John, I told Mama that he had rode off early to go huntin' with his brothers. 'Jest as well,' she said. 'Menfolk ain't worth a hill o' beans when hit comes to birthin' a child. Oh, one or two might come through and be mighty helpful, but that ain't true fer the vast majority. Ever' man I know thinks nothin' of pullin' a calf from hits mama or a foal from a mare, but when a man is watchin' his own wife strugglin' to bring his child into the world, he's more'n likely to throw up or faint dead away, one or the other, sometimes both. Ye and yer mama can handle whatever comes down the pike, so don't ye be afeard. Ye ain't the first woman to have a child and ye won't be the last.'

"Mama was talkin' to me as we walked back and forth in the kitchen and then out to the garden whar she started commentin' on the trees and the birds, the flowers that was still bloomin', and the gourds a scattered about the withered up vines. While she kept me movin', she would sing a hymn or recite scripture. Then she'd throw in a story havin' to do with me and the boys while we was young'uns and we'd begin to turn up special memories of our days on the farm. The pains was gittin' stronger and comin' closer together, but Mama was doin' what she could to take my mind off the waves of pain I was attemptin' to ignore. Finally I pleaded with her to let me lay down and rest a bit:

"Hit ain't goin' to do ye no good to lay down on that bed. The pains will be that much worser, Aulene. I promise ye though I'm not sayin' sech to make hit harder on ye, child. When that baby is ready to join the rest of us on this earth, he'll do hit on his own terms and I'll be here ready to catch him when he comes out."

"Are ye tellin' me that this baby is a boy, Mama? I know John wants a son so bad after we've been waitin' so long. I don't want to disappoint him."

"Shush, child. First off, two or three years ain't that long. Ye both still had some growin' up to do. And to my mind, war time ain't a good time to be startin' a family. Course I suppose the gover'ment sees hit as a woman's duty to replace the souls that done been lost on the battlefields of both sides."

"Mama! How kin ye be so harsh in yer thinkin'?" The tone of my mother's voice reminded me how preachers read the words of Old Testament prophets with fingers pointed and shrill condemnations spewin' forth. Mama would've made a good prophet, I thought, if God had called women to be preachers. Ye must be hallucinatin' in yer pain, Orlene Puckett, I chastised myself, to have the devil put sech thoughts in yer head. Even so, one last perverted idee rushed into my muddled brain. Iffen this baby turns out to be a girl, maybe God will put His hand on her and send her out to preach the gospel.

I had promised myself that I would not yell or carry on sech as I had been told about other women durin' the birthin' process. "No," I vowed, "I will be brave and not make Mama ashamed of me." Still, I was aware that some mightly powerful yells was comin' from nearby, while my mama was kneelin' in front of me as I crouched on the edge of the bed.

"Push, Aulene, push easy but strong. Put yer whole weight behind ye. Push, then breathe. Push, then breathe. Hold on to my shoulders and look straight at yer mama. Concentrate on what I'll tellin' ye to do. Yer baby will be here 'fore ye know hit."

How long the two of us worked together that day, I kin not tell. Hit seemed like hours, though more'n likely hit was jest a matter of minutes. When I thought I could not hold out or on to Mama fer another second, she reached down and called out with great satisfaction, "Well, look at this, a purty little girl, jest like her mama!" and she was holdin' a misshapen bundle of shriveled blue, covered with blood, up to my eyes.

"Oh, Mama, iffen she looks like me, she ain't purty," and at first glance I wasn't even sure she was human, "so's the bestest thing ye kin do is send her back." We laughed as Mama begun cleanin' her up. By the time I got the second look, I took heart. No, not like her mama, I felt right satisfied. She's got her papa's dark hair and her grandmama's button nose with that big dimple in her chin. John didn't git his son, but look what I got, a right purty little girl named Julie Ann!

Without thinkin' the words popped right out of my mouth. "Mama, do ye think hit's possible that God would call a woman to go out into the world and preach the gospel?"

"Aulene, ye do have the strangest notions. And that ain't one that the elders of our church would find favorable."

"And why not, Mama? Some of Jesus's best friends were women like Mary and Martha. They stood by him at the cross and waited fer him at the tomb. Ye told me so, yerself, Mama. Ain't hit true that some of 'em took the good news that Jesus was gone from the tomb to the disciples? I always thought that a Christian could tell the good news of Jesus to any body that come along."

"What has come over ye, child? Ye must be a bit out of yer head with all the hard work of bornin' this here baby. Though I will say to ye in confidence that I've had the same thoughts throughout my own life. But to keep the peace and not git the menfolk riled up, I reckon hit's best iffen us womenfolk turn the matter over to the Lord and let Him deal with hit in His own good time. As fer ye, Aulene, ye need yer rest. Tomorrow will be yer first day as a mama in yer own right. I'll be here with ye fer a day or so, but from here on out, life's goin' to be mighty different."

And in more ways than she could have foretold, my mama was as usual right as the rain that was a comin' down o'er our heads.

Soon me and Julie Ann was snuggled down in the bed, as Mama snoozed in front of the fire, all three of us plumb wore out. The sun was long gone behind the horizon.

Then John come a bustin' in the house, shoutin' at the top of his lungs, "Whar's that new Puckett boy? Whar's my son?" I woke to see him peerin' down at me, the baby in my arms. "Is that our baby?" he asked, and I wondered iffen he'd been in the whiskey agin.

"Hit ain't a son, John. Hit's a little girl. I'm namin' her Julie Ann. I hope ye ain't disappointed."

"No, I ain't disappointed, Orlene, and I'm right proud of ye fer givin' me this sweet looking child. Thar's enough Puckett men in these parts. A little girl will make us proud and give us reason to spoil her in a special way. Thank ye fer bein' here, Mother Hawks. Yer daughter's full of spunk, I kin tell ye that fer sure, and I reckon ye're responsible fer Orlene Hawks turnin' into the finest wife and mother to be found in these parts."

"I was sure I was hearin' the whiskey talkin', but John's words was balm fer my wore out body and soul. Maybe John was a hard man at times, but fer that minute I knowed fer sure that he had a good heart and would take care of me and our new baby."

October 7, 1939

SOMEONE WAS SAYIN' MY NAME but fer the life of me I couldn't seem to open my eyes. I wasn't sure whar I was or what time of day hit was. I was tryin' to lift my arms to push myself up from my bed, but my arms didn't seem to be workin'. The voice was comin' closer and I thought I knowed the person speakin to me. Confused, I could not say whether I was awake or dreamin'.

"Aunt Orlene, are ye alright? Hit's yer niece, Tavia. Ye've been asleep goin' on thirteen hours and I've been a frettin' over ye. Are ye dry? Do ye need to use the chamber pot? I don't think ye kin make hit to the outhouse even iffen I kin help you git up from the bed."

"I ain't a child and I ain't a invalid, Tavia. What I am is tired—tired of livin', tired of bein' old, tired of bein' a burden to ye and yer family, and tired of the racket that's bein' made whar that road is a goin'. Iffen I want to sleep thirteen hours or fifteen or even twenty-four, hit ain't no one's concern 'cause by my reckonin', hit won't be long 'fore I'll be a sleepin' right through eternity, and I've heerd that's a mightly long time."

"Aunt Orlene! That sounds like blasphemy to me! Ye're supposed to be a Christian and believe in the resurrection. We ain't goin' to be sleepin' in heaven; we'll be walkin' with Jesus and askin' God the questions we couldn't git no answers to down here, and in the in-between times, we'll be holdin' reunions with all the kinfolk that's gone on 'fore us. Don't ye believe in yer own resurrection, jest like Jesus come back from the dead after He was crucified and placed in that tomb? Ain't ye grateful that ye've been saved and whenever yer time comes, you will be with Jesus in heaven?"

"Yes, I do believe, and I am lookin' forward to seein' Mama and Papa and my brothers and sisters and each one of my precious children when I finally cross over the world that's waitin' fer me. Thar is one part of the business that's worrisome fer me and that's meetin' up with John Puckett in heaven. Iffen John Puckett kin make hit into heaven, hit raises the question in my mind as to the Lord's judgment when hit comes to the character of a man and I ain't so sure I want to be thar myself!"

"Aunt Orlene!" Tavia was so het up she was sputterin' forth words that did not make no sense. By this time, I was a laughin' at the way I had pulled that girl's leg. She shook her finger at me. "Iffen ye had not already wet yerself when ye woke up, hit's fer sure I'm goin' to have to change yer bed 'fore ye git back in hit come evenin.'"

Hit took a while fer Tavia to git me cleaned up and the bed changed. "I reckin ye'll have to be puttin' diddies on me from this time on. One minute ye're a child growin' up, the next minute ye're a growed woman havin' yer own babies, then the next thing ye knowed ye're a baby agin, without a tooth in yer head, crawlin' around 'cause ye cain't stand up straight, wettin' yerself and dependin' on whoever happens to be around to tend to yer needs. I don't like hit much, Tavia. I'm mighty obliged to ye fer takin' me in but I'm mighty sorrowful that I'm causin' ye so much trouble. How long have I been here with ye? Time seems like one big blur, one minute runnin' into the next and the hours are either too slow or too fast. I've done lost cost of the days jest the same as I lost count of all them years that's gone past. Hit's hard gittin' old, Tavia. Take my word fer hit and avoid hit like the plague iffen ye kin. A hot biscuit with a cup of coffee would do me fine about now, if hit ain't too much trouble. Then we kin start in on what took place after Julie Ann was borned iffen I'm recollectin' whar we left off last."

"One thing at a time, Aunt Orlene, one thing at a time. That rest of yers surely did put ye in a talkin' mood. Ye've been here with me almost two weeks as of yesterdy. As fer ye a bein' touble to me, I ain't goin' to hear no more about hit. Ye're company to me with my children scattered to the four corners of the earth and not seein' any one of 'em more'n a few times or so durin' the year. While ye're tellin' yer stories, I'm larnin' about the history of these here mountains and the families that settled in these parts. The past may well be surroundin' us but hit's fast disappearin' from memory as well as from sight. Outsiders is a crowdin' in and children growin' up without a sense of what hit was like to work the land and live as hard as our ancestors and us had to live.

"Ye talk about how hit is to turn old and feeble but the truth, Aunt Orlene, as ye well know, is that we ain't in control of our own destiny as far as how many years the good Lord portions out to us. When the day comes that we've outlived our usefulness to Him and to others, He will call us home. I'm countin' on him givin' me enough time to write down what you have to say so's I kin pass hit on to the Hawks and Puckett families and the other families that ye helped in their time of need.

"As fer whar we left off when we was havin' our last talk, and fer the record hit was yesterday mornin' right after ye had a bowl of hot grits

{ *October 7, 1939* }

and yer coffee, yer baby Julie Ann had made her appearance with the help of yer mama. Then John had come home from huntin' with his brothers to discover that he was the proud daddy of a little girl."

"Well, Tavia, here's my recollection of what come to pass after Julie Ann was borned in September of eighteen hundred and sixty-two. That is one year that is fixed as firm in my head as any of the others that have come and gone. Mama stayed with us for four or five days, makin' sure that I had my strength back and the baby was healthy and gittin' enough nourishment. Sech was common practice in them days. Whether hit was a granny woman or a mama, a neighbor or other relative, a new mother and her baby was not left until hit appeared to be certain that both was in good health and thrivin'.

"John appeared to be takin' his new responsibility of being a daddy right serious and Mama told me 'fore she left, 'That young husband is comin' along faster than I thought possible bein' that Sarah Puckett has spoiled him to death. See to hit that he keeps away from the whiskey, though. Hit has a way of poisonin' a man's brain and bringin' out a mean streak in some of 'em. I ain't sayin' hit's true fer 'em all. I ain't never seed yer papa drunk nor one of yer brothers. They's been brought up with a healthy respect fer theirselves and what liquor kin do and they control their appetites fer hit, but hit ain't the same fer some of the men. John comes from a hard-drinkin' family, but he's got a good heart. Keep him away from the wild ones and he'll be a good husband to ye and a up-standin' papa to his children.'

"I thanked Mama fer her advice and her kindness to me and my new baby. She left me with a store of provisions, clothes fer the baby, and a bright and shinin' clean house. Supper was cookin' on the stove when one of the neighbor men headin' to Rocksburg come by to pick her up in his wagon. We said our goodbyes with brave smiles while the tears flowed freely. Hit was always hard when family visits would come to the end because travel was hard in them days due to long distances, rough roads, if a body could call 'em roads, and few means of transportation. Ye might be able to make two or three miles in a hour's time by foot, if the weather was kind to ye and the road well traveled and not too steep goin' up or down. A horse or mule might git ye thar in half or a third of the time and a wagon in good shape might do better or worser, dependin' on how many was in the wagon or iffen goods or crops was loaded into hit. Regardless, five or six miles could put a heap a distance atween family members. We was never sure when we took our partin' when or under what circumstances we would be together agin.

"As I stood in the doorway holdin' Julie Ann, Mama turned and waved one more time 'fore the wagon headed down the hill. I looked down at my baby with the sudden realization that I was no longer a young bride, unlarned in the ways of the world. I was a growed up woman with a child of my own, livin' not only in a place still strange to me with neighbors and relatives of John's that I hardly knowed, but I was also livin' in a dark time fer the land I loved so dear, with danger and uncertainty closin' in tighter ever' day and night.

"Julie Ann was not even one month old the day that John busted in the door carryin' a old gunnysack over his shoulder, hustlin' and bustlin' about, throwin' clothes and food from the cupboard into the sack:

"Whar's them wool socks ye done knit fer me last winter?" John shouted at me. "Is thar any fatback in the smoke house?"

I was holdin' Julie Ann to my breast, tryin' to nurse her and keep her from cryin' through the racket he was a makin', all the time a followin' him around and askin', "What are ye doin', John? What's this ruckus about? Ye're makin' sech noise as to scare the baby. The milk will turn on her iffen she's upset while she's a nursin'. Set down a spell and tell me what's happenin.'"

"I'll tell ye what's happenin'. The Yankees is a makin' a show of headin' this way. Word has come to the 50th Infantry to git ourselves over to Blacksburg and turn 'em around from these parts. Me and the boys is leavin' as soon as we kin git our gear together. I need warm garments and enough food fer a couple of days until we kin set up the encampment and ready ourselves fer battle." John's face was as red as fire. His voice bellowed through the little house like a raging bull. Julie Ann was cryin' at full force while I was tryin' to take in John's words.

"John," I pleaded, "we got a new baby. She ain't even a month old. Winter's comin' on and the crops ain't in yet. Ye ain't even started cuttin' the firewood fer the cold weather. The colt ain't weaned and ye and the neighbors is supposed to be butcherin' the hogs in a week or so. How kin ye be leavin' today? Ye cain't jest go off like this without no warnin' nor no preparations fer gittin' yer wife and yer child through the winter.

"So many menfolk done left these parts fer the war, John. Why, thar's farms all about with just womenfolk and children left to do the chores and take care of the animals. What are we supposed to do with the husbands and brothers, uncles and cousins gone off and not knowin' when they's goin' to be back? When the war started, ye men was tellin' ever'body that would listen that hit would be over in six months—six months!—and hit's into the second year with things gittin' worser and worser. I cain't believe ye're up and leavin' yer wife and new baby with winter comin' on. Hit don't seem like the Christian thing to do, John Puckett!"

"Hell fire and damnation, Orlene Puckett! Bein' a Christian and fightin' a war ain't got one thing to do with one another. Hit's my duty to go fight fer my country and my country is Virginia and she's part of the Confederate States of America. That's what ole Robert E. Lee said. Said he couldn't take up arms aginst his Virginia kin and iffen's that's good enough fer Robert E. Lee, hit's good enough fer me!" He slapped fifty Confederate dollars on the table as he headed out the door.

"Whar did ye come by this money, John?" I called after him.

He laughed. "Me and the boys signed up agin two days ago down at Stuart!"

Jest then Churchill and Elijah rode up, pulling another horse behind them. John jumped into the saddle, wheeled the horse around and faced me jest as his two brothers rode up. He tipped his hat to me. "Hang in thar, ole gal," he called out. "Ye'll make hit, Orlene. I know ye will. We'll be back 'fore ye know hit. We're goin' to run them Yankees right over the border into Canada and then us Johnny Rebs will take over the whole god-damn territory so's we won't have to see 'em or live with 'em or have any dealins' with 'em from here to eternity! Take care of yer mama, Julie Ann!"

I didn't so much as git a word out of my mouth 'fore the three of them was gone, leavin' me and my baby alone, with a farm to take care of and winter jest around the corner."

I cain't recall how much of the day that part of the story took fer tellin'. The next thing that come to me was Tavia tuckin' me into the bed as she was a whisperin', "Poor old thing. Ye are plumb wore out with relivin' them hard days after John took off and left ye and Julie by yerselves. A good night's rest will do yer mind and yer body a right smart favor. People's always talkin' about that 'tight-lipped' Aunt Orlene, but I reckon when ye's wound up tight like ye was today, they'd change their minds real fast and see the world in a whole new light to top hit off."

Tavia's voice drifted far, far away until I warn't sure that hit was her voice I'd been hearin'. Maybe hit was the wind rustlin' through the pine trees. Or hit were the doves cooin' on the fence near the spring. Maybe hit warn't nothin' but a dream that would go on and on. Maybe my whole life was one big dream that God was havin' and I was not real flesh and blood but jest a bein' that was part of his imagination.

"Oh, Aulene," I heerd my mama say, "Yer mind ne'er stops workin', does hit? Fer sech a little girl, ye got mighty powerful idees runnin' back and forth in thar, seems twenty-four hours a day. Yer dreams must take ye on some grand adventures, I reckon."

"How do ye know sech, Mama? I ain't ne'er told anybody, not even William, and he loves stories more'n anything in the world. But yer stories are his favorites and he's always tellin' 'em back to me and the neighbor children, so I jest keep mine to myself. Hit's hard to imagine God, ain't hit Mama? That's the hardest thing for me. The next hardest thing is livin'. Sometimes I don't seem to git the meanin' of hit all. Do ye, Mama? I know ye are always sayin' to us that life is life, not matter how ye look at hit, but know what, Mama? Sometimes I cain't bear to look at hit, like when we found the baby deer shot in the head in the meader and sometimes I cain't look at hit hard enough, like the time we come upon the nest of baby mice in the barn and the mother stayed right thar lookin' at us and wouldn't leave her babies 'cause she was afraid somethin' would happen to 'em."

"Child, ye are about to wear me out with yer idees and yer questions, most of which we must figure out fer ourselves as we go through this life. What we cain't figure out, we'll have to wait fer till we git to heaven, when I reckon God can answer each one of 'em to our satisfaction."

"I don't think I kin wait that long, Mama." I could hear myself sayin' the words and hit come to me real clear that the waitin' hadn't been so long after all. As the warmth of the downy feather bed settled down into my cold old bones, a soft voice whispered into my good ear, "Hit won't be long now," and I took comfort in knowing that life and the mysteries that come with hit would soon be clear to me.

The next day and the ones that come after is all fuzzy in my mind. I knowed that Tavia was nearby, takin' care of my needs, preparin' food she thought I might take a likin' to and tuckin' me in at night fer a good night's rest as if I warn't goin' to be restin' enough in the time to come. Time hitself seemed to have lost all meanin'. Thar was no separatin' day

{ *October 7, 1939* }

and night, hours and minutes. So many seasons had done come and gone that I thought of 'em only in terms of colors, bright green fer spring, blindin' yeller fer summer time, bright oranges and reds fer the fall and shiny white fer winter. Even so, hit seemed like my mind was only seein' a faded picture of what had been so dear to me in the days that was long gone.

I could hear my voice talkin' to Tavia recitin' remembrances of the past but the when's or the how long's was no clearer than the creek turned muddy when the thunderstorms sneaked up on us and overflowed the banks, washin' away new planted seeds and bringin' giant old timey trees down to be chopped into firewood. Whether I was sayin' the words out loud or only hearin' the memories in my head, I could not rightly tell, but in one form or the other, the story kept on tellin' hitself in my mind.

After John left, times went from bad to worse. Most of the menfolk had gone off to fight, except fer the old men and young boys, although some boys as young as eleven, twelve, or thirteen would sneak off and join up lyin' about their age 'cause they wanted "in on the action" as they called hit. The women was left to take care of the farms and the children, but they had to work theirselves nearly to death with no men to put in the crops or tend to the animals. The farms went downhill fast and food was hard to come by. Soldiers from both sides was all over these parts. Some of 'em was lost, some was deserters, some was wounded; most of 'em was jest tryin' to make hit back home. They might have fought in a battle or two and that was enough fer 'em to realize that the war wasn't goin' to be endin' any time soon.

Soldiers would come by the farmhouses wantin' somethin' to eat or maybe needin' a wound cared for or a bandage changed. People around these parts helped out however they could. Hit didn't much matter what color uniform a soldier was wearin' iffen that could be decided. The uniforms was so thin and raggedy hit was hard to set one aginst the other but no matter. I ne'er begrudged a person a bit of food. Iffen thar was somethin' on the stove, a piece of cornbread, a cold biscuit or a spoonful of thin soup, that soldier was welcome to share what I had. As time passed and winter was a comin' on, I figured hit would not take long fer my food to run out that was feedin' me so's I could provide milk fer my baby. I took to hidin' food wherever I could think that no one would look, like puttin' eggs in the toes of my shoes or cabbages under the pillers on the bed. Thar was a trapdoor that went down to the cellar whar I had hid some shriveled up apples and root vegetables. Hit was covered by an old rag rug and I prayed ever time one of the soldiers come by the house that no one would suspect that somethin' was hid underneath.

One day two of them Johnny Rebs stopped by and asked if I had anything to eat. I asked 'em to come in and set two bowls of thin soup made from chick peas down in front of 'em. Well, they set thar long after the soup was done gone and after a spell I saw 'em lookin' at me in a way that made my skin start to crawl. My granddaddy's old rifle was hangin' over the fireplace and I knowed how to fire a gun, but I warn't sure I was up to shootin' a human bein' or even if the gun was in workin' order. While all the turmoil was goin' on in my head, Julie Ann started whimperin' in her cradle, so I picked her up, wrapped a blanket about her and told the men that a sickness had been goin' round the farms that caused a high fever, vomitin', and a bad rash and that the baby had seemed feverish and sickly durin' the night. I told 'em that I was goin' to take her out fer some fresh air and walk her about a bit to settle her stomach. 'Fore they could stop me, I was out the door and into the woods behind the house that led down to a outcroppin' of rocks whar I could watch the house without bein' seen. I stayed thar till finally I see'd the two of 'em come out the door and head on down the hill in the opposite direction. I waited till hit was almost dark 'fore takin' Julie Ann back to the house. Onct I was inside, I bolted the door and started gittin' me and the baby settled down fer the night, but I noticed that the quilt my mama had made fer my weddin' day was missin' from my bedstead and the old iron pot that was my grandmama's was gone from the stove. I knowed that times was hard and that people, no matter who they are or whar they're from, will do whatever needs to be done in order to survive. But the things that hold ye to yer family cain't ever be replaced in yer mind or in yer heart. Life is full of sorrowful lessons and whether we like hit or not, thar are days when we have to larn more than what seems to be our rightful share.

October 8, 1939

"WHAT DAY IS HIT, TAVIA? And how many days have I spent with ye here in yer cabin since they took me away from my cabin over thar on the ridge?"

"Lord a mercy, Aunt Orlene! I ain't got ye out of yer bed yet and here ye go askin' the same questions I've been hearin' mostly ever'day since ye come to stay with me. I believe hit's Thursday and hit's been closet to two weeks come this Monday that you've been here in my house, though hit seems no more'n a day or two."

"Have we done gone through the war yet? I cain't recall what I was a tellin' ye jest 'fore I shet my eyes, was hit last evenin'?"

"Ye was talkin' about the hardships ye had to bear after John left ye and Julie Ann to go off and fight once the Yankees started makin' their way towards these parts. The last thing ye told was when them two soldiers come to the house and was a lookin' ye over; ye skidaddled out to the woods with the baby till they left. That was mighty smart thinkin' when ye told 'em about a sickness goin' round amongst the neighbor farms. I reckon hit skeered 'em enough to hightail hit outa thar 'fore they caught whatever hit was. I'll say this much, Aunt Orlene. Folks that knows ye, whether kin or stranger, gives ye credit fer bein' quick on yer feet when hit comes to thinkin' through a problem. 'Ye take Orlene Puckett,' they's always sayin', 'she's as quick-witted as they come. Ain't nobody, not even a man, can outsmart that woman, no sirree.' I've heerd sech fer as long as I kin recall."

"Well, that's right kind of them that thinks so and fer ye to pass along to me, Tavia. No soul on earth knows all thar is to know about any other man or woman that travels this earth. Each person has his own truth, hit seems to me, and the onliest person who knows hit a hunderd percent is the Lord Hisself, since most of us wind up deceivin' our own selves a good part of the ways. I've made mistakes, but they was my own and I ain't goin' to pretend that I ain't been afeard or ashamed or confused or downright ornery when hit comes down to confessin' my sins, but I will tell ye this and be as honest as I know how to be, I was a quick study. I larned my lessons about life from all my fallin' downs 'cause, ye see, I ne'er could stay down. I'd fight as hard as I could to git back up even when one of my brothers knocked me down and threatened to bloody my nose iffen I got up and run to tell Papa. The first time hit happened, I got up all right but I didn't go runnin' off to Papa or to Mama. I jest turned around and slung the biggest rock I could git my hand on right at his privates—I had a right smart throwin' arm—and that was the end of that. From that day on, I reckoned I could take care of myself if and when trouble showed up. Course I own the truth that I ain't in full charge of my life these days, but I'll fight till my last breath to stand on my own two feet and not be a burden though I know fer sure that I am beholden to ye, Tavia."

"Ye've jest about talked the mornin' away, Aunt Orlene, and ye ain't had no breakfast to speak of, one biscuit and a cup of coffee. Hit's sunny and warm outside. Ain't goin' to be many days like this left 'fore winter sets in. Would ye like me to take ye a chair outside in the sun and wrap ye up in yer quilt? Ye kin go on with yer story about how ye made hit through the winter with John gone and I'll write hit down while we're takin' in the sunshine. Ye seem plumb wore out when evenin' comes, so's maybe the mornin' time after ye've done had a night's rest is the bestest time to do the talkin' and the recordin'. Then ye kin take a little nap and I kin do my chores after we've had our dinner and put the leftovers away fer supper. The days is gittin' shorter and seems like I'm ready fer bed almost as soon as the sun sets."

"I reckon ye're ready fer bed from bein' wore out takin' care of this old woman who's settin' here in front of ye. A soakin' of bright sunshine might go a long way in heatin' up these cold old bones. I reckon some fresh air mighten perk me up a bit so's I kin git back to the next happenin' in my story.

"Julie Ann and me somehow made hit through the winter. Then one morning when hit seemed like I could smell spring not far off, I walked out and looked down the path to see an ole man comin' towards the house. He was all bent over, his left arm in a bloody bandage, his clothes all tattered and worn thin. Who is that ole man? I was thinkin'. He don't look like nobody from these parts. He kept on walkin' towards where I was a standin'.

"And then, John Puckett was right there in front of my eyes, lookin' like some poor starvin' animal. 'Orlene, I'm home. I ain't a goin' back.' Then he walked into the house, fallin' dead asleep on the bed. I'd already heared all the rumors about him and his brothers desertin' and runnin' from the Home Guard. Word was passed from farm to farm that John and his brothers was hidin' out in the barn of a farmer who lived four miles or so up toward Floyd. I even managed to send some food by some of the neighbors who was headed that way. When John and his brothers finally made up their minds to make a run fer home, they was so many bullets fired at 'em as they tried to cross the Ararat, the banks of the river collapsed. Even to this day, people won't own up that the Guard would shoot their own not to let 'em desert.

"Knowin' my own husband was a deserter, was I ashamed? All I know is that the war was goin' mighty bad fer the South and most of us had lost everything that could be lost. The men jest wanted to run away from the horrors they seen and endured, not from the duty of fightin' fer their cause. I decided long ago that I could not condemn a body fer what I hadn't lived through and could ne'er understand.

"John tried to stay out of sight, lest somebody turn him into the Home Guard, but the war turned more terrible. Hit seemed that the days of misery and hopelessness was jest beginnin' with a vengeance towards anybody that was in the way. By that time, Julie Ann was six months old, sunny dispositioned, with curly blonde hair and big blue eyes. John and that baby took to one another right smart. At night, he'd hold her on his knee, rocking her to sleep in Grandmama's ole chair with songs we had larned as children. I could of been jealous of my own child as he showed her so more attention than he did me, but I could see the softness comin' back to his face and the burden seemed to be liftin' from his shoulders. I could not deprive my husband of the joy of his little girl.

"But fate ain't in our hands. People is right to admonish us not to go puttin' too much hope in knowin' the future, 'cause if we did, we couldn't stand hit. John had hardly been home a month 'fore the baby took real sick. Her fever went right high and she seemed not to be able to swaller. I sent John to get Mama. When she come the next morning, she took one look at Julie Ann and said, 'She's got the diptherier. They ain't nothin' to do fer hit but to try to keep the fever down and keep her throat from closin' and pray as hard as ye kin.'

"In spite of everythin' we done, in less than a week our precious baby was dead. I recall wakin' up and seein' her face pale, not flushed with fever. I felt her head and hit was cool to the touch. 'Wake up, John,' I called to him. 'I reckon our baby's done passed the crisis.' But when John stood up and leaned over my shoulder to touch her, he jest shook his head. 'No, she's gone, Orlene. She's gone.'

"I couldn't take hit in. My precious baby was dead. Then John went out of the house and in a few minutes I heerd hammerin' and sawin' and I knowed that he was building a coffin fer my baby. He come in later and said he was sendin' word by the neighbors fer the family to meet us the next day at the Baptist church where we was married. John helped me bathe Julie Ann and put her in a little pink dress that Mama had made fer her first birthday. I don't recall the rest of hit, even puttin' on my dress and shoes and walkin' down to the church where we gathered, mostly womenfolk and children, the next noon to put our baby to rest. I couldn't believe hit. The sky was like a crystal blue spring and the air was warm and soft around me. I was tryin' to pray and listen to the scripture, but all I could think was, Lord, how can this be? How can hit be such a glorious day when my heart is breakin' into a hunderd million pieces. I'm about to put my precious baby into that cold, dark ground and she ain't goin' to like hit. When the funeral was over, John called fer me to come on back to the house, but I couldn't go back and see that empty cradle waitin' fer my baby. Instead, my mama took my hand and I followed her and Papa back to the farm where I had spent happier days. They left me alone to grieve in my own way but whoever come into this world knowin' how to grieve? We have to do the bestest we kin to work through the emptiness that takes over our hearts and our souls.

"When winter seemed about spent, Mama chided me to head on home and be a wife to my husband, as I wasn't the only one that had lost a child. I was hoping that our grief would bring John and me together, but he was tore up inside and couldn't stop drinkin' whiskey. I remember when ever'thing came to a head."

> One evening at supper, he banged his cup down and demanded more whiskey.
> "Don't you think you've had enough, John?"
> "No I ain't had enough. I need somethin' to take my pain away!"
> "And what about me" What do I have to make my pain go away?"
> "I'll give ye somethin' to make the pain go way," he yelled, "and iffen that ain't enough, thar's more where that come from." Then he jumped up and hit me in the face, knockin' me to my knees, as he headed out the door.

"After that, I didn't see him agin fer near to a year. But we wasn't the only ones who had suffered the loss of someone they loved. Most families lost kinfolk. Husbands, fathers, brothers, even grandfathers died in the war. The ones that come back was wounded and maimed. Ye didn't want to see them, some blind, some deaf. One young'un lost both his hands when the cannon misfired. Some made hit home only to die in their beds. The womenfolk had to do the nursin' and buryin', while tryin' to feed their families after the soldiers come through, takin' the livestock and crops, whatever hit was, fer food. The farms was gone, the land destroyed, families uprooted. Hit warn't a matter of livin' from day to day or hour to hour, hit come down to livin' from minute to minute. I'd go out into the woods, scratchin' in the dirt and leaves fer seeds or acorns that I could mash up and turn into a thin soup or a make-do coffee. I could hear Mama tellin' us to never let the hard times git the best of us, that God would provide. Many a day there was considerable doubt in my mind, but one thing I larned, a human bein' will do jest about anything to survive.

"One day a farmer come up the hill and knocked on my door. 'Orlene, do you think you could plow a field? My son's gone off to the war and we ain't heerd from him fer over five months. My daughter-in-law and her six children is a livin' with me as her papa and mama has been dead many a year now. My mule died three days ago and I need to get a crop of corn in 'fore hit rains. I'll share my last piece of fatback with you if you can get that field plowed.'

"Next mornin' I was in that field 'fore the sun came up, the plow strapped around my waist. I finished sometime 'fore the stars come out. The ole man appeared, carryin' a piece of meat no bigger than my palm. When he started to cut hit in half, I said, 'No, jest cut off the end. Hit'll do with some beans my mama brung me.' He was old. I was still young and strong enough to hold out a little longer.

"When the food was gone, Mama and Papa, who didn't have much theirselves, come to my rescue. By the end of winter, the South was in hits death throes. Nothin' could change the fact. When I looked at the ruined farms and starvin' friends and family of my childhood, I thought, I could've told ye so. Any of us women could've done told ye the truth about war and hits doin's. Some of the women that knowed readin' and writin' wrote to both Abraham Lincoln and Jefferson Davis beggin' fer their husbands to be let go so's they could come home and put in a crop to feed their children. One of the neighbors read her letter to me, sayin' that her and the children was starvin' and that iffen her husband didn't come back real soon, he'd find his whole family dead. She was cryin' so pitiful the whole time she was a readin' hit to me, I broke down and cried right alongside of her. But who was listenin' to the wives, mothers, sisters, and sweethearts of all them poor men, young and old, who was bein' shot up and killed from one end of the country to another? No one. When menfolk take the first step to go to war, others will follow …until ever last one is gone.

"I wisht I could of wrote hit down, but my eyesight was poor, so I could hardly read my own name much less put hit in writin'. Even if I could a done the writin', when would I of had the time? There was no time in them days to spend on a person's own wants. Them days was about survivin' and I ain't jest talkin' about the men that joined up to fight. I'm talkin' about the old folks, the children, and the women that was left behind to take care of 'em, hopin' and prayin' all the while that a body with some sense would put a end to the killin' and the maimin', the thievin' and burnin' of houses and crops that brought us to our tables hungry and to our beds cold and desperate. Between times, hit brought us to our knees, but we didn't stay long 'cause the children and the animals was starvin' and everything else fallin' apart.

"Don't be tellin' me about all the glory and honor. I don't want to hear no more lies. Them that talks about sech ain't seen the truth 'cause I lived hit. When ye been in the midst of all the horror and pain, hit comes out different. If a woman's done seen her papa, her brother, or husband go off to war, she knows in her heart they ain't no reasonin' behind hit. If she's seen him comin' home without his hands or a leg or arm, she knows fer sure what's real and what's jest pretend on the outside. If she's watched some stranger comin' up the hillside with a body slung over a broken down ole nag, she has the right to scream and rail mighty long and strong at the powers that be. And mark my words, if she's washed and cleaned that mangled body that nobody else recognizes, she has the right to keep on making her voice heard, even if hit falls away to a bare whisper, as long as there's breath left in her body, though nairy a soul be listenin'.

"Another winter was a comin' and I had no food left. One more time I made the trek back to the farm in Rocksburg. I walked most of the way till a old man with a broken down mule and wagon picked me up and carried me part of the way. Mama and Papa didn't have much food left fer theirselves but they shared what they had with me. The boys had left their farms to go off to fight and their wives had gone back to live in their own homes.

{ *October 8, 1939* }

"I was angry and bitter over the loss of my baby and John's leavin'. Whar he was and what he was a doin', nobody knowed or iffen they did know, they warn't a tellin'. One day my sour disposition got hold of me and I brought up the subject of John and his disappointin' ways:

"John'll ne'er be the man Papa is," I noted as we set 'fore the fire, tryin' to draw some warmth from broken limbs that had come down in a wind storm. Mama put forth her usual Bible-based optimism.

"I know ye're hurtin', Aulene, but some good will come out of this. Jest wait and see."

"Oh, Mama, people always said ye had the sight, but this time I'm a thinkin' hit's failed John and me."

"Hold on, child. Have patience. This ain't no time to be bringin' children into the world. Ye and John are young still. Ye have plenty of time to have that family when times is better. Wait and see."

"I'm tired of waitin', Mama. Fer all I know, John Puckett is dead or run off out West to start a new life. What does that leave me but a plain widow with no skills or prospects, bein' that most of the young men are dead or maimed, some beyond even knowin' what they look like or who they belong to." I was in no mood fer someone to be tryin' to lighten up the darkness that had done took over my soul.

"Listen to me, Aulene. Here is God's truth, whether ye want to accept hit or not. The sun is always in that sky, even if ye cain't see hit fer the clouds, the fog, or the rain. The sun is goin' to shine agin one of these days, even down to the deep part of that dark soul of yers."

How did my mama know the battle that was goin' on inside of me? But she always knowed me fer what I was and ne'er did she give up on me, even when I come down so hard on myself wallerin' in my own doubts. One mornin' I woke up and smelled spring in the air, though hit seemed a far distance away. I washed my face, put on my dress and shoes and headed into the kitchen.

"Iffen I could have me a bit of breakfast, I reckon I'll be headin' back to the house. Maybe the rains will hold off a bit and I kin start plowin' up the summer garden."

Mama give me a bag of vegetable seeds to take with me, though I was wonderin' if the soil had any life left to nurture another generation. I spent the night with some of the neighbor folk since hit was a good two days' walk back to the foothills of the Blue Ridge. Comin' up the hill later the next afternoon, I spied a figure, hoe in hand, working the garden. John Puckett turned and throwed up his hand. "Orlene, I'm home. Get on up here, woman. There's greens growin' on the hillside, a bag of meal is there on the table with four eggs from a nest out in the field. Ye can make a man some dinner, cain't ye? No time to waste, Orlene. We've got a family to be startin'."

I never asked him whar he had been or what he had done while he had been gone. Some folks said he had gone to Gettsyburg with the 50th Virginia Infantry and that he had come back after the battle determined not to fight ever again. I ain't sure about that 'cause he never told me nothin' about hit, but I know whatever hit was that he witnessed, hit left hits mark on him fer the rest of his life.

Maybe the war was finally over but one thing seemed fer sure. The weariness would linger fer a mighty good spell. And somethin' seemed to be whisperin' in my head that there was other battles we'd have to fight waitin' somewhere over the top of the next hill.

By the time I come to the end of that part of the story, I was feelin' like I'd fought in that war myself, drained and battle weary from hunger, no sleep, and the constant sounds of rifles and cannons firin', men and horses screamin' from pain and tryin' to run from death. In my head I was hearin' John's words when he come home 'fore Julie Ann died. He was wore out and turned into a broken old man way 'fore his time.

"I cain't do no more talkin' about the war today, Tavia. Hit hurts this old heart of mine to be goin' over hit agin. Let me jest set here fer a bit and rest. I'll have me my supper early and go on to bed, iffen ye won't be mindin'."

"Aunt Orlene, ye know what is fer yer own good. I ain't plannin' to make hit wearisome fer ye to find yer way to the past. Ye rest there fer a spell and when ye're up to hit, we'll have us some supper. I'll fix up yer bed and ye kin sleep all ye need. When tomorrow comes, ye kin make up yer own mind what ye want to tell and when ye want to tell hit."

"Ye're a good and kind woman, Tavia. I reckon thar ain't a body around that would do fer me what ye're doin'."

"Oh, I reckon that ain't so, Aunt Orlene. Us kinfolk done wrote our names on slips of paper to draw the one who would have the honor of takin' ye in when they come to move ye from yer cabin."

"Well, hit pleasures me to know that when ye're tired of takin' care of this old woman, thar's another one or two standin' by who'd be willin' to put up with me fer a day or so. But I ain't plannin' to live forever, and ye kin pass the word on to the others iffen ye've a mind to do so."

"The world ain't goin' to be the same without you, Orlene Puckett. Ain't nobody that I've heerd of ready to see ye go. Hit'll be a mighty sad day fer yer kinfolk and neighbors when the Lord calls ye home and that's fer certain, but we ain't goin' to talk about this no more this day. I have chores to do and ye're needin' to rest up so's we kin git back to the recallin' of them long past days."

"One thing's fer certain, Tavia, the past is clearer to me right now than what happened yesterday. I cain't recall the day of the week or even this year that we're livin' fer the life of me. I don't recall how old I am today or even iffen I've had me my breakfast. The days since I left my cabin seem to have been swallered up in a fog, like them that follers the ridges of the mountains. But the memories of my growin' up days and bein' married to John, livin' through the war, losin' my babies, why, they's clear pictures painted in strong colors on my mind. They ain't ne'er goin' to leave me as long as I have a breath left. Iffen I could only write the words that goes with all them pictures, I could leave this earth with no regrets. Maybe that's why yer name was on that paper. Hit's up to ye, Tavia, to put the words to the memories stored in this old head."

October 9, 1939

"Are ye awake, Tavia? Are ye up?"

"Land's sakes, Aunt Orlene, I've been up since the first rooster crowed his wake-up call. The coffee's on the stove and hot biscuits in the oven. My pencil and paper is layin' thar on the table ready to commence with this mighty important piece of history that we're workin' on fer the world to read and marvel at."

"Don't be makin' fun of me. Jest git me up and open the door so's I kin go outside fer my mornin' business. Ye kin put my breakfast thar on the table so's we don't waste no time dilly dallyin' about."

"Ye ain't been outside fer three or four days now. Ye've been usin' the pot right thar aside of the bed."

"Might be so, but the sun is shinin' iffen I ain't mistook whar all the brightness done come from. I've a hankerin' to hear a bit of hymn singin' from the birds, so's I'm headin' out fer a little talk with the Lord. I'll be back in a short time, don't ye worry none except as to whar we was when we left off our talkin' yesterdy."

"Ye was sayin' how hit was when John come back from the war. Ye was glad that John had come home and the war had come to the end, even iffen hit meant that the Confederate States had lost the war and had to be pulled back into the Union. Course I understand how some folks ain't ne'er got over the whole thing, even after so many years has done passed. Them's the ones that walk around with their heads in the sand, thinkin' to theirselves that the South is goin' to rise agin. Then they kin have ever'thing their way without nobody tellin' 'em what to do or how they's supposed to behave, especially when hit comes to loyalty to their kinfolk and the place they come from. Seems like some jest cain't let go of the past and move on to the hope that the future might offer. How do ye see hit, Aunt Orlene? I know I ain't got the wisdom or the common sense that ye are knowed fer, but am I makin' some sense?"

"Ye got as many smarts as the next person, Tavia. Don't be hard on yerself 'cause others will be hard enough in dealin' with ye. That's what Mama always told us children. As fer the past, I kin see hit both ways. Life can put ye through some mighty terrible times so's hit's right easy to keep lookin' back and thinkin', though ye know hit's plumb foolish, that somehow what happened to tear yer world apart warn't true or that ye'll wake up and find hit was jest a bad dream. I've been thar and I've done my share of wishin', hopin', and a prayin' but in the end nothin' changes or kin be changed. We keep ourselves tore up with vain regrets, as Mama called 'em, and stay bogged down in our sins and sorrows till we ain't of no use to one person, not to ourself or to the ones we love or who love us.

"I was prayin' ever'day durin' the war when John was away that the Lord would take care of him and send him home to me. We could start over, bring the farm back to life, and have us a family. Still I will confess to ye, Tavia, that iffen I could of knowed what the future would bring after John come back, I ain't sure that I would not have prayed that the Lord would take me on home to be with Him. Hit was not in me to pray that harm of any kind would come to another human bein', least of all John Puckett. Course some might have been so unkind as to say that John was deservin' of whatever hardship or punishment that the Lord sent his way, seein' that he had not walked the straight and narrow path, along with havin' done harm to his wife as well. I was never one to air my troubles to the world but hit was common knowledge in these parts that John took his fists to me from time to time, mostly after a bout of heavy drinkin', and commenced to brag about hit to his brothers and any ne'er do well that would listen.

"Ain't nobody alive who don't know the stories about all the Puckett babies that died down thar at the foot of the mountain as well as the four that is buried up here on top of the Groundhog. One by one they come into this world and one by one they left in a hurry. They was some that lived a day or two, some that lived a few weeks. Three or four of 'em was dead right when they come from my body. Others, maybe five or six, was what was called misconceptions. They wasn't complete in their human form so's we didn't even know whether they was a boy or a girl. Not a one of them babies lived as long as Julie Ann and she was jest about seven months old when she died.

"The first one that come along after Julie Ann was another girl. I called her Matilda after my mama, but she lived only three weeks. Then come a boy. John was mighty proud that he had hisself a son and named him Jacob, after his papa. That baby was gone in six days, but we kept tryin' and hopin' that the bad luck that was follerin' us would git tired of houndin' us and move on elsewheres. But nothin' could drive hit away, not my prayin' nor John's cussin'.

"Ever' time one of them died, hit would seem like I was buryin' Julie Ann all over agin. Hit come to the point that I could not give the baby a name knowin' that death was waitin' round the corner. We put a stone into the ground at the cemetery fer each one, markin' hit 'Baby Puckett' even fer the ones that ne'er become a complete human bein'. I don't have the words to describe what I endured durin' them years I was workin' so hard to have my own baby. There was one of the misconceptions that come near the end and my womb was so mangled and wore out, hit come out of me and I used all the strength I had to push hit back into my body so's I could have one more hope of keepin' my own child to raise.

"But hope run out time after time. I knowed that John was goin' through some sufferin' on his part since his brothers and sisters was havin' young'uns right and left. I done told ye that John was not a man fer talkin' through his troubles. No, he'd go after the jug of whiskey and try to drown his sorrows in drinkin' and carousin' around with his brothers. Sometimes the heavy drinkin' would turn hits way towards me and I'd have to run away from his bad temper and his fists. I took many a beatin' fer a long time and others, even John's folks, knowed about hit, but I managed to keep the secret from my mama and papa since they was a good distance from whar we was a livin'.

"Do ye know, Tavia, and I'm sure that ye do, that folks around startin' gossipin' about John hurtin' our babies. Some come out puttin' me in the business of bringin' harm to the children in one way or another. Why that come about I cain't say. Seems like people will start a rumor and keep on addin' to hit when they ain't nothin' else to do, as iffen they ain't enough work on a farm with raisin' a family to keep most folks from mischief. Still they's always one or two that makes hit their business to mind the business of others, whether they know the truth of the matter or not. I kin hear the words in my head right this day that one of John's cousins reported back to me after the death of our tenth child, a boy that come out lookin' pink and healthy but died within three days. 'People are sayin' that iffen ye want to see the new Puckett baby, ye better git over to the house 'fore John gits home.' I asked him what he meant. 'I don't want to hurt yer feelin's, Orlene, but the word is that John is smotherin' them babies right after they's born 'cause he's afeard that they's goin' to die anyways and he don't want ye to git too attached to one of 'em.'

"I could not sanction that a body could be so cruel, Tavia, not fer the life of me. But after I had me three misconceptions in a row over the next four years, Mama come up from the farm to stay with me fer a visit and said that one of the neighbor women related to her that folks was tellin' that I was makin' up potions to kill the babies 'fore they was borned. I cain't hardly convey to ye how sech talk wounded not only my heart but went down into the depths of my soul. I suffered heartbreak from losin' each of my babies and then suffered more from the meanness of so-called Christian folks who should of knowed better than to keep on hurtin' a person with the hard lashes of words that come from evil intentions.

"Still I kept on believin', and I knowed that some would call hit foolishness, that the Lord was with me in ways I could not determine or hope to understand. Mama's words come back to me over and over to not give up and to have faith that He would show me in His own time how my sufferin' could lead me to the purpose He had laid up in store fer me. Keepin' them thoughts in my head warn't never easy fer me, I will confess to ye. They kept me from losin' my faith and my mind so's I could hang on through them days when I was thinkin' that life weren't worth the livin' and I wanted to die with my babies that couldn't live.

"Aunt Orlene, durin' them years that ye was havin' the babies was thar help fer ye when yer time was near? Was thar a granny woman at the foot of the mountain whar ye and John was a livin'? Ye borned me, I was told, and right many of the folks livin' up in these parts, but how did women make hit through bearin' a child, or havin' a misconception, as ye call hit, in them days so long ago? Seems to me us womenfolk was mighty ignorant of sech things, when ye come down to hit. I kin attest that the home remedies and ways of helpin' the process along was out thar in abundance but hit does seem from my own memory that catchin' a baby, as people offen calls hit, was fer the most part a hit-or-miss proposition."

"Thar's truth to that fer sure. Mama come to be with me fer many of the births, iffen word come to her in time or the weather allowed fer hit. Womenfolk mostly took care of one another. We was brought up on farms and the ways of animals, of how the young come to be borned. Life and death was part of one another. Sometimes a family would send us off to be with other kinfolk or a neighbor when a mama was expectin' a new brother or sister and then bring us back home to admire the baby as if hit had been dropped off on the doorstep, but children are smarter and understand more about the mysteries of life than most give 'em credit fer. Iffen ye growed up on a farm, the secrets of the birds and the bees, as they call hit these days, ain't so secret as far as I kin tell.

"As fer helpin' git the baby into the world, ever' woman had her own methods, handed down from one generation to the next, grandmama to mama to daughter, over and over. Iffen one thing, sech as puttin' a knife under the mattress to cut the pain, appeared to do the trick, the next woman would swear by that. A granny woman might use snuff or a feather to git a girl to a sneezin', hopin' the force would push the baby out. So on and so on. One would say how sech and sech would work. Another mama or grandmama would tell how the women in her family would do this or that to help the birthin' along. Iffen hit happened that a baby come along soon after, why hit was took to be a remedy fer passin' on to the next generation.

"Even though ever' one of my babies that come out whole died, some come easy. Some took mighty hard work. One or two of 'em brung me two or three days and nights of sech pain and misery I was fer sure that I was a dyin'. The misconceptions come along at different stages of the expectin' time. The longer I carried each baby, the greater was my hope that the child would survive. I ne'er gave up hopin', Tavia, not even after the last one was buried up here on the mountain. Time jest run out fer me and I had to accept the fact onct hit was made plain to me that bein' a mama to my own child wasn't part of God's plan.

"I think that's enough story tellin' fer one day. Whatever ye're cookin' on that stove does smell right good to this old nose of mine even iffen my appetite ain't what hit uset to be. I'll have me a bite to eat and then have a little nap while ye go about doin' yer chores. I need to rest up a bit after birthin' all them children. I'm feelin' a mite stronger today. If the good Lord is willin', I'll make hit to one hunderd years to spite all them gossipy people that told sech meanness about John and me. The Lord has his own way of gittin' even, Tavia. We best not forgit hit ain't in our hands."

October 10, 1939

"HIT'S COLDER'N YESTERDY this mornin', Aunt Orlene. We'll jest keep ye wrapped up tight right thar in front of that fire after ye done used the pot. I'll bring yer breakfast to ye, some hot grits and a biscuit. When you've a mind to talk a bit we'll take up whar ye left off talkin' about havin' yer babies that didn't live. It seems to me that a body ne'er gits o'er sech grief. I reckon hit's been the same with ye. Iffen sech had been my lot in life, I think I would of jest laid down one day and willed myself to die."

"Ye kin will hit all ye want, Tavia, but iffen hit ain't what the Lord's got in his mind, hit ain't goin' to happen. I dreamed about movin' up to this mountain durin' the night. Hit was as clear to me as the sky is bright this mornin'. Course I ne'er wanted to leave the foot of the mountain fer the top of the ridge but onct John had his mind made up, thar was no turnin' his sight from follerin' what he called his dream. I kin recall that day some ten years after the war was over and recollect his words to me jest as iffen hit was yesterday.

"I was headin' out to the garden to dig taters to put up in the celler when John come ridin' up towards the house, a shoutin' my name:

"Orlene, Orlene, these is the last taters ye'll be diggin' on this spot of ground, I'm a tellin' ye. Come spring, we's headed to the top of Groundhog to start a new life up on the Blue Ridge!"

He was a whoopin' and a hollerin'. A body could of heerd him all the way to the Buffalo! Swooped down from the horse and grabbed me by the waist, pickin' me right off the ground and swingin' me from side to side like some wild Injun on the warpath.

"Stop, John!" I yelled and started kickin' at him, but he jest laughed all the more while he was a huggin' me and peckin' at my face like a riled-up hen.

"Put me down," I squealed, but he seemed to take my protests as a license to keep on tormentin' 'me. I changed my tactics by implorin' him to show some concern fer the new baby that was a comin' in the spring.

"By springtime, honey, this baby will be wakin' up in a brand new cabin on top of the mountain built strong enough fer the mightiest winds that ever a body did see. Papa and the boys is already workin' up thar. I bought over two hundred acres near what they call Strawberry Ridge. They's fellin' the trees fer the logs and clearin' the land fer the crops we'll be plantin'. This son of mine is goin' to live, I'm sure of hit, and we'll have a new life together right up thar at the top of the mountain." He pointed straight up in the direction of the mountain that could not be seen fer the fog that covered the hillside.

But the dream was his'n, not of my choosin'. I didn't want no part of hit and I told him so onct he set me down on the ground and my breath come back to me. Anger was boilin' up inside of me and I could not hold hit back. Fer the most part I am a person of mild disposition but iffen ye git me to stewin' over a matter, I kin be right hard to handle. At least that's what my papa uset to tell folks. On occasion, when I stood up to John, he'd say a cuss word or two that I ain't repeatin', pull off his hat, throw hit on the floor, and go stompin' out the door.

"That woman is more'n I kin bear," he would mutter over and over, whilst I was thinkin' the very same words about the man who was my husband.

"What are ye sayin', John Puckett? That ye're takin' me to live on top of that mountain, the one we cain't see hardly more'n a few days out of the year fer all the fog and clouds that creep over and around, keepin' hit out of sight. Have ye looked up thar? When hit snows, hit don't go away. When the storms come, the trees is twistin' and turnin' and the winds they are a howlin' like wolves hungry fer a kill, which they well might be, along with coyotes and bears and bobcats and sech. All kinds of wild beasts are a roamin' them mountains. Hit's a wilderness up thar. How near will my closest neighbor be?" I was a gittin' more whiney and pitiful as my thoughts come pourin' out in words of protest. John managed to sneak in a word or two whilst I was catchin' my breath.

"I ain't sure. Maybe two or three miles. Some of my brothers are already puttin' in crops up thar and they's a farmhouse or two goin' up not all that far from whar they's buildin' our cabin."

I didn't want to hear nothin' about the whole business and as soon as I had my voice back, I picked up on another set of arguments and threw 'em at John.

"My babies is buried down here, at the cemetery near the church where we was married. Ye cain't take me away from my babies, John. I ain't goin' to stand fer hit."

"We need to start over, Orlene. Thar's too much sorrow holdin' on to us down here. This is our chancet to take this new life up to the mountain and give him some clear air to breathe, so's he won't be suffocated by the hardships of the past. This baby will live, Orlene. I kin feel hit in my bones iffen we give him a new beginnin' and let go of the tears we done shed fer his brothers and sisters."

But I wasn't about to give in without another argument or two. "Mama and Papa live over in Rocksburg, almost a day's journey from this place. They ain't gitting no younger, John. They won't be makin' no trips up the mountain iffen we go thar to live. And hit won't be easy fer me to make the time nor the effort to head down their way even when the weather is passable. Don't ye see what ye're doin' to me, John? Ye're takin' me away from my family, from my babies, from the only life I've even knowed to go to a wilderness full of loneliness and danger. I ain't goin', John Puckett. I'll jest lay down and die right here and now. Iffen ye want to take me with ye, ye'll have to carry me or drag me up the mountain. Dead or alive, hit don't make no difference to me. Hit's fer sure I'll be dead by the time I git thar, dead from a broke heart and a mind gone crazy with misery and pain."

John looked at me and shook his head. "Orlene, ye never let up, do ye? Should have been one of them actor persons they's always talkin' about that moves about and puts on shows in some of them big cities like Stuart or Washington or New York City. Ye might have made a name fer yerself with all that play-actin' in yer blood. But hit don't change nothin', ye see, 'cause ye're fergittin' what the Bible teaches about women bein' obedient to their husbands. A woman is s'pose to listen to her husband and do what he says. That's in the Bible and that's how hit's goin' to be, like hit or not. When spring comes, we're loadin' up what's in this here place that we call our home and we're movin' up on top of the mountain. Papa and the boys will have us the beginnin's of a fine cabin that'll be a right smart bigger'n this 'un and we're goin' to live happily ever after jest like all them fairytales yer mama done told ye durin' yer growin' up days."

"Don't go preachin' the Bible to me, John Puckett. My mama was teachin' me Bible stories 'fore I could walk and as fer the fairy stories, they was a lot better'n any one that ye told me all these years. And one more thing fer ye to think on, John. The Bible says that a man is supposed to love his wife the way that Jesus loves the church, and iffen ye loved me, ye wouldn't be takin' me up to the god-forsaken mountain!" I was so mad by that time I was almost spittin' the words at John.

That time John come to have the last word. "Ye's a Puckett and ye've been one fer twenty-some years. Puckett women foller their men, plain and simple. Come spring, after the rains and the floodin' is o'er, I'm a headin' up the mountain and ye'll be with me, along with our new baby."

"So John had his way. In April, we loaded up one of the neighbor's old farm wagons, borrowed a couple of mules, and with the help of our brothers and their wives, we struggled up the mountain. Hit took two whole days 'cause the ground was muddy, the path all warshed out, and the mules was old and not in any mood for heavy pullin'. We had to stop halfway up and make camp fer the night. The men was in foul moods, cussin' the mules and each other. The women was tryin' to keep the children from wanderin' off and gittin' into mischief while fixin' vittles to keep our stomachs full fer the hard work of climbin' the mountain. I cried so hard, thinkin' of leavin' my family and my dead babies behind, I was sick most of them two days, but by the middle of the third day we had made hit to the top of the mountain, I could see the frame of our home, a two-story sturdy log cabin, in a small clearin' right near the crest of Groundhog Mountain.

"John had made his dream come true and I was standin' thar aside of him, but one thing was missin'. Our baby, the son he was so sure of, was not with us. He had been borned too early. We buried him a month 'fore we made our way up the mountain.

"Hit was a right smart cabin, bigger'n the little house, what folks would proclaim to be a shack, whar we was livin' down near Ararat at the foot of the mountain. The logs was made from virgin trees, the trunks as big around as was the height of the tallest man in these parts, one of John's cousins on his mama's side. They was two rooms fer the ground floor, one fer sleepin' and the other fer cookin' and visitin' or jest settin' in front of the fireplace like we's doin' this evenin'. My grandmama's old spinnin' wheel was settin' in the corner and I had a plan to grow me a plot of flax fer spinnin' yarn and workin' hit on a small loom that was put up on one of the kitchen walls.

"They was stairs that took ye to the top with one big room that was divided into another room fer sleepin' and the other space fer storin' goods along with a quiltin' frame that my papa made fer me when we come up to the mountain. John was right proud of that cabin as was his papa and brothers and mine that had come together to build hit fer us.

"We was ready to start a new life up on the mountain. The war was behind us and the farms was comin' back though the workin's seemed as slow as molasses and thar was folks that could not and would not never, as far as I could reckon, accept the fact that the Confederacy had lost the war and no longer was in existence. Still the battles was fought over and over agin whenever menfolk got together and pulled out the whiskey jugs. Hit seemed that John and me had ever'thing we needed to live a good life except fer a family of our own.

"John tried to cheer me. 'She's strong enough to stand up aginst any wind or storm that the Lord sends our way, by God. And she'll be standin' here long after we are dead and gone, Orlene. One of our children will live in this cabin and his children and his children's children on into eternity. I kin see hit in my mind right this minute, Puckett after Puckett takin' his place in the roll call of life. Hit's a grand thing, Orlene, fer a man to build somethin' that will take hits place in the history of the world.'

"His ramblin's was all well and good. I was glad that John Puckett had his dream standin' right in front of him, but my heart carried a burden that I could not put down. I looked at my bright, shiny new home with them sturdy walls and spacious plenty of room fer more'n two people so's once more I prayed as hard as I knowed how that the Lord would allow me the privilege of bein' a mother to my own child:

Lord, jest one livin' baby, jest one. That's all I'm askin' of ye. Jest let him or her, I don't care one way or the other, live to grow up and be a man or woman 'fore John and me passes on. I ain't askin' fer the child to be handsome or purty, or smarter than the next child, or to be a success in the way the world views sech. I ain't askin' fer grandchildren or great-grandchildren to be part of the package. John and me's gittin' too old to put much stock in the years we have left. Ye've been good to us and I ain't complainin' though I know ye're thinkin' I ain't bein' truthful in that matter. Yer word says that hit rains on the unjust as well as on the just, so's all I'm prayin' is that ye'll send us a child, jest as ye send the rain, even iffen we ain't been the Christians ye've called us to be or walked in yer way when ye was expectin' more of us.

Iffen ye've been sendin' punishment our way fer our sins and misbehavin', I think we done been punished enough. I will admit to my own stubbornness and willfulness and I kin testify that John has done his share of follerin' after the ways of the world. Hit's hurtin' him, Lord, even iffen he don't show or talk about hit, that he ain't had no child to bear his name, especially since his brothers and sisters have produced baby after baby, almost at the drop of a hat, fer his mama and papa to brag on and parade around to our friends and neighbors.

I'm askin' ye to give us another chancet to be a family with a child of our own. I understand from the teachin's of my mama and the preachers hereabouts that hit's suppose't to be in yer will as sech but I reckon ye kin make hit yer will if ye want to. I'm askin' this one favor of ye in as humble a spirit as I have in me and I promise, Lord, that I will do my bestest to be yer servant in this place that ye brung us no matter what answer ye send our way. Amen.

October 11, 1939

"Are ye awake, Aunt Orlene? Why hit's almost the middle of the day. Ye've been sleepin' so hard I was afeard to wake ye up, but we need to check yer bedclothes and git ye somethin' to eat though hit's near time fer dinner to be put on the table. Kin ye hear me, Aunt Orlene? Do ye want me to help ye up so's ye kin wash up and put on a fresh nightshirt?"

Tavia's voice seems far off in the distance. I try to say words that would answer her questions but I cain't hear my own voice. The straw mattress under me feels cold and wet. My hands are twitchin' at the covers pulled over me. I strain hard to lift my head from the piller, but I cannot move. A dampness fills the corners of my eyes and trickles down my cheeks. My mouth is hot and dry.

"Are ye tryin' to tell me somethin', Aunt Orlene? Ye're movin' yer mouth but I cain't hear nothin'. Yer niece, Wavy Quesinberry, is comin' over to help me this mornin'. She'll help me git ye cleaned up and yer bed changed. Ye don't seem to have no strength in ye like ye did yesterday. Maybe we need to send fer that doctor that's down thar in Mt. Airy to come and take a look at ye. Ye look mighty pale to me."

Well, of course, I look mighty pale. I'm somewheres atween ninety-nine and 102 years old, dependin' on who's doin' the talkin'. I'm a dyin' right here in front of yer eyes. We're all of us a dyin', Tavia, even ye, ever' day of our lives, but hit don't take hold in our brains till hit's a mite too late to do anything about hit. But thar's more to tell ye 'fore I move on into the next world. Movin' up here to the mountain ain't the end of my story.

"What's that ye're sayin'? Somethin' about movin' to the mountain? Ye need to conserve yer strength, Aunt Orlene. Have yerself a bite to eat. We got time to go on with yer story after ye're cleaned up and rested a bit."

No. Time's a runnin' out fer me. Time ain't on my side and hit ain't on your'n nor anybody's else side fer that matter. We cain't be wastin' our time on what don't amount to a hill o' beans, sech as cleanin' and cookin' and gossipin' with the neighbors. There's work to be done, Tavia. Work to be done fer the Lord. We cain't stop till He's finished with us.

Hit ain't us that does the finishin', Tavia. Hit's the Lord that says, "That's enough. Ye've served yer purpose and I'm takin' ye home." I'm waitin', Tavia, fer the Lord to take me home but hit ain't goin' to happen till He's fer sure onct and fer all that I've served my purpose. Some of this was only said in my mind, but other words found their way aloud.

"Aunt Orlene, ye're mumblin' words that ain't makin' no sense. Ye must be dreamin' though yer eyes is wide open and tears is runnin' down yer cheeks. I wisht I knowed what is goin' on in that head of yers, but hit'll be alright. Wavy will be here in a bit, and we'll git ye cleaned up and comfortable in a fresh-made bed. Here's some broth from that chicken stew I made up fer our dinner. Try to eat a spoonful or two to warm ye up and bring ye more to yer senses."

My senses are servin' me jest fine, thank you, exceptin' fer the fact that I cain't seem to speak loud enough fer ye to hear me or move these old bones around on this hard old bed. Give me some time and I'll be out and about goin' up and down these hills same as I was a doin' the years me and John was a livin' in that cabin o'er the way whar they's a buildin' that new road. With the noise they's a makin', cuttin' the trees, movin' the boulders and bringin' in them new fangled machines to clear a road bed, hit's a wonder a body kin git a good night's rest anywhar's near these parts. I took a breath and said what sounded loud and clear to my ears, "Is my cabin still standin'?"

"What's that ye're sayin', Aunt Orlene? Don't try to talk with yer mouth full. The words come out soundin' like mush."

I'm losin' my patience with ye, Tavia, even iffen ye are John's niece. That ain't no way to be showin' respect fer an elder, correctin' and criticizin' the way I talk. Yer mama should of larned ye better manners.

"Have another spoonful of broth, Aunt Orlene. Yer color's comin' back and I think I detected a word or two that had somethin' to do with yer cabin. They took one of them bulldozer machines to hit three days ago the cousins over that way are sayin'. They's tearin' down a lot of the old outbuildin's and people's heerd from some of the men workin' on the road that they's goin' to be rebuildin' a few of 'em that is of some historical interest. Ain't no uset to frettin' about hit, Aunt Orlene, what's done is done. I myself kin testify that I've heerd yer own mama say many a time to anybody who would listen, 'Hit ain't what hit could be. Hit ain't what hit should be. Hit is what hit is. Hit's best to move on and put the past behind.'"

Quotin' my own mama back to me. Iffen that don't take the cake. Hit ain't that I don't appreciate yer kindness and caretakin', Tavia, but I tell ye the truth, iffen I could git up and clear out of this place, I would be on my way in a flick of my wrist. I reckon ye cain't hear these words neither and hit's jest as well. I don't want to leave no hard feelin's behind when I'm gone and I might as well jest be on my way as far as I'm concerned. Hit pains me to wake up in a cold, wet bed and know that I cain't make hit to the outhouse or the pot on my own. Hit seems I cain't feed myself and I cain't talk so's a body can understand what I'm wantin' to tell 'em. When ye ain't no uset to no one nor to yerself, I reckon hit's time to give yerself over to the Lord and let Him do with ye as He wills. Iffen ye's a listenin' Lord, what I'm prayin' is that ye'll finish up with me, the sooner the better, and take me to be with ye and my family so's I won't burden my niece Tavia and my other kinfolk no longer.

"Wavy's here, Aunt Orlene, and we's goin' to git ye up, clean ye up a bit, and put ye in a fresh nightshirt to set thar 'fore the fire whilst we change yer bedclothes and fluff up that mattress and yer pillers. Kin ye hear me talkin' to ye? She's been sleepin' most of the past two days, Wavy, and she ain't hardly eat a thing, part of a biscuit, a spoonful or two of soup. And she's jest about stopped talkin', though she's makin' some sounds and movin' her mouth. To tell the truth, I ain't understood one word that she's uttered since yesterday. She's been relivin' her life, tellin' stories about her mama and growin' up in Rocksburg, marryin' John, the war, havin' all them babies that died, and wanderin' off here and thar to throw in parts I ne'er even heerd about whilst I've been tryin' to write down the main parts so's the family would have a record of sech, don't ye know. But she appears to be weakenin' right fast in the past day or so. I don't think we're goin' to make hit to the end of the story."

"Do ye think Aunt Orlene is a dyin', Aunt Tavia? She borned me, ye know, and my mama and my grandmama," Wavy said. "I've follered her up and down this here mountain since I kin recall, like many another boy or girl she done brung into the world. Why, she'd be comin' up the path, carryin' that medicine bag, after one of the farmers brung her nearby in his wagon and us children would run after her wantin' to find out whar hit was she was goin' to catch a baby! And now's the road is comin' through, her cabin's done gone, and Aunt Orlene looks weaker than a newborn pup that's the runt of the litter and cain't find a teat to suck on."

"Wavy Quesinberry! Whar in the world did ye pick up sech talk? Yer mama would be plain mortified to hear ye speak so!"

"Oh, Aunt Tavia, I growed up on a farm and been around menfolk since I was a baby. Do ye think girls kin grow up to be all sweet and innocent when ye's out and about workin' alongside yer papa and grandpapa, brothers and cousins? Ye cain't keep yer ears or yer eyes closed ever' minute of the day. Ye kin guard yer tongue and practice real hard bein' a lady but onct in a while somethin' lets loose and the words jest pop out. Besides, hit's good fer provokin' a fit or two of laughter from them that ain't all that uset to hit. Course, hit's also good fer a few smacks acrost my backside but sometimes I jest cain't help myself!"

"Shush, child, the old woman might not be a talkin' any, but that don't mean she ain't hearin' ever' word we say. We don't need to go agitatin' her or gittin' her worked up when she's needin' her rest. Make sure she's bundled up right good and put another log or two on the fire. The days are turnin' chilly with the nights takin' on more and more of the cold air. I'll see if she kin eat a bite or two while she's settin' up fer a while. Mabe ye kin talk to her a bit and she'll respond to ye, Wavy. Ye always was one of her favorite great-nieces although she has so many about these parts I don't see how she kin separate one from the other. I ain't meanin' no disparagement to ye.

"Anyways, she's told me how hit was to come to live up here on the mountain in that fine cabin John and his papa built that she's been so proud of and that's about as far as I've got with the story. She don't rightly recall all the dates, says hit's run together like rain fallin' into the creek and makin' hits way to the river and on to the ocean. As best as she kin recollect, they come to the cabin somewhars in the 1880s. The census records might help us out a bit iffen a family member took hit upon hisself to do a little researchin', but most people don't have the time to go lookin' into the past 'cause the present takes up all our energy."

Hit sure does, I'm thinkin' to myself as Wavy set herself down in front of me to offer me a spoonful or two of the chicken soup that Tavia had put on the stove to cook earlier that mornin'. I am tryin' to smile at my favorite great-niece, admirin' her silky golden hair and her bright blue eyes. She is no blood kin of mine, related to me only through one of John's brothers, but if my memory is honest and true, I kin see a resemblance to myself as a young girl near to her age. Whar have the years gone? I wonder only to myself and doubt that Aulene Hawks, as named by her mother and father, was ever so young and as comely as the great-niece who is carefully spoonin' warm broth into my mouth and tenderly wipin' away the droplets that run down my chin. I could cry fer my helplessness and my inability to communicate my gratefulness fer her presence and her kindness, along with that of Tavia, another niece by marriage, but the tears have dried up of their own accord. They don't come in spite of the terrible sadness that has come o'er me. I'm leavin' this world, maybe not this minute or even within a day, but I'm leavin' hit fer sure and hit won't be long, Wavy. The woman that done borned ye will be dead and gone and ye'll be sorrowful fer a while along with the rest of 'em, but life will go on the way hit always has fer thousands and thousands of years till after a while yer Aunt Orlene will be jest a memory. Maybe they'll put up a marker with my name on hit. Maybe hit'll be jest a piece of that white mountain rock like the ones John and me set in the ground fer our babies. Sooner or later, the earth takes back what belongs to her with or without a name, and Orlene Puckett will be no more, only a ghost from the past. I ain't got no regrets, Wavy, and iffen I could tell hit to ye aloud right this minute with ye settin' here aside me, I would. I reach my hand towards her and she takes hold, puttin' hit to her cheek.

"Thank ye, Aunt Orlene, fer helping me come into this world and fer takin' care of me and my mama. She told me she put ye through a mightly hard time with her hollerin' and carryin' on due to the fact that I was her first young'un. Ye calmed her down and got her through what she told me was the greatest pain she ever felt in her whole life. She thought she was goin' to die, but ye shamed her into bein' brave fer the sake of my papa who was beside hisself fer causin' her so much misery. I ain't goin' to fergit ye, Aunt Orlene. All them times I walked aside the wagon bringin' ye our way to help another mama with birthin' her baby, I was proud that ye was jest not *my* Aunt Orlene but Aunt Orlene to most ever' family that lived in these parts. Still we ain't ready to let ye go. There's more to yer story that ye ain't told to Tavia and we're hopin' that ye'll have some of yer strength back tomorrow."

I'd be hopin' the same iffen I thought hit would do any good. What part of my story hasn't been told, I wonder. Who's out thar who hasn't heerd or been told a story of Orlene Puckett, the midwife, and the babies she brung into this world durin' her years livin' on top of Groundhog Mountain?

When John moved us to our new cabin over my vain protests, did I have any idee of how that hard journey though short in time would change my life? No, I was mired down in my own despair, thinkin' only of my wants and feelin's. With sech a state of mind, we kin only see the bad that is waitin' fer us around the bend. The good that kin come from our misery and lack of faith ain't ever part of the vision. The promised land ain't a part of what we's imaginin' due to the fact that our imagination has done been stomped on and beat into the ground.

A discouragin' feelin' comes creepin' over me as iffen the weariness of my old bones is not enough to push a woman old as Methusaleh right on into the grave. I can hear my mama exhortin' me to "take heart and keep on goin'," but she didn't live near as long as I'd been on this earth. Fine fer ye to say, Mama. Talkin' back to her seems a mite easier now that she is gone and I am makin' my way to join her.

I manage to croak out Tavia's name and point to the bed signalin' that I am tired and want to rest from my day's labors though I could not fer the life of me recollect whether I have gone up or down the mountain this mornin' to catch a neighbor's new baby. Which neighbor was hit? I do not recall and as Tavia helps me to the chamber pot afore puttin' me into my bed, I work real hard at askin' her whar I have been and whether the baby is a boy or a girl.

She does not understand my words and keeps shakin' her head, sayin', "No, Aunt Orlene, since ye've been here with me ye ain't been out any mornin' or any evenin' helpin' a mama with the bornin' of her child. The last child ye done borned was little Maxwell, and that was closet to a year ago. I reckon them days are behind ye and ye best be glad of hit at yer age. Ye know thar's another granny woman up towards Fancy Gap and that new doctor down in Mt. Airy, the one that come up here to talk with ye and take ye around with him to meet some of our kinfolk, is the one that's catchin' most of the babies these days.

"Time's is a changin' and I reckon fer the better. Why, thar ain't nobody that I kin think of who'd go so far or brave the worstest kind of weather, storms, sleet, cold, lightnin', creeks overflowin', what have ye, to be a help to so many women and their babies over sech a long time. 'How did she manage to go so many places and borne all them babies?' people's always askin' one another. Ever'one comes up with the same answer: 'Must be the Lord was with her ever' step of the way.' And I kin testify that I've heerd ye tell hit more than onct that the Lord was by yer side each time ye set out and ever' time ye reached down to catch that baby, no matter whether he come easy or give his mama a right bit of trouble gittin' here. Ye always give the Lord the praise and the glory fer the good ye done and people hereabouts ain't ne'er goin' to fergit hit.

Yer life is a testimony to turnin' the bad into good and I'm thinkin' that's why the Lord has blessed ye with a strong body and a long life."

Well and good fer ye to say, now that I'm hardly able to lift my head from my piller or make hit to the pot afore I wet myself. But once upon a time, I was a strong and able woman. I could walk miles up and down the hills and valleys without stoppin', except to take in the long range views or watch a doe and her fawn cross the path. I rode a mule when I was in my seventies. Have I told Tavia the story of how I come to have that mule? I cain't recollect whar we left off afore my words got all tangled up and they come out like sounds that only the wind roamin' through the woods kin make.

Seems to me thar warn't no choice but to be strong durin' the war years when we had no food, the animals was taken away, and our menfolk was off fightin', some of 'em dyin', ne'er to come back home. The fields and woods is filled with the bones of dead soldiers from both sides, left behind in a battle, lost and bleedin' to death, runnin' away from fear, maybe plain anger. The thoughts come to me long after the war was over when I'd be out in my garden or up on the hill pickin' blackberries or headed to the spring fer fresh water. Sech a waste of flesh and blood, hearts and minds. Maybe that was the reason the Lord led me to the birthin' business after I lost my own children. He had to make up fer all His precious children the world took away with no thought as to how hit would cause Him grief. At least's that's how I come to view the war and the doin's of them that couldn't have hit no other way. And then one day He said, "Orlene Puckett, how about ye watchin' out fer the women who might need some help when a new baby is comin' their way. Ye know how hit is. Ye been thar. With faith, ye kin turn yer troubles into triumphs fer others."

Maybe He didn't call me with them exact words but the idee was put in my head and hit come clear to me that I could do what He was askin' of me. But sometimes hit takes a while 'fore a vision turns into somethin' you kin reach out and touch.

October 12, 1939

"AUNT ORLENE, YE'VE BEEN mumblin' in yer sleep most of last evenin' and late into the night. What ye was sayin' come out clearer than what I was hearin' yesterdy mornin' and the evenin' afore. I took notes and wrote down some of what ye was sayin' jest to give me somethin' to fall back on iffen ye come back to yerself and want to try tellin' more of yer story. Kin ye hear me? Do ye know what I'm sayin'?"

"Is this the daytime or has the night done come 'round? Am I speakin' clear to ye? My bed and clothes feels warm and dry so's I ain't wet myself since Wavy done left, have I? How long has the child been gone? When is she comin' back? Is thar somethin' on the stove fer me to eat? I'm feelin' a mite hungry."

"My, my, Aunt Orlene, ye done turned into a miracle! Wavy and me was sure as rain that ye was on yer way to leavin' us 'fore this day come and here ye are talkin' up a storm and askin' fer food when hit's been near two days since ye took a spoonful of broth. Yer speakin' in mostly a whisper that's a bit mushed up but I reckon we kin make sense of what we need to. I'll bring the pot right to the edge of the bed if ye're willin' to try hit but Wavy and me put some diddies on ye and we've been changin' em so's ye don't have to wear yerself out with the effort of gittin' up outa yer bed.

"Wavy will be comin' this noon time. Ye've been here fer over two weeks now, sixteen days to be exact. I'll warm up a biscuit and put a bit of the butter I churned on hit with some of that sourwood honey that ye brought with ye from yer cabin.

"They took my cabin down? Right to the ground? And the farm? What's happenin' to my land? Is the spring house a standin' or the chicken house?"

"Wavy says ever'thing's been tore up, the logs layin' in piles, off to the side whar the road's a goin', right through the middle of yer land, Aunt Orlene. The gover'ment paid ye fer hit, paid ever'body somethin' fer what they took but hit warn't much so they say. Course some says people around here ain't ne'er had any money so somethin' is better'n nothin' and most of the land ain't fit fer farmin' no ways. Others is as mad as hornets. Whether the land is fit fer farmin' ain't the bottom line, they says. Hit's the principle of hit. No gover'ment has the right to take a man's land without he's agreein' to hit. That's what the war was about, warn't hit? Both the wars, when hit comes to the truth of the matter. I tell ye, Aunt Orlene, they's folks in these here parts won't ever let go of their bad feelin's o'er the matter. Ye best be glad ye won't be around to see the bad business comin' down the pike cause of this here road."

"Tavia, they told me hit would be good fer the people up here, that hit would bring work and prosperity to the folks durin' these hard times. Hit would open up new communities and help build schools and bring the world in so's we wouldn't be so isolated, they was sayin', one from the other. I have no children to leave my land to as ye know. What they didn't take will go to ye and others of John's and my brothers' nieces and nephews. But as fer my cabin hit sorrows me to know that the hard work of buildin' hit and all them years of livin' in hit with John and then by myself has come to a pile of logs layin' aside the road. My life, pure and simple, has come down to a pile of old logs that will soon rot and decay and turn back to the rocky soil of these old mountains. And the same thing's waitin' fer me, Tavia. This old body's waitin' fer the same fate as them old logs. Might make hit a mite richer. As the Bible tells us, ashes to ashes and dust to dust."

"Aunt Orlene, thar ye go turnin' to yer dark ways! Shame on ye. The Lord's give ye one more day, so's ye best make some use of hit. Are ye up to tellin' more of yer story as to what happened after ye and John come up to live in the cabin? Ye started in on that part in the evenin' three days ago but we didn't git all that far. Hit was still a time 'fore ye was called to help with the birthin' of that first child, warn't hit?"

"After we come up the mountain, John settled in to make a farm off'n this poor old rocky land. Him and his brothers cut down trees to clear fields fer plantin'—corn mostly. That was the crop to count on in them days. Ye had corn fer grindin' into meal, cornstalks fer fodder fer any cows or horses or mules ye might have to feed, and corn fer makin' whiskey, or shine, as most of the folks around here called hit. When times was real hard, that whiskey brought money into the house. Farmers called hit their bestest cash crop so when the revenuers come around to shut down the stills and put a tax on hit, the menfolk got their selves all riled up and some of 'em turned as mean as snakes.

"But that's another story fer another day, though I will mention to ye that whilst thar's some disputin' o'er whether I took a jug with me on my birthin' missions, I kin tell ye that most ever' farmhouse had a stash put back somewhars fer what was called 'medicinal purposes.' Iffen a woman was in terrible pain when the baby was makin' hits way into the world, a swig of whiskey might be the onliest thing on hand to help her through the ordeal. When that doctor man come up from Mt. Airy, he was quick to pronounce whiskey as a remedy to be avoided at all costs due to harm hit might cause the baby, but that was not somethin' we knowed of in the ole day.

"We had us a cow fer milkin', a yardful of chickens, two or three sows, and more'n a dozen sheep that a farmer traded to John fer two fine hound dogs fer huntin'. I brung up the spinnin' wheel that belonged to my grandmama, and Mama give me some flaxseed that took hold in the garden that John dug up fer me to raise vegetables and herbs fer cookin'. I pulled the bark from chestnut trees and boiled hit till hit was like a dye fer colorin' leather goods that John and some of the menfolk made fer theirselves and others. Fer the most part we relied on our own selves to survive as did most of the families that settled up here on the mountains and in the foothills below.

"What we didn't grow or make fer ourselves, we traded with our neighbors. Say I made baskets and Mr. Smith over on the next farm was a wood worker; John might take him two or three sturdy baskets in return fer a plain work table or a milkin' stool. As the years passed, they was stores set up fer buyin' and tradin' goods. The Keno store was over the next hill and others like the Marshall or the Kinzer stores provided goods that come from far off places. We managed to git by, though John ne'er seemed to have a true bent fer farmin'. Our crops was meager by the standards of his papa and our neighbors but John would proclaim that the next year we'd come out in the black. Somehow we managed to put food on the table, even when kinfolks or neighbors come by. Course when that happened, whether hit was a whole family or a single neighbor, they always brung along some kind of food, whether a pie or a plate of cornbread or vegetables from the garden and they always asked me did I have a fresh sweet tater cobbler in the oven. I had my own store-bought stove that John had brung by wagon one year when the crops turned out some extra money.

"Mountain folks was always real proud people. They won't take somethin' without givin' in return. We was mostly poor, but we shared what we had with any human bein' in need. I think the war left a mark on our lives that wouldn't go away. Not a soul escaped bein' hungry to the point of almost starvin' so's food took on hits own special worth fer each person who set down to eat a meal. I reckon fer most of us havin' food on the table was more valuable than havin' money in a bank, which was an idee that most of us had not run into anyways since money in them days was mighty hard to come by.

"Ye recall that I told ye how I argued with John about movin' up to the mountain, callin' to his attention the hardships we'd be meetin' onct we was here. Well, hit don't give me no pleasure to relate to ye that hit was even more of a trial than I could've imagined. The first summer was hot and drier than cornbread without butter. I planted a garden and John put in a half acre of corn but the rains didn't come. John's family and some of the neighbors brung us stores of food to git through the first winter.

"Then winter come in early November, with a vengeance hit seemed. The wind howled day and night and when the snow come, ye couldn't see yer nose in front of yer face. John had built part of a barn and hit was all he could do to git the animals in out of the cold and git 'em feed and water ever' day. The firewood he cut from the trees that he cleared fer plowin' was gone in no time. The water in the spring froze over and the hens cackled and clucked and carried on but wouldn't lay no eggs. At night we could hear coyotes off in the woods and cows would start bawlin', along with the hogs a squealin', and I couldn't help but shed a few tears fer myself in my misery. When the snow let up one day after about a week of temperatures cold enough to freeze yer toes off in spite of heavy boots, John took down his gun, saddled up the horse, and went off huntin' fer fresh meat. When he come back late in the day, he was carryin' in the carcass of a skinny little rabbit and two ole crows with most of the feathers stripped away. I told him, 'John, I cain't eat that. I don't even know how to go about cookin' somethin' like crow meat.' Tears was dribblin' down my cheeks.

"He was too hungry for arguing. 'Hell, Orlene, I'll fry the rabbit myself. Put some water on the stove to heat, scald the rest of the feathers off'n them birds and then I'll git rid of the innards. Put 'em in a pot of water, throw in a onion and a tater or two, and we'll have us a right fancy supper even iffen we have to take my razor to shave the meat off the bones!'

"He was tryin' to humor the both of us through a bad situation, but I didn't take kindly to his efforts. I did his biddin', but a few bites of taters with the onions and one of the rabbit legs was about all I could stomach. There's more I could tell ye about that first winter but the one lesson that comes to me is this: if ye expect the worst, that's probably what will come to ye.

"The other ills I had ranted and raved about was true as well. Wild beasts roamed through the woods, comin' right into the farms theirselves seekin' prey in the barns and outbuildin's. Hit warn't unusual to lose chickens to foxes that raided the coops or find a new born calf carcass that had been dragged off by a bear or coyote. Hawks and eagles swooped down from the sky fer a tasty young pig, duck, or rabbit that some of the farmers raised fer cookin'. Onct I watched a hawk come nose-divin' down to snatch a trout that John had brung up from the creek and was cleanin' on a workbench out in the yard.

"Neighbors and kinfolk was spread out fer as a body could walk in one day. Riley, one of John's brothers, was buildin' a house three or four miles maybe from whar our cabin stood; another brother had a farm up near the top of Groundhog Mountain. But gittin' from one place to another was mighty tryin'. Wagon paths was rough and narrow with rocks and boulders, makin' travel a hard predicament fer horse or mule and the driver, not to mention the wear and tear on them farm wagons. Most people walked to wherever they was goin', fer the conductin' of whatever business had to be done. Visitin' neighbors was occasions of need, sech as a death in the family, or celebrations of a weddin' or the comin' of a new member of the family.

"Churches, mostly Primitive Baptist, was built near whar members of a family had settled and was buildin' houses closet to one another. Preachers traveled from one church to the other on a rotatin' basis, doin' marriages, baptisms, and funerals in one well sweep, if circumstances allowed fer sech. Folks might come together durin' the harvest time or fer a barn raisin' or a revival meetin' at the church, but fer the mostest part hit was a mighty lonely place to be and fearful as well. I did not take easy to the mountain life, at least fer the first three or four years. I was a brave child, accordin' to my papa, but the storms skeered me with all the lightnin' flashin' and bringin' down trees, the thunder boom-boomin' over and over till my ears hurt and the wind blowin' and screamin' so hard ye couldn't stand aginst hit or hear yer own voices yellin' to each other to git the animals undercover.

"On top of them miseries, at the beginnin' of the October after our first spring on top of the mountain, I lost another baby. I was out in the garden when I felt somethin' wet runnin' down my leg. I looked down and see'd hit was blood and then bits of pink and red-colored matter was droppin' on top of the ground. I give one big cry and fell down right thar in a patch of punkins John had planted fer me. Thar was no need to call fer John 'cause he'd headed over to Riley's place early that mornin'. The baby warn't that far along by my calculations, maybe four months at most. I hadn't said nary a word to John due to not wantin' him to get his hopes up another time and end up with nothin' to show fer hit.

"Well, Tavia, thar I was layin' thar and another whoppin' big pain hit me so hard I was sure that I was a dyin'. I reached down between my legs—I know this ain't pleasant to be hearin' but the truth ain't always a purty thing—and I could feel somethin' thick and rubbery at the end of my private parts. I knowed right then that my womb had done come out and that would be the end of my hope to be a mother and give John a child of our own. I done the only thing I could think to do. I gathered my womb up in my hands, holdin' hit closet to me, walked to the house, hit was mighty slow goin', put some water on the stove to heat so's I could wash the dirt offen hit and my hands real good, then got out some clean rags and stuffed 'em in place fer hit to heal good and strong agin. I reckon hit's part of the story beyond the belief of any person who would hear hit, but that's what I willed myself to do jest fer another try at havin' a child.

"I laid down to rest after my ordeal, which hit was; no mistakin' the pain I was sufferin'. When John come home, I told him I'd taken on a terrible ache in my back and legs, which was also God's truth, and needed to stay in bed. I thank the Lord that he hadn't been into the whiskey that day or I might have been in fer another bad time. He lit a fire on the stove, put a pot of stew on to warm up, and headed out to the barn to milk the cow and feed the animals. I drifted off into a restless sleep due to the terrible pain runnin' through my body, but the next mornin', though I stayed in the bed later than was usual, I was able to git up and at least pretend to be goin' about my chores. John took off towards Riley's place, sayin' they wanted to do a little huntin' fer a bear that had been movin' about them parts and fer me not to bother myself with fixin' his dinner or supper as he might stay over fer the night. I took that to be a blessin' in disguise as I would make myself do only what was necessary and rest up fer the rest of the day and night.

"Speakin' of sech. I'm feelin' a mite weary. Ye know, relivin' the hard times does seem in some ways to be worser that they was the first time around. I ain't got no idee of the time, but I'm needin' a nap fer sure.

Help me git to the outhouse and fix me a bowl of soup, then I'll be layin' myself down fer a while. Might jest sleep through the night onct I'm settled in."

"Aunt Orlene, ye ain't been out of this house fer over a week. Usin' the pot ain't no big chore fer me. Besides, hit's a mite chilly today. I don't think hit's warm enough to be takin' ye outside. Iffen ye catch *pneumonier* not a soul in yer family or mine will forgive me."

"Catch *pneumonier*? Don't that take the cake? Tavia, listen to yer old Aunt Orlene. What I done catched is old age. Hit ain't near as excitin' as catchin' one of my babies, but hit happens to most human bein's, exceptin' fer the fortunate ones who die when they're young and don't have to go through the wrinkles, the aches and pains of failin' limbs, the fallin' out of yer teeth, yer hair turnin' white, iffen thar's any of hit left, and ever' piece of yer body wearin' out and not workin'. I ain't complainin'. I done my share already, but fer whar I'm settin', I'd say the Lord has done planned the whole business of life on this earth fer his own pleasure. I kin hear Him now. 'I brung ye into this world all helpless and dependin' on others fer yer survival and that's how I'm takin' ye out, only hits Me ye better be dependin' on since ye spent most of yer life believin' ye was capable of goin' hit alone, takin' care of yerself. Well, ye kin fool yerself fer jest so long.'

"That's what I've done, Tavia, and what the human race keeps on believin' about hitself. We kin go hit alone, do hit all by ourselves. I believed hit, tried hit fer myself, but I've lived long enough to know better. When we say our prayers, hit seems to me that at the top of the list, we'd best be askin' the Lord to forgive us fer our foolish pride that we flung in His face ever' step of the way.

"Now iffen ye don't mind, I'll use a bit of what life I got left to ask ye to take me to the outhouse onct more. I need some sunshine warmin' my shoulders and some quiet time to myself. When I was a growin' up, that was the place whar I did my clearest thinkin'."

"But—"

"No need to be arguin' about hit. I'm headin' out the door with or without ye. Course hit would go a mite easier with a little help. Then I'll rest up a bit fer tellin' the next part of the story iffen ye're willin' to do some more listenin' and writin' down in that book of␣your'n. Are ye certain that hit'll make fer good readin' somewhars down the road or will this chit-chatterin' about the past come to nary but a speck of dust on the wall of time?"

{ *October 12, 1939* }

"That's about as purty as poety, Aunt Orlene. Maybe ye ain't got the education that ye hankered fer when ye was a young'un goin' off to school that first day as far as readin' and writin' goes, but ye know the facts about livin' life on yer own term. I reckon in the long run that beats the education that comes only from books and has no common sense to go along with hit. Ye was always braggin' about yer mama and how smart she was; I reckon if Julie Ann and yer other girls had lived, they'd grow up braggin' about ye in the same way."

Onct Tavia got me settled in the outhouse and wrapped a blanket around me real tight I set thar fer a good while and contemplated the worth of a sunny day, a blue sky, and the solitude of a sturdy, strong outhouse whar a body could think her own thoughts and not be obliged to share 'em with a single soul. When Tavia come to git me the sun had drifted off behind heavy clouds and I was ready fer a good long nap.

"Rain's comin'. Not only kin I smell hit closin' in around us, but I kin feel hit in my bones. Ain't nothin' like a hard, steady rain to stir up the achin' in my knees and ankles."

"Do ye want somethin' to eat 'fore ye take yer nap? The lastest time ye took to yer bed in the middle of the day hit was noontime the next day when ye waked up. Ye hadn't had no supper and ye said ye was hungry, but ye didn't eat enough to keep a new hatched chick alive."

I kin hear Tavia's voice floatin' around about me so's I am bound to answer her questions and put her in a mind of ease but what words come out of my mouth don't fly all the way to her ears.

"Ye've tired yerself plumb out, Aunt Orlene. I told ye goin' to the outhouse was not a good idee. Ye have to conserve yer strength these days and not put so much of a burden on that wore-out body of your'n."

I know my niece don't mean no harm by her words. She is as honest and plain speakin' a woman as kin be found in my family, or John's, fer that matter. Still mostest women is right sensitive about their age and remindin' 'em of their frailty and uselessness don't amount to what could pass fer kindness from whar I was watchin' the world go by. The understandin' that death is a comin' is one thing. Acceptin' hit without throwin' up a protest or two or three is another. I kin recall plenty of days when I had hit in my mind to jest lay me down and give up my ghost, mostly after each of my babies died or come out as bits of bloody matter, but now that the hourglass is down to hits last grains of sand, I seem not to have the will to jest let go.

Sleep comes easy but the livin' goin' on in my dreams brings nothin' but torment and hard times. Mama uset to say that dreams was a way of takin' ye away from the harsh realities that life made ye face right thar in the mirrer starin' at ye. In yer dreams ye could visit faraway lands and live the life of a princess or a famous person that was wrote about or people talked about in stories and poems. But my imagination ne'er traveled that far. I was a plain farm girl who growed up to be a plain farm wife livin' among farmers and their families, all of 'em workin' at the same chores, seein' the same sights, mornin' and night, summer and winter, eatin' the same kinds of foods, endurin' the same struggles, day after day, year after year. If thar was romance—my mama actually talked about the 'romance' of the simple life—thar warn't no evidence of hit in my life that I could tell. So how could hit come to bein' in my dreams? Another question fer the Lord, I am thinkin' to myself. I surely hope He's settin' aside a mighty big block of time fer our first conversation beyond the "How d'ye do? I'm mighty glad to make yer acquaintance, Orlene Puckett." That's plain foolishness. He's made my acquaintance, nigh to a hunderd years ago. I wonder if the Lord ever forgits one of His children, as to whar they wound up or how long they've been hangin' around waitin' fer their invite to come join Him in heaven. Maybe He's forgot that I'm still alive, iffen ye kin call hit that, and He's searchin' around fer me in heaven, which I will grant is takin' a lot fer granted.

If hit's jest the same with ye, Lord, shut down this wicked old mind of mine and give me a good night's sleep. That's about as far as prayin' I kin work up to fer now. I hope ye're still listenin' and while ye're at hit, ye kin stop lookin' fer me up thar in heaven. I'm still here as far as I kin tell even though I don't know the reason. I reckon hit's up to ye to make the next move.

October 13, 1939

"I'M STILL IN MY BED AND makin' some attempt to talk to Tavia, but she keeps on shakin' her head and mutterin' to herself whilst she's changin' my bedclothes. All the time she's tryin' to help me hold up my head so's I kin drink her good, hot coffee. My voice, what I kin hear of hit, sounds hoarse and whispery, like wind blowin' acrost a field of hay all gone to seed.

"I cain't understand ye, Aunt Orlene. Conserve yer strength. After ye's had some coffee, I'll make ye a bowl of thin grits with lots of butter and some hot milk, jest like ye like. Wavy'll be here in a short time and she kin sit here with ye whilst I milk my cow, git the eggs from the hen house, and cut some more firewood. October is fer sure goin' out in a spell of right cold weather. The frost is heavy this mornin'. Wisht ye could see how purty hit is, shinin' acrost the fence and coverin' the ground like snow.

"Iffen thar's any talkin' to be done, provided yer mind and yer mouth'll work together, I reckon Wavy can do the listenin' and the writin'—she made hit all the way to the fifth level, ye know—I reckon she kin take over fer a while so's I kin peel and slice a basket of apples fer dryin', maybe even put a cobbler in the oven fer our supper tonight. Do ye think ye might take to a piece of fresh apple pie? I'm takin' yer noddin' to be in the affirmative, so's I'll make the crust right after we have our dinner and ye're takin' a nap."

The girl do talk on and on, I'll tell ye. Course she's gittin' up in years, maybe even to her thirties, I suppose, but any woman that ain't reached her nineties seems like a young'un to me. I recall the night she come into this world, pink and peaceful as kin be. She was smilin', happy to be a part of this big, wide world. I handed her to her mama, and even though hit warn't her first child, she carried on, cooin' and tellin' that Tavia was the purtiest baby she done see'd. But ever' mother feels that way about each child that she's brung into the world, whether hit's the first or the seventeenth. I kin testify to that truth, 'cause I've been a witness to many a mama seein' her newborn child. Ye kin see the hope, the pride, the prayers and happy wishes fer the future all come together in the eyes fastened on that baby. Nothin' comes closet to kindlin' sech feelin's as come over them that's watchin' hit all come to pass.

Remind me of the story of Mary and Joseph and the night that baby Jesus was borned in Bethlehem. No matter what time of day or year, birthin' a baby was like havin' Christmas come round agin fer this old granny woman. Hit was and still is the bestest present in the whole world, at least until they start growin' up and causin' ever' soul that stands in their way trouble and turmoil. Bringin' a child into the world is a right joyous occasion but thar was days I wondered how me and the children might have fared iffen they had lived long enough to grow up and have minds of their own. John was set in his ways and when he took to drink, he was meaner'n a snake. I was stubborn and proud, sure of what was right and what was wrong. That added to a child decidin' to stand up and make his own way in spite of what his mama and papa says fer him to do seems to point to jest one thing—an explosion of one kind or 'nother.

"Aunt Orlene, I've come to set with ye a spell whilst Aunt Tavia does a few chores. She says she's goin' to make a apple cobbler fer dinner and I kin stay through the evenin' if I've a mind to 'cause Mama don't need me to help her up at the house. Kin ye hear me, Aunt Orlene? Aunt Tavia says ye ain't into talkin' much this mornin'. She says she don't know if ye ain't able or jest ain't in the mind to be bothered.

"I'm goin' to feed ye some of the grits she done fixed. She says that's yer favorite eatin's these days since ye done lost most of yer teeth, but we ain't goin' to force ye to do what ye ain't up to. I'll hold the spoon up to yer lips and if ye want a bite, jest open yer mouth and I'll feed hit to ye."

Oh, Lord, is this what my life done come to? Cain't speak on my own behalf, wettin' my bed, and bein' fed like a baby by my great-niece, Wavy Quesinberry? Once upon a time, I changed her diapers and held a bottle to her mouth when her mama's milk dried up. Now the tables is turned and I'm not likin' it one bit. I always thought that hit was the livin' of these days that was the hard part. Dyin' would come quiet and easy and carry our minds along with hit. Our old bodies would jest wind down like a clock, one tick tock at a time, and sooner or later the hand would stop and that would be the end of Orlene Hawks Puckett. Don't seem to be workin' out that way, Lord. I told ye I warn't goin' to complain and I'm tryin' mighty hard to accept things the way they is, but thar's a lot of onery bones left in this ole body.

Yer Word tells us that hit is appointed once fer ever' man to die. I am guessin' that includes ever' woman as well, and after that comes the

{ October 13, 1939 }

judgment. From whar I am today, I reckon I done faced the judgment right here on this earth. First off, bein' married to John. The second bein' the bearin' and buryin' of our twenty-four children. Iffen ye ain't counted 'em fer yerself, Lord, I'm askin' ye to do the recallin' right this minute. In the middle of hit all was the war, that terrible war that took our men, our farms, our animals, our crops, and our children. Iff ye don't see nary of that as judgment upon yer children, that's yer privilege, but as fer me I witness hit was judgment upon me and them that was a part of me ever' step we took along the way.

After we come up to live on top of this mountain, five more years went by and four more babies died. They's buried up at the cemetery on Renfro Ridge. Ain't no use lookin' fer markers with names. No, they's layin' thar under big stones that was dug up and moved to make way fer plantin' crops. Seems right sensible when ye think about hit.

Waste not, want not. That's what my mama would tell us. When ye're as poor as we was, thar warn't nothin' to waste. No sirree. A sheet that was wearin' out was turned into a shirt fer Papa. When the sleeves got all raggedy and thin, Mama cut that down to a shirt fer one of the little boys. Bits of clothes that was wore out and too small fer sewin' into another garment become a quilt or a rag fer washin' dishes. Same way with food. Meat was boiled right to the bone and cooked with taters or other vegetables to make a stew. What was left over was put in a pot with milk or cream iffen we had any or water from the spring fer soup. Nothin' was throwed away. Hit was fed to the hogs or the chickens when feed was scarce. We made do with what we had. Didn't do no good to complain. That was our life and survivin' depended on us workin' together. Papa would call up to us to "rise and shine" at five o'clock in the mornin' and that's what we done.

"How's she doin', Wavy?"

"I don't know, Aunt Tavia. Fer the most part she's been sleepin' but ever' onct in a while, she starts talkin' though hit's hard to understand what she's sayin'. Right off, she was tellin' about comin' to the mountain and havin' them four more babies that died. Next thing I make out she's talkin' about her mama and papa and the hardships of growin' up poor, but how they worked together as a family to survive. Has she done spoke about her growin' up down near Rocksburg on her papa's farm?"

"That's whar she started when she first come here. From the way I'm lookin' at things, hit don't seem probable that she's goin' to live much longer, maybe two or three days. Course she's still got to make hit through the night first. She don't look like she's hardly takin' a breath and we ain't even made hit to that cold winter's night when Laurie Bowman's husband come a poundin' at the cabin door wanting Aunt Orlene to go on up to Groundhog Mountain fer to catch Laurie's first baby. And after that they kept on comin' to take her up and down round and about these mountain peaks and valleys to catch one baby after another fer nigh onto the next forty-four or forty-five years. Some will swear by the Bible she's been at hit fer no less than fifty years. Why, ye cain't call the name of nary a family in these parts that ain't had Aunt Orlene to show up fer the birthin' of at least one child, but more'n likely they's more than kin be counted if ye start with the nieces and nephews of John's brothers and sisters, then add the ones belongin' to Orlene's brothers. Next comes the grand nieces and nephews and their children, not to mention the cousins that come from marryin' outside the two families.

"They's people who cain't or won't believe that one old woman could have borned over one thousand babies without losin' a mama or a young'un but they ain't lookin' at the whole picture. I reckon iffen a body kin do the figurin' of say twenty or twenty-five children a year over a period of forty-plus years, hit would add up to a thousand or even more. Would ye reason the same, Wavy? Yer mama says ye got a head fer readin' and doin' numbers.

"Speakin' of yer mama, Aunt Orlene was thar when she got borned. When yer grandmama Hawks called out what was to be her name, Iduna, nary a soul knowed how to spell what she was a sayin' and then some twenty years later thar was Iduna, married to a Quesinberry, about to bring her own child into the world. Yer mama was a cryin' and carryin' on somethin' terrible when Aunt Orlene come to the house. She shook her finger in that girl's face and told her to hush up and git herself under control 'cause hit was doin' harm to her and her baby, and she warn't going to put up with hit. I heerd her say so right in front of yer daddy and the rest of the kinfolks gathered on the inside and circled round the house. Sure enough, yer mama stopped all her snivelin' and squealin' and got down to the business of pushin' ye out into the world with the supervision of that old woman layin' thar beside ye. Ye owe ye life to Orlene Puckett, Wavy, as is true fer many of the generations of families that live in these here parts.

"Us children have follered her up and down the mountain paths when she was goin' out to take a new brother or sister to one of the farmhouses. Least ways that was the story we was told, how Aunt Orlene would find a new baby whilst she was out walkin' and carry hit to a mama and papa who was wantin' their first child or another one to play with the ones they already had, or even take the place of one that had died. We knowed better fer sure but we made out like we believed ever' word they was a tellin' us 'cause hit did fill our lives with a touch of mystery and give us somethin' excitin' to pass round instead of jest plain ole gossip with no outcome to speak of."

"Is she dyin', Aunt Tavia? Jest watchin' her layin' thar in the bed, she don't seem like she's got no life left in her. Look at the skin on her face and her hands, all thin and white like the paper in my mama's Bible. Ye kin see the veins runnin' underneath. Her breathin' is raspy soundin', when ye kin hear hit. I'm fifteen years old, Aunt Tavia, and I cain't recall many days to go by without walkin' with her to pick blackberries or fox grapes fer makin' preserves or follerin' her down the mountain to the tradin' post. Sometimes I'd go to the cabin and she'd set in her rockin' chair tellin' stories of how hit was when she was growin' up. When I saw they tore down her cabin, I cried and cried till the tears jest dried up and no more would come. I'm of the understandin' that she's earned her rest. Still I cain't imagine livin' up on this mountain without having her about to parcel out all the larnin' she took in whilst she was makin' a life, not jest fer herself, ye see, but fer the children like me that she brung into the world."

"Hit's the truth, Wavy. She's dyin', but not a one of us kin say fer sure when that's goin' to happen. She's been sorta up and down the past few days. One day she has the strength to set up and take a bite to eat, maybe say a word or two or recollect some event of import to her. The next day she ain't movin', jest layin' thar pickin' at the threads of her quilt, mutterin' sounds that might be words or not. We'll do the best we kin to keep her clean and comfortable. I'm hopin' fer a little more time to spend with her while her mind is still clear. I'm also prayin' the Lord will take her quick and easy when the time comes. Run on home, child, afore darkness sets in. When Orlene Puckett is gone, the news will travel right fast. I reckon hit'll even be wrote up in one of the local papers."

Ye both reckon I cain't hear a word that ye're sayin', but the old-timers had a sayin' that the hearin' is the last to go. I'm tellin' ye not to give up on me. I ain't seein' angels yet. A good night's rest and I'll be up and about, maybe even fix my own breakfast fer a change. This ain't the first time I've looked Death in the face and lived to tell about hit. Them last babies brung me to Death's door but he took the two of them instead of me. I asked the Lord to spare each one but He had his mind already made up on the matter. One was a boy, the other a girl. John would've had his family but hit warn't to be. I lost so much blood with each birthin', John sent fer my mama and papa, but they was so old by that time, they couldn't make the trip up from Rocksburg. His sisters come to help out and nurse me back to health, but I knowed in my heart my child bearin' years was over and done with. I allow I was too sickly to turn my hurt into anger. I had argued with the Lord and His way of doin' things ever' step of the way. When the last baby was buried, and I knowed fer certin he was the last, the fight left me. Fer whatever reason, the Lord had made hit plain and clear that John and me would ne'er have a child of our own.

October 14, 1939

HERE I AM, OPENIN' MY EYES to another day even though I kin hardly believe that I made hit through the night. Accordin' to what Tavia and Wavy was sayin', I was expectin' to wake up and be standin' afore them pearly gates that the preacher man's always talkin' about. But hit goes to show ye that ye cain't count on nothin' from one minute to the next whilst ye're makin' yer way along the pathway that turns out to be yer life. No, sirree. Ye cain't count on nothin'.

"What is hit that ye cain't count on, Aunt Orlene? Or are ye mumblin' in yer sleep like ye been doin' since late last evenin' and fer the most part of the night? Ye been mighty fidgety in that bed of your'n as well, tossin' and turnin', raisin' yer hands in the air and callin out a name ever' onct in a while, includin' that of the Lord, but I kin assure ye, Aunt Orlene, that thar was no blasphemin' or takin' His name in vain in yer rantin's as far as I could tell. Now, don't ye be thinkin' that ye're goin' to be tryin' to git up from that bed so's ye kin move about. Hit ain't goin' to happen, Aunt Orlene. Ye ain't got the strength of a butterfly."

"And what kind of butterfly would ye be referrin' to, Tavia? I heerd hit told by one of the schoolmasters down in The Holler that the ones called monarchs can fly from up north in Canada to somewhars way down in Mexico. That's strength fer ye, Tavia, strength beyond milkin' or plowin' or carryin' water from the spring."

"Land's sakes, Aunt Orlene, fer two days now ye ain't said one word that a body could understand. Now ye wake up with a sermon jest pourin' out of ye mouth and ever' word as clear as a bell! Still, that don't mean ye're fit to git up on yer own. Ye was all Wavy and me could handle fer the past two days. Changin' yer bedclothes and yer diddies and purty near forcin' food down yer throat. Though ye appeared to be sleepin', ye was orderin' us to do this and not to do that till the both of us was plumb wore out."

"That so? Well this day I aim to be settin' in front of that thar fire and tellin' more of my story iffen I ain't done finished hit already. Course I ain't finished yet 'cause I'm still alive and a kickin' as far as I kin tell. When I come to the end, I'll let ye put me into my bed so's I kin die in peace. Recordin' the whar, I suppose that ain't goin' to change none, but the when and the how will be up to ye, Tavia. Ye'll have the last word as far as my story goes. Don't seem fair to me that a body cain't speak at her own funeral or that a stranger writes down the history of yer life and ye ain't around to help 'em git the facts straight. Does hit seem fair to ye, Tavia, even iffen ye do have a few years left to think about hit?"

"Orlene Puckett, ye do beat all! Hit ain't been twenty-four hours since Wavy and me was fer sure that ye was at Death's door. Now ye're settin' thar orderin' me about and talkin' that high falutin' talk like ye was some professor come from Charlottesville or tharabouts. Give me a bit of time to help ye up iffen yer heart's set on bein' in front of the fire. I'll change the bed and find ye a bite to eat. Then ye kin go on with yer story and I'll take my notes though I'm jest about to run out of the paper that Iduna give me when ye come here last month."

"Since ye brung hit up, how long has hit been since I come to live with ye?"

"More'n two weeks I believe."

"And how many years has come and gone since I come to yer door?"

"I jest told ye that hit was near to—"

"No. No, that ain't what I mean. What ye're writin' down—about growin' up and marryin' John, havin' the babies, the stories I've been tellin' ye about my life—how far have we come on that journey?"

"Well, that's a interestin' way of puttin' hit, I suppose. Let me see what I wrote down on my copy book. Ye was tellin' about the first years after ye come up on the mountain and how ye had four more babies up here and they died jest like the rest and was buried up at the little cemetery near the Primitive Baptist church. Ye said ye come near to dyin' yerself with the last two and then ye realized yer childbearin' years was over. Ye quit yer arguin' with the Lord about the matter 'cause the fight wasn't in ye no more and come to the acceptance that John and ye would ne'er have a child of yer own. That's the last thing I wrote down."

"Did ye ever hear about how people went 'round tellin' that John and me had somethin' to do with our babies dyin'?"

"I heerd them stories, Aunt Orlene, but not one soul that knowed ye face to face would e'er think sech a terrible thing. Not one soul. Nothin' but ignorance is how I see hit. Take a body that's ignorant and add a mite of meanness to go along with hit and what ye end up with is mighty hurtful to them that gits a full dose."

"Oh, hit done hurt alright, hurt a right long time as well. After so many babies died, I was fer certain that the sorrow and the gossip was what brung John to his breakin' point, so's he commenced to drinkin' more and more of that shine and takin' his fists to me in his anger. Many a time I run out and hid from him, even crawlin' under the cabin, all the time hopin' he'd pass out and forgit that hit was me he was after. Sure 'nough, when he come to, he'd come to the door and start callin' fer me. 'Orlene, honey, come on back. I ain't goin' to hurt ye.'

"And back I'd go. What else was I to do? We stood up in front of that preacher man and vowed to stay together fer better or worse, richer or poorer, through sickness and health, and that's what we done; what ever husband and wife done in them days. We stuck together 'cause thar warn't no other way to go. The gossip and the rumors stayed with us even after we come up to the cabin. Over time, John and me had fewer and fewer words atween us but we worked together on the farm and made a life fer ourselves up here on the mountain.

"Ye don't have to answer me, Aunt Orlene, 'cause maybe I don't have the right to be askin' to begin with, but did ye love John Puckett after the way he took his fists to ye, along with his drinkin' and leavin' ye alone to fend fer yerself when the war was a goin' on? Seems like he warn't the man to bring ye comfort and help keep yer spirits up."

"I figured out long time ago, Tavia, that ever'body's got his own truth. I kin tell my story from how I recall hit happenin', in sech and sech a way, but another person standin' thar watchin' the events of the day, jest might see hit from another angle and tell hit his way. Thar's only one person who knows the hunderd percent truth about you or me, and that's the Lord. The rest has only one piece of the puzzle.

"Supposin' hit was John settin' here tellin' his side. Do ye think he might say somethin' to the effect that I warn't no saint to try to live with so's that's how come he turned to drink? Or maybe he might open up and own to the disappointment and frustration of watchin' child after child die while his brothers and sisters was havin' so many children that his mama and papa couldn't recall their names when they stopped by fer a visit. Ever' boy and girl inherits a world that is different from the world that their mama and papa come into and the same thing will happen when their children come along, which makes the bridgin' of the gap atween 'em that much harder. Same goes fer people, I reckon. Two women can relate to bein' married and the business of havin' a husband, but aside from that, the differences keep pilin' up as years go by.

"I'm goin' to take me a nap settin' here by this warm fire. Sure does feel good to these weary old bones holdin' me together. Ye go on with yer chores and by and by I'll be pert enough to tell ye what happened after we lost our last baby."

"Ye ain't hardly been awake no hour and ye're already needin' a nap?"

"Iffen I'm goin' on with my story, I need all the rest I kin provide fer this ole body. Them years made fer a long, tiresome journey and I reckon pullin' hit out of my memory ain't goin' to be no easier. I might need more'n one nap or two to help me through the tellin'. Ye might need a little nap yerself to provide the strength to keep that pencil of yers a movin'!

"I wisht I'd larned readin' and writin' so's I could of wrote hit down on paper fer myself at the time the names of the families and their babies. The dates when I was thar to help 'em make their grand entrance into this mostly wonderful and sometimes pitiful world. Nowadays hit all runs together like the rain fallin' into the creek and the creek findin' the river that leads on to that big ocean out thar somewhars. Cain't separate one drop of water from the other. The children would foller me from one farm to the next, up the mountain and down, askin' me if I could recollect their names or who they belonged to. Most times they couldn't wait and hit would bust out 'fore I had to put my old memory to work. 'Do ye recall me, Aunt Orlene? My papa told me he give ye a pig fer me. The fattest one 'cause he thought I was the purtiest newborn baby he ever done seen.' Child after child, story after story. Iffen I'd got me that education and wrote hit down durin' them years I'd had me some memories to keep me company as the years was passin' by and old age was catchin' up with me. Maybe I could of put hit together like a book or had a reporter fer a newspaper write hit fer me. Wouldn't that be somethin'? To be settin' in a chair in front of a warm fire and readin' from a book that has yer own words wrote in hit?

"Mama and Papa was always makin' excuses fer me, talkin' about my poor eyesight due to, they would explain, the eye that seemed to wander off by hisself. They should of made me work harder and not let me off so easy. Markin' one X on a paper ain't nothin' to brag about, that's fer sure. I kin hear John tellin' me ever' time I set out with Roadie, 'Orlene Puckett, ye's near to bein' as blind as a bat. How ye goin' to make hit down to The Holler?'

"By that time I was at least in my mid-sixties. Still I would muster up determination and the pride that Mama scolded me about when I was a young girl to tell him, 'Roadie'll git me whar I need to go. He knows ever' path and wagon track within ten miles of this place.' Then John would say, 'But how does he know whar the Marshalls live?' Or the Cullers or the Martins, whoever had sent word fer me to come. And I would answer, 'He jest seems to have a sixth sense. Smartest animal I ever knowed. Smarter than most people 'round these parts. Even the menfolk and I could name ye one or two iffen ye've a mind fer hit.' I'd smile to myself when I said them words, wonderin' if John knowed I was teasin' him a bit. Then I'd climb up on Roadie's back, John would hand me my medicine bag and off I'd go. Oft times I'd looked back and see John standin' thar, watchin' me and shakin' his head back and forth, worryin' that I might git lost or fall off the mountain."

I closed my eyes:

Jest atween us, Lord, I ain't sure I ever sent up a "thank you" fer sendin' Coy Hawks to the cabin that day all them years ago pullin' Roadie behind him. I kin hear him a callin', "Aunt Orlene, Aunt Orlene, come on out here!" and when I stepped out of the cabin, he smiled and asked me how would I like to have that ole mule. You know, I'd been a pesterin' John fer years about buyin' me a mule due to my knees and ankles bein' all swolled up and hurtin' with the rheumatism from walkin' up and down the mountain and hereabouts catching all them babies. We'd been livin' on the mountain near to ten years and one day when I went to the spring fer a cup of cold water, I leaned over and thar was a white-haired stranger a lookin' back at me. My eyes was so dim I warn't fer sure what I was a seein' so I backed up 'cause hit startled me so, then moved up to take another look. Well, hit come to me then and I had to laugh at myself. Orlene Puckett, I said to my reflection starin' at me, ye done turned into an old woman, and fer the first time in my life, Lord, with them aches and pains runnin' through me, I could feel the weight of the years that had passed by with all thar hardships and heartaches.

So when Coy come to the cabin with that old mule, I understood what hit was to covet somethin' that belonged to my neighbor. I told him, Lord, that me and John didn't have no money to buy a mule, leastways accordin' to John, who was as tight-fisted as they come. Ye know hit to be the truth, Lord. But Coy offered fer me to pay a little then and the rest later over a good, long time. Said he knowed I was helpin' minister to them women and their babies so he wanted to be on the side of the angels even iffen he warn't no man of religion. I knowed Hit was ye, Lord, that put hit all in place. I ain't certain, even to this day, that he was ever paid all the money that we owed him. I kin hear

Uncle Coy a sayin' to me, 'Ye know I bought him fer plowin' and he ne'er took a likin' to hit. Ye put him to a better use, Aunt Orlene.'

So, Lord, ye brung me Roadie and we was together all them years, goin' wherever I was supposed to be, I reckon. I kin see that old mule stickin' his head in the cabin winder whilst I was doin' my chores or cookin' the meals, lookin' at me like he wanted to know iffen we was headin' out that day. I'd shake my head and he'd back out and go on munchin' on the hay John put out fer him.

I knowed I give John a hard time all them years ago when he come in and told me, told me mind ye, that we was goin' up the mountain to live. I was mad as a hornet, but ye know all that and the rest of hit, fer that matter. I didn't want to trade bein' with my family to live amongst John's family, the Pucketts. I could not bear to think of leavin' my babies thar in the cemetery at the foot of the mountain, though hit warn't too far to walk to visit 'em onct in a while. Course the trek up the mountain was another story 'cause I'd be cryin' so hard that my eyes turned blurry and was swolled together by the time I made hit back to the cabin. John would take one look at me and shake his head. "Put hit behind ye, Orlene. Put hit behind ye. We'll have that baby yet."

He was right and wrong at the same time. We had them four babies up here on the Blue Ridge and we give 'em back to whar they come from. I took to visitin' them instead of walkin' down to the cemetery at the church whar we was married. As time went by, I pushed that part of my past little by little to the back of my mind. Oh, I ne'er forgot them children, but hit give me peace to know they was lyin' thar in the shadow of yer presence.

Do ye recall, Lord, that October day when I was headin' back to the cabin after catchin' one of the Pruitt girls? I stopped to take in the valley below me and the far off mountains streaked with colors of red, orange, and gold. Hit looked like a paintin' stretched out as far as the eye could see. Hit come to me like a vision that I was standin' on the purtiest piece of land ye done made, Lord. I repented right then and thar fer my weepin', wailin', and whinin' that I put John through when he told me we was movin' into a cabin him and his papa and brothers was a buildin' fer us near Renfro Ridge.

I knowed fer sure, Lord, that this was part of yer plan fer me, and even iffen that that meant hard and difficult times during the days and nights, ye put me in a glorious place whar I could do my work surrounded by my own garden of Eden. Ye didn't send me out. Ye brought *me in and I'm mighty grateful fer yer mercy and yer patience. Ye could of brung me home that day or any day after 'cause hit was fer certain that the glory of yer presence was lightin' up the world around me. Right now I'll stop botherin' ye fer a while so's I kin wake up with my mind all cleared out and go on with my story.*

I opened my eyes and Tavia was still right there, smilin' at me. I don't know if she knew I was havin' a talk with the Lord or iffen she just thought I'd drifted off to sleep.

"Ever'body tells about the first time ye was called to go catch a baby, Aunt Orlene, but I ain't ne'er heerd ye say a word about how ye come to be a granny woman after John moved ye to the new cabin. Maybe hit warn't to yer satisfaction, but my mama told me when I was a young'un that the womenfolk was green with envy when they see'd how big yer cabin was with its large room on the ground floor that was divided like to make a sleepin' area separate from the kitchen and them two big rooms up the stairs. Hit was virgin forest them timbers come from and Uncle John and his papa set to braggin' about how no wind, even iffen hit come from the North Pole, would be strong enough to bring that house down! I reckon the good Lord took 'em on home years ago to spare 'em the grief of seein' the farm taken out from under 'em fer that new road, not to mention witnessin' with their own eyes the tearin' down of that fine cabin."

"Hit ain't helpin' me none to hear ye keep remindin' me about 'em tearin' my cabin down. What's done is done. That's what Mama always told us. No uset to cryin' over spilt milk, she'd say. Never let up with them proverbs she had stored up in her head:

One day I looked up at her and proclaimed innocent like, "I ain't spilt no milk, Mama. I cain't recollect ever spilling no milk, neither. Ain't thar another piece of wisdom ye kin impart to us fer a change?"

"Oh, I'll impart another piece of wisdom to ye, young lady. Maybe two or three iffen ye're up to listenin' fer a spell. The first one is that ye are gittin' too big fer yer britches. And ye know what I've told ye about that. Pride goes 'fore a fall. Yes, ma'am. Hit sure does. The second one is that ye are settin' yerself up fer a run-in with yer papa and that will come to no good on yer behalf. As the Bible says, Honor thy father and thy mother. Hit don't appear that ye're doin' yer part to honor me or yer papa when ye go questionin' the advice I'm handin' out to ye so's ye kin avoid the pitfalls that's comin' yer way."

"What pitfalls would that be, Mama? And what's a pitfall anyhow?"

"Are ye makin' fun of yer mama, Aulene?" She looked straight at me with them piercin' blue eyes and I felt my knees turn to jelly.

"No, ma'am. I really want to know and I'm ready to give hit a good listenin' to, iffen ye'll take the time to explain sech to me."

"Oh, go on with ye, child. Thar are times when I ain't sure but that the devil done got ahold of ye fer the main reason of aggravatin' yer papa and me. Ye're a good girl, Aulene, and right smart. Too smart fer yer own good from whar I'm standin'. Iffen all things works fer good fer them that love the Lord, that schoolmarm that give ye that whippin' must surely love Him in a mighty way. Otherwise ye'd be in that schoolhouse today givin' her a run fer her money. And I mighten have me a few minutes of peace without yer play-actin' through yer chores and spreadin' mischief about to yer brothers, which is somethin' they cain't git enough of as hit is.'"

"Thar ye go, Aunt Orlene, talkin' about yer mama when we was jest gittin' to the part about how ye come to catch that first baby. I knowed yer mama was a real special lady to ye and yer family. I reckon that havin' good memories of them that was responsible fer bringin' ye into the world is worth more than rubies and gold. That's what my mama told me when I was a growin' up. Why, Aunt Orlene, are ye laughin' at me?"

"Have ye noticed, Tavia, how when one person starts tellin' a story about somethin' that happened in their life, ever'body who's listenin' jumps in with a story that they been reminded of concernin' the same subject matter. And the stories go on and on jest like logs rollin' down a hill. People kin set around the supper table or after the church meeting or barn raisin' and hit's the bestest thing in the world to hear the words a spillin' out like whiskey from a jug—which mighten be one of the reasons fer all them loose tongues—and ever'one's laughin' or cryin' or caught up in a spell of some kind 'cause hit's like actors in a play and fer a while at least hit takes their minds of their own troubles.

"My mama could tell a story all right, make ye laugh till ye was about to wet yer underpants or give ye goosebumps that stayed with ye all night. And she could sing. Such a purty voice. I ne'er heerd no one sing so pure and true. Not even them that sung in the church choir. Why some of 'em had voices that crackled like layin' hens. I done got off the path agin, Tavia. Tell me whar we was so's I kin git back to my story. I ain't feelin' so wore out today, so's I reckon hit won't hurt me none to keep on talkin', provided I don't wander off no more.

"Here's how hit come to be that I become a granny woman. And hit's right fittin' that my mama keeps showin' up whilst I've been recitin' the events of my life. Ye see, she was the one who sent me out into the cold that winter of 1889, when I borned Laurie Bowman's little boy. I was settin' in front of the fire at my cabin, jest like we're a doin' this very minute. John was already asleep as he usually climbed into the bed early when he put in a good day's work. I was piecin' blocks fer a quilt that some of us women was makin' fer one of John's nieces who was bein' married in the spring. The wind was blowin' so hard the tree limbs rattled aginst the winder with a steady beat almost like a drum. Next thing I knowed here come Bynum Bowman knockin' on my door, askin' me to come tend to his wife Laurie, who was tryin' to have her baby but not makin' no progress.

"I asked him did he know who he was talkin' to and he replied that he was thinkin' he was talkin' to Orlene Puckett, John Puckett's wife. 'I'm the one who done lost twenty-four babies,' I told him. 'Ye don't want me comin' to help yer wife. Fer all I know, I'm a cursed woman. I ain't plannin' to take that curse with me to some unsuspectin' woman who wants to have a baby that will live. No, ye go on, Bynum. Find someone else to help ye in yer time of trouble. Hit fer sure ain't me.'

"But he wouldn't leave. Said thar warn't no granny woman nor doctor to be found. He stood thar beggin' me take pity on him fer his wife's sake. Then he said, 'We reckoned that ye have some knowledge of what was needed seein' ye been through this ordeal so many times yerself. We'd be mighty obliged to ye fer yer trouble. If ye don't come, I'm afraid I'll lose my baby and my wife.'

"He was lookin' so pitiful I could hardly stand watchin' him. I was shakin' my head and sayin', 'No, I cain't do hit,' when I heerd a voice say, 'Go on now, Aulene. Ye go with that man to help his wife. This is the work that the Lord wants ye to do fer him. That's why He brought ye up here on the mountain. As long as ye live, ye will not lose one child or one mother if ye jest follow wherever He leads.'

"It startled me. 'Mama?' I said 'cause hit was my mama's voice I was hearin' even though she'd been dead for many years. 'Hit's yer mama's voice ye're listenin' to fer sure but hit's the Lord tellin' me what to say. Get that old bag from under the bed that belonged to Doctor Floyd'—that was John's brother who died over in Richmond durin' the war—'and get them little scissors I give ye fer yer weddin' day and that camphor oil in the cupboard along with some clean strips of linen that ye'll be needin' to help with the baby. And while ye're at hit, take along them biscuits and any other vittles ye can carry, 'cause the folks might need some nourishment while they's a waitin.'

"While she was tellin' me what to do I was goin' through the motions of doin' as she told me. Then I throwed a old blanket over my shoulders and me and Bynum headed up to Groundhog Mountain to catch Laurie's baby. When I got to the house, the poor girl was plumb wore out with workin' so hard and to be truthful, I cain't recall what I done or how I done hit. She was moanin' somethin' terrible with pain. I asked one of the men iffen thar was peach or apple brandy at hand to dull the pain. He shook his head that he didn't know but one of the men pulled out a jug of blackberry wine and I give her a teaspoon two or three times to ease her misery. I didn't approve of whiskey fer drinkin'. I see'd too many men ruined by hit, still most families kept whiskey, homemade wine or brandy in the house fer medicinal purposes, or at least that's the excuse that was give out.

"Fer a minute or two, I jest stood thar, not able to move a muscle. Well, without warnin', a powerful force took over my mind and body and 'fore I knowed what was happenin', that baby dropped into my hands and I was holdin' him up to show to his mama while I cut the cord with the scissors. I wiped out his little mouth with a clean rag and give him a pat or two between his shoulders and he started to cry. The family begun clappin' and oohin' and ahhin' while me and Bynum's sister cleaned him up, wrapped him in a crocheted blanket that Laurie's mama had made for him, and handed him to his mama. His papa said they was namin' him Kinny. Laurie said she was cold and I asked one of her cousins to heat up some water so's we could make her some tea. My mama uset to make mint tea with lots of sugar to build up our strength, she said, when we was feelin' poorly.

"Then the celebratin' started when two or three of the menfolk took out their jugs of whisky and passed 'em around. One of 'em even offered me a swig. 'I reckon ye've earned yerself a good swaller after bein' out in the cold and workin' so hard to save Laurie and her baby. We appreciate ye, Orlene Puckett, and what ye done. As far as I'm concerned, ye done sech a good job, hit won't surprise me none iffen ye don't have the callin' to be a granny woman. Hit's fer sure we could use a woman with yer skills in this neck of the woods. Why don't we make ye a pallet over thar

{ *October 14, 1939* }

by the fire so's ye kin spend the night? Hit's way too late and too cold fer ye to be headin' back to yer cabin this night. John knows whar ye are and that we'll take care of ye and see that ye git back home tomorrow safe and sound.'

"That's how I come to catch my first baby. Hit seemed to come natural to me. Course thar was times when I was alone when my own babies come so quick, full term or not, and I had no choicet but to handle the situation, whatever hit turned out to be, by myself. The womenfolk took care of each other 'cause they was hardly no doctors in these parts, at least when I first come up the mountain.

"When I held that baby in my arms and handed him to his mama, I tell ye, Tavia, hit was like I was seein' my own child but I knowed right then without one doubt that Kinny Bowman was goin' to live. I cain't take no credit fer hit or for any of the other babies that come after. The Lord give me the strength and the knowledge to do whatever had to be done. I'm jest a poor, ignorant woman but I kin tell ye one thing I know to be fer certain in this world. When the Lord calls a body out fer a special purpose, whether great or small, He will walk beside ye and git ye through hit, no matter how hard the task or how long hit takes to git hit done. The Lord has always been on my side even when I deserted Him. And don't ye forgit what I'm tellin' ye, 'specially now that ye're stuck with havin' to take care of this old, dyin' woman.

"I need to be takin' a rest after I've had me some supper. Well, I reckon hit's time fer supper though I cain't tell ye how long we've been at this story tellin' business. A bowl of crumbled up cornbread with some buttermilk would be right pleasin'. This day has lasted fer about a week. The older ye git, the faster the time goes by. At least that's what they tell me. But I've set fer hours at my cabin wishin' fer the end of a day that was goin' as slow as pourin' molasses. Plumb foolish fer any human to be wishin' fer time to speed up. Seems like hit was only yesterdy when I was wonderin' how my life would turn out, what I'd be when I growed up. Now I'm closet to a hunderd and I'm still mullin' hit over as to what I'll be when I'm a growed woman. We ne'er git to the point whar we sees ourselves as growed up. That's the problem of hit all. On the outside, we are wrinkled up skin and bones. On the inside, we're still the little girl who played with dolls and listened to her mama's songs and stories. I'll finish my supper and ye can help put me to bed. I reckon ye're as wore out from the listenin' and writin' down of my life as I am from the actual livin' of it."

October 15, 1939

"AUNT ORLENE, ARE YE AWAKE? Ye've been in the bed since about seven o'clock last evenin' and hit's the next day with noon time done passed. Wavy's here a helpin' me. We've turned ye over and changed yer sheets, washed yer face and hands, and got ye into a fresh nightshirt. Yer eyes keep on openin' and closin' so's we ain't sure whether you kin hear us or not. Iffen ye want to keep on layin' in the bed, we ain't goin' to bother ye, but I'll git ye some good hot coffee and a biscuit iffen ye're hungry. Appears to me, Wavy, that either she cain't hear us or she's jest too weak to try to talk. I knowed she was usin' up all her strength yesterdy when she went on and on about that first baby she borned up thar near the Groundhog. Kin ye imagine her bein' able to recollect what happened with all them other thousand babies that she was responsible fer bringin' into the world? From whar I'm standin' I'd say she's a prime example of how a human bein' can take misery and hardship and turn hit into somethin' good and of lastin' value that reaches out to so far thar ain't no end to hit."

"Aunt Tavia, do ye think she'll live long enough to tell the rest of her story so's ye kin write hit down 'fore ever'body starts forgittin' who she was and what she did? My mama says she's ministered to others besides the mothers and their babies. She told me that sick people would stop by the cabin and Aunt Orlene would give 'em medicine fer jest about any ailment ye kin name 'cause she made her own medicines from the plants that grows in these here mountains. And she cooked food and took hit to them that was sick or had a death in the family or a new baby to look after. She hardly ever took time to do fer herself 'cause she was too busy takin' care of others. Busiest woman she ever knowed, my mama said, and on top of that, she kept the cleanest house fer miles around. People would stop by the cabin to visit or ask fer advice jest so's they could git a good look at the cabin and how purty hit was with the way Aunt Orlene put the furnishin's together, sewin' curtains and braidin' rugs, crochetin' and knittin' afghans and coverlets. Ye name hit, she could do hit. Sayin' was that Aunt Orlene Puckett's hands was always workin' at somethin' useful.

"I asked her about what Mama told me one day when I come over to bring her a jar of sourwood honey and she was settin' in her rockin' chair, sewin' pockets on her apron. 'Mama says that yer hands ne'er stay still, Aunt Orlene. Is that the truth? Do ye have the fidgets or somethin'?' She said, 'No I ain't got the fidgets, Wavy, but I'll tell ye this. My mama always told us children that idle hands and minds was the devil's workshop. I believed her when she said them words and I believe hit still. Thar's jest too much work to be done in this world fer any body to set around and waste time, 'cause hit ain't jest time that's goin' to waste, hit's smarts and talent and good intentions that's goin' to waste along with the time.' Then she started in on the Bible, 'Jest like that story Jesus told about the master who gives his servants so much money and two of 'em put hit to good use and hit multiplies the worth of hit, but the last one is a lazy scardy cat, so he goes off and buries the money in the ground. When the master comes back, he ain't got nothin' to show in the way of extry earnin's so the master sends him a packin' and gives his money to the one who done the most with hit. Maybe that's hard to understand now, but as ye grow into womanhood, ye'll begin to sort hit out and make sense of what I'm tellin' ye. Ye cain't beat the stories that Jesus told as far as gittin' to the bottom line of livin'.'

"Thar's one thing fer sure, Aunt Tavia, when ye asked Aunt Orlene a question, she didn't hold nothin' back. She give ye the full measure of what she had stored up in her head. Mama said that she could talk about most anything in the world a body could name, but iffen she was lackin' knowledge of the matter bein' discussed, she didn't mind sayin' she didn't know and to go find somebody who could shed some knowledge, and maybe a smidgeon of wisdom, on the subject at hand. She told me one day that thar warn't no excuse fer a person to go through life ignorant, with or without the benefit of education. 'People who wants to larn, kin,' she said. 'Hit's as simple as openin' up a book or a mind of a man or a woman who has the knowledge ye're searchin' for. I cain't read or write, Wavy, but I reckon no person in these parts would proposition that I'm ignorant as far as common sense goes or in the ability to make hit through each day doin' whatever has to be done.' And with that said, she walked out the cabin door and started choppin' firewood fer the stove. Aunt Tavia, do ye think she's goin' to wake up today? She ain't moved a muscle or so much as made a sound whilst we been standin' her watchin' her. Is she breathin', kin ye tell?"

I'm a breathin' all right. As fer talkin', even iffen I was tryin', I don't think I'd git a word in edgewise. And ye're talkin' about me jest the same as I ain't even in the room. Not that hit ain't a common occurrence as far as old people is concerned. People think ye're deaf most of the time. As far as the rest of the time, supposin' ye kin hear? Well, they tell theirselves, ye ain't goin' to understand what they're talkin' about anyway. Set ye up in a chair in the corner or put ye in the bed and kivver ye up to yer ears. Hit's all the same to them that has the burden of takin' care of folks. And hit is a burden, no matter how they go around denyin' the inconvenience and the tediousness of hit all. Might as well be dead as far as I'm concerned.

Oh, they's prayin' that the Lord will spare Mama or Papa or Grandpapa or Aunt Josie fer one more day but hit's all fer show. They'd be ashamed to admit that they's plumb wore out with the washin' of the shriveled up old body and the cleanin' up of the puddles and the spoon feedin' that ends up in drool runnin' down the chin, the liftin' and turnin' and strugglin' to pay attention to ever' sound that comes from the dried up mouth that coughs and spits and gurgles with ever' raspy breath. The plain truth of the matter is that them that's doin' the caretakin' as well as them that's on the receivin' end are good and tired of the whole business. Both sides keep wonderin' when the waitin' be over. One is askin' the Lord when He's goin' to stop the foolishness and take her on home to her new life while the other is askin' the Lord when He's goin' to stop the foolishness and let her go on with her own life here and now. Hit's a sorry state of affairs as I see hit. Ye're supposed to know what's best, Lord, so I'm leavin' hit up to ye to act on yer promise, but could ye quit dilly dallyin' about and jest git on with hit?

The two had stopped talkin' so I decided to give it a try. "Could ye git me a drink of water, Wavy? My mouth feels like hit's full of cotton. I reckon I've been in this bed a good while, but I'm confessin' to ye both that I don't believe I'll be gittin' up today. My dreamin' done worked me as hard as carryin' that twenty-five pound bag of cornmeal up from the Martin store all them years ago when the war fought hitself out. That's about how I'm feelin' right now. My old body's been fightin' a war to stay alive, but we know how hit's goin' to turn out. We ain't goin' to win this one. Don't git yerselves all worked up. The white flag ain't gone up yet, not today, maybe not tomorrow but one thing is fer certain, surrender is comin'. Them that's been defeated, they cain't deny hit but in the end they make the final decision as to when to put their weapons down and ask fer mercy from the enemy.

"Set down here beside me and I'll tell ye about the famous preacher

{ October 15, 1939 }

man that was borned down in The Holler on the coldest and bitterest night ye kin imagine in January of 1890. Thar was a blizzard blowin' up on the mountain that night and I recall that John said to me whilst he was makin' ready fer a good night's sleep, 'Orlene, ye know I'm not much at prayin' but I've been prayin' all this day, ever since that wind and snow started up, that ye'd not be called out fer a birthin' this night. The mama might be in a bad way but ye'd be in right much danger yerself goin' out in sech a storm. Come on to bed. Thar's nary a soul could find his way anywhars with the snow fallin' so hard ye cain't see two inches in front of yer face. And I know ye ain't asked me to, but this mornin' I put some nails in them old brogans of your'n to keep ye from slippin' and slidin' in the snow and the ice when ye venture out in bad weather. The soldiers fixed their boots thataway come winter time durin' the war and hit worked most of the time. Seemed like a good idee to me seein' ye's out when the ground's mostly froze over from November till the end of March. But I reckon ye won't be worryin' about sech when the temperature's below freezin' and as far as ye kin see ever'thing is covered with ice. Put yer sewin' away and come on to bed to help keep yer man warm, ole woman.'

"That was almost a speech as far as John Puckett's attempts at conversin' went, and he took great delight in callin' me 'ole woman'. I was still on this side of bein' fifty when he commenced his needlin' of me, more oft than not in the company of other menfolk who had took the same perverse pleasure in referrin' to their wives as iffen they'd walked this earth more years than the men theirselves. Well, the truth is that women was broken down and wore out from the hard work and the constant carryin' and birthin' of children, one after the other. Did we know what caused them babes to be springin' forth at the drop of a hat? Fer certain we did, since hit usually occurred right after the hat was dropped, along with a few other garments we won't mention. Could we do anything about hit? Maybe we could, maybe we couldn't."

"Aunt Orlene! Wavy is right here listenin' to ever' word that ye're whisperin'. Ye shouldn't be tellin' hit in sech a coarse manner."

"Oh, hush up, Tavia," I laughed. "The child understands more than adults give her credit fer, as is true of most children. What she don't know, she'd best be larnin', not goin' into the marriage state as ignorant as all getout, which is one of the main problems that's causin' these poor mountain women to be havin' one baby right after another, with no let up. Menfolk don't care. Oh, maybe at first, when the wife dies on 'em and takes the baby with her, while leavin' an orphan or two or three behind. They cry and moan and carry on fer a week or two, but 'fore long, they're out lookin' fer some young thing that's got her head in the clouds, waitin' fer Prince Charmin' to show up. And would ye believe, when he comes along, ridin' a mule and sportin' a beard turnin' gray, with a small army of runny-nosed orphans trailin' behind, she thinks she's done struck gold!

"As fer as I kin tell, people took the comin' of a child as a gift from the Lord, regardless of the circumstances, and big families was a way of life. Children was needed to work the farms and keep the families fed. The motto of these mountain men come down to 'The Lord giveth and He taketh away. Blessed be the name of the Lord.' When the first wife dies, with her back done broke and her teeth gone, make room fer the next one to take away our sorrow and our tom-cattin' ways and keep on sendin' them children to lighten the load at the end of the plow. Amen."

"Aunt Orlene, here ye was leadin' us to the story of the bornin' of that preacher man, Bob Childress, and ye done led us down the paths of sin and degredation. I think ye need to rest up a bit and settle yer nerves so's ye don't fill Wavy's head with no more of yer Satan filled talk."

"Satan kin show up wearin' a suit or a pair of overalls. He does his business and moves on. Don't go makin' me out to be one of his handmaids, Tavia. The truth is the truth and the sooner that Wavy finds hit out, the better off she'll be. And the truth fer me at the moment is that I've been ramblin' on without sayin' much to be of any uset to ye and I'm sorry to be a wearyin' ye so. There'll be time enough tomorrow to tell the story of the Childress family and how that young'un made his way into the world. Give me some of that good hot soup that's been simmerin' on the stove all day, help me to the pot, and wrap me up tight in them quilts. The Bible tells us that each day is sufficient unto hisself and I believe hit to be true. Even though I ne'er larned to read, Mama made us memorize one verse each day whilst we was growin' up. When times was hard, one of 'em fer sure would pop into my head jest like the Lord was talkin' to me in a personal way. Thar ain't no finer education in all the world than what kin be larned from the Bible. That's my testimony fer this day and I'll be tellin' ye both good night even iffen the sun ain't gone down behind the hills. Them soft colors creepin' through the winder will be enough to ease my bones and set my mind to a peaceful rest. If the Lord is willin', he will grant me another day. If hit ain't a part of His plan, I'll be seein' the two of ye agin when we meet in heaven."

{ October 15, 1939 }

"Could ye hear what she was sayin' thar at the end, Aunt Tavia? Her voice was mighty weak, comin' and goin' all whispery like."

"Somethin' about gettin' her rest and meetin' in heaven. I reckon she's preparin' herself to leave us, Wavy. How any more days or more'n likely hours she has left ain't fer us to say. One thing we kin say. The likes of sech a woman we ain't likely to see agin in our lifetime. Ye head on home now. Come back in the mornin' if ye kin. Our time to be in her company is slippin' away mighty fast."

October 16, 1939

"Have I done told the story of Bob Childress yet? Is Wavy with ye, Tavia?"

"Land's sakes, Aunt Orlene! Ye ain't even opened yer eyes and here comes words spewin' out of yer mouth without a bit of warnin'. Ye was sleepin' so soft I was jest about to lean down to check to see—"

"If I was still breathin'? I reckon I kin figure what's goin' through yer mind when hit comes to Orlene Puckett lyin' here in yer bed. Well, hit seems to me that I'm still alive, though my limbs feel like they's not got no life to 'em. I've been tryin' fer the longest time to raise one of my hands to git yer attention but thar's not so much as a finger twitchin' on the one or th'other. Kin ye hear what I'm sayin' to ye? I cain't hardy hear a word I'm sayin', that is, iffen I'm makin' sounds that might be words."

"Wavy's here, and we kin hear ye, but the words is comin' and goin' like the water runnin' o'er the rocks in the creek down the hill. Ye need to conserve yer strength, Aunt Orlene, till I kin git some hot coffee in ye and maybe a biscuit with some honey. Does that sound good to ye? I kin hold the cup to yer mouth while Wavy holds ye up against the piller thar. Jest nod when ye want a bite of the biscuit and I'll put a bit of hit in yer mouth and give ye time to swaller."

"Oh, my. This life is done come full circle. I come into the world without a tooth in my head dependin' on my mama and others to feed me and clean me and take me one place to another and hit done seem like I'm headin' out of this world in the same tiresome way. Onliest difference is that this time I know how the whole thing will turn out."

"Here. Take yer coffee and yer biscuit so ye kin build up yer strength a bit."

"Tavia, ye are a foolish child, but I thank ye fer yer carin' and yer patience. When ye're finished doin' fer the least of these, that would be yer ole Aunt Orlene, ye and Wavy kin help me to the rockin' chair in front of the fire. I want the pleasure of hits warmth and comfort one more time while I tell ye about the night Bob Childress, poor, sickly child that he was, made his entrance into this world. Kin ye hear me?"

"Yer voice is mostly a hoarse whisper, but me and Wavy is pullin' chairs up real closet to ye so's we kin hear ye. Take yer time. Thar ain't no hurry. I'm writin' hit down and Wavy will repeat what ye say iffen I git behind or lose the words."

"Ye're wrong about one thing, Tavia, and I apologize fer havin' to correct ye 'cause, ye see, thar *is* a hurry and I cain't take my time since the Lord has made hit clear to me that I ain't goin' to be on this earth come this time next week. That's a fact that should be as plain to ye and Wavy as the nose on yer face."

"No one knows the time or the place."

"But them that's got common sense kin make a mighty good guess, I reckon. I was settin' 'fore the fire, jest like right now, one cold bitter night in January of eighteen hunderd and ninety, almost a year to the day when Kinny Bowman was borned up on Groundhog Mountain, when thar come a knockin' on the cabin door. John was asleep. In the winter time, he turned in about the same time as the chickens, and I called out fer whoever hit was to come in.

"Hasten Childress was standin' thar lookin' fer all the world like he was already froze to death. 'My papa sent me fer ye, Aunt Orlene, to come down and help my mama. Thar's a baby a comin' and havin' a mighty hard time of hit. Don't seem like she's got no strength left. Papa wouldn't say hit in front of the younger ones, but he called me aside and told me he was afeard that Mama was dyin' and the baby would be dead as well. Please come and help her. My papa loves my mama more'n his own life and us children ain't goin' to make hit without her.'

"He was cryin' so hard, he was sputterin' all the time he was talkin' and I thought he would nigh choke to death. Well, I knowed the Childress family. Like most of the families up and down the mountain, they was poor but they was proud. They lived in a tiny old two-room shack that was hardly big enough to turn around in. They was already six children, with Hasten bein' the oldest, and the new baby would make another mouth to feed. 'Son,' I said. 'Thar's a blizzard outside. I cain't believe ye made hit up the mountain with the wind a blowin' so hard and the snow comin' down so thick ye cain't see yer own hands in front of ye. We's goin' to have to wait till mornin' 'fore we strike out in sech weather and hope hit takes a turn fer the better.'

"The child broke down in tears, beggin' and pleadin' fer me to come with him. 'I'll git ye down thar, Aunt Orlene. If I kin make hit up the mountain by myself, hit's fer sure the two of us kin make hit down together.'

"I could not look that young boy in the face and tell him I would not go with him. No, I did not have the heart fer hurtin' Hasten Childress any more'n he was already hurtin'. I pointed towards my bag and told him what needed to go in hit whilst I pulled on my old boots, nails and all, and pulled John's coat around me. Then I picked up two quilts from the bed, handed one to Hasten and gathered the other around me. I pulled a wool scarf over my head and face, opened the door, grabbed the boy's hand, and we headed down the mountain right into a blizzard the likes of which I ain't seen since.

"We could not see the sky above us. Thar was no moon nor stars. Hasten's tracks comin' up the mountain was done covered up with snow so deep hit come almost up to our knees. Still, by the grace of God, we made hit down the mountain and found our way to the Childress farmhouse, if ye could call hit a house. Inside, Mr. Childress and the children was huddled in a corner whilst Lum, the mama, was stretched out on a rickety old bedframe that the papa had pulled in front of a poor excuse of a fire; they was no firewood left to burn. Mrs. Childress looked up at me and thanked me fer comin'. She was all skin and bones. Ye couldn't believe sech a thin creature was carryin' a child, much less in the act of bringin' hit into the world.

"I knelt down aside of her, helped her into a half-standin', half-settin' position to take the burden off her back all the time a talkin' to her to give her encouragement and keep her calm. I was thinkin' that fer sure this was one baby that would not come out alive, but he proved me wrong. When I caught that baby, he was long and skinny, didn't seem to have no weight to him at all. He squalled whilst I was cleanin' him up and I heerd Mr. Childress break into a half-sobbin', half-laughin' kind of sound and the children clapped and started askin' iffen they could see their new brother. I told 'em to hold off a while while I settled him down to begin to take some nourishment from his mama. But her milk warn't comin' in and as I looked around and turned my eyes on Mr. Childress, hit struck me real hard that him and his wife had been starvin' theirselves to feed them children. That's why the baby was sech a shriveled up little thing and why Lum didn't have no milk.

"I called to Hasten and told him to head out to git some milk fer his mama and little brother as soon as hit was light enough to see. I recall tellin' him that I didn't care what kind, goat, cow, whatever a neighbor'd give him, jest to git some milk back as fast as he could, which he did. I stayed with the family fer nigh to a week, makin' sure that both Mrs. Childress and the baby was gainin' strength. I sent Hasten out to ask the neighbors to send food fer the family, told 'em that Mr. Childress would pay 'em back soon as he got his crops in come summer or early fall. I did the cookin' and lookin' after them other children till Lum was back on her feet. By the time she was able to git up and start doin' the chores of runnin' the house, the snow was meltin' and so early one mornin' I started on up the mountain. Hit weren't as cold that day but I spent most of my time slippin' and slidin' in the slushy snow.

"When I got to the cabin, John was settin' inside in front of a blazin' fire, smokin' his pipe."

"Whar ye been, Orlene?" he wanted to know.

"Down to the Childress farm to catch a baby," I told him. "I been gone over a week now, since the night of the big blizzard. Have ye had plenty to eat whilst I been away?"

"Reckon so," he answered. "After the blizzard died down, I headed over to Riley's place and I jest come back this afternoon. What ye plannin' fer us to have fer supper?"

"I'm plannin' to have whatever ye're plannin' to have," I told him. "What's on the stove?"

"Some cornbread I brought from Riley's and a big slice of ham. Thar's a few eggs I brought in from the hen house. We could have us some breakfast fer supper, then we wouldn't have to fix hit in the mornin.'" He was laughin' so hard at his own jokin', he turned all red in his face.

"Sounds like a mighty good idee to me, John. I'm goin' to take off my boots and warm my feet by the fire. Let me know when ye got hit on the table."

"Ye ain't funnin' me, are ye?" he asked, a wary look of his face.

"No, I ain't funnin' ye," I answered, bitin' down hard on the words. He started pickin' the eggs out of the basket while I set myself in front of the fire, tryin' to bring the warmth back to my cold, wet feet.

Years later, when that boy become a preacher man up and down and around the parts that faced the Buffalo, he come to see me up at the cabin. Knocked at the door and walked right in. Tipped his hat and looked me straight in the eye.

"Mornin', Ms. Puckett,' he said. "My mama told me that you were the granny woman that delivered me on a cold winter's night in late January of eighteen ninety. I was passing by on the way to one of my churches and wanted to stop and thank you for saving the lives of my mother and me when that terrible blizzard was raging all about. I owe my life and my ministry to you and the Lord; I've always be sure that God sent you to us on that night. My mother lived to take care of us children and my father turned out to be a pretty good farmer in the end."

He went on afore I could say anything. "From what I've heard, you've been a godsend to many a family for miles in any direction to be taken. As a minister, I should be asking you if you've been saved and have taken Jesus as your savior, but hearing about your ministry makes me believe that you're indeed a true believer and that God has blessed your life and your work and that you take that blessing with you wherever you go."

"Thank ye fer stoppin' by, Pastor Childress. I've heerd tell of ye and the good things that ye've been doin' as well, buildin' churches and schools fer the children. People have a mighty high regard fer ye. At least, if they ain't tryin' to stir up moonshine and run hit down the mountain."

We both laughed and he turned to go but I called him back. "As far back as I kin recall, I was baptized when I was jest a young girl, but most of them that would recall the day have moved on to other places. Thar's some that's still aggravatin' me about goin' down to the creek fer another baptizin' to make sure that I'm headed fer heaven and me goin' to be ninety or somewhar's about thar dependin' on who ye talk to."

"Don't fret, young lady. The Lord knows your heart. I'm carrying a jar of water with me in case I need to do a baptizing when I'm visiting members of my churches, but I'm not sure your Baptist brothers and sisters would take to a sprinkling from a Presbyterian as a sign of salvation. Whether or not you make it back down to the creek, there is no doubt in my mind that the Lord is waiting to receive you with His arms open wide. Thank you again, dear lady, for your kind and compassionate heart. I'll make hit a point to stop the next time I'm passing by. May the Lord continue to bless you and keep you so long as you continue to serve Him for the rest of your days."

"That was a fine day and I will ne'er forget the kindness that was shinin' from Pastor Childress's face or the twinklin' of them steel blue eyes as he stood thar talkin' in sech a grand way as iffen I was a body of high rank. As he started up that wore-out old automobile that someone

{ *October 16, 1939* }

had give him, I said to myself, Orlene Puckett, ye are jest a poor, ignorant mountain woman who kin hardly write her own name, but when the Lord opens a door, He expects ye to walk through hit, 'cause He's plannin' to walk through hit with ye. And He will stay right thar aside ye makin' yer way plain and straight as long as ye put yer faith in Him.

"I still believe that today and have found hit to be true. Now, hit seems to me, we've done a good day's work gittin' that preacher borned and sendin' him out into the world. I'm of a mind that iffen ye touch one person's life for the right, and that man or woman touches another, and so on, somethin' good will come of hit on into whatever eternity might be. I kin recall my brothers skippin' stones acrost the neighor's pond. When one of 'em hit the water, hit caused a ripple. Then come one after hit, then another till the ripples of one little old rock reached all the way to the edge of the pond. Lookin' out fer yer neighbor leads to lookin' out fer the next one up the road. We jest keep passin' the carin' on from one to the other. In time, I reckon, this life up here in these mountains will be the better fer the like of a man like Pastor Childress. Course hit ain't goin' to happen over night or even in a body's lifetime, but hit does provide a mighty big dose of hope to the rest of us.

"Right now I cain't hardly hear my own voice. A cup of hot sassafras tea would go down mighty smooth and maybe let me rest easy tonight. Don't want no supper. No appetite. I'll drink my tea and ye kin help me into my bed, then ye head on home, Wavy, 'fore the sunset finishes driftin' behind the mountains.

"Hit's a mighty purty world, ain't hit, girls? Ye reckon heaven is more wonderful than what surrounds us as far as our eyes kin see? Even with streets paved with gold and angels flyin' around with silvery wings, I'd be hard pressed to hold them things above a field ablaze with goldenrod or the bustin' open of a milkweed pod. But farther along, we'll know more about hit. That was one of Mama's favorite songs. Iffen ye know the words, Tavia and Wavy, I'd be mighty obliged to hear a verse or two whilst ye're dressin' me fer bed. Thar ain't nothin' like the singin' of a hymn to settle yer mind and bring peace to yer soul. The Lord willin', tomorrow will bring another day. Should I not live to see hit, at least ye'll know whar to find me!"

"Aunt Tavia, seems like she's talkin' about dyin' more'n more in the past two or three days and laughs about hit. Don't seem right to me. And she's sleepin' more in the mornin' and goin' to bed afore the sun goes down. Why, this time a year ago, she was goin' over to the farm to born little Maxwell Hawks. She was up 'fore the roosters crowed and settin' up in her chair mendin' or stitchin' a piece fer a quilt, even with them bad eyes of hers."

"Ye need to understand, Wavy, that the body starts shuttin' down when death's around the corner. Old people sleep more and more cause they's restin' up fer the hard work of dyin', at least that's what the old-timers say. The body don't need food fer workin' so they stop eatin' and that goes fer the rest of what's inside keepin' us alive, the heart, our lungs, the kidneys and bowels. The blood ain't flowin' so fast and hard, and the breathin' slows down. The body fights to go on livin', but sooner or later hit winds down jest like the clock on the mantle.

"If ye plan to come over here ever' day till she's passed on over, hit might be this night or a day or two from now. She might even last a week or more. Yer Aunt Orlene is a tough old bird. I heerd John call her that one day afore he passed on, but she has a tender heart and lovin' hands. Ye need to prepare yerself fer what's comin' and be calm in yer own heart and mind. However long she lives, she's earned her reward in heaven, even though us Baptists don't believe in earnin' salvation. She knows who her savior is whether or not anyone else accepts the when or where or how that hit come to be. Go on home, child. She's sound asleep. Maybe she'll be pert and lively enough on the morrow to go on with her story."

"What iffen she don't live, Aunt Tavia? What iffen she don't tell us the rest of the stories about bein' a granny woman and tendin' to the womenfolk as they was havin' their babies? The school marm talks about how a country's history is important fer citizens to know and how hit's the little bits of people's own histories, like whar they come from and whar they settled and how they come to make their livin' that make up the big story of a state like Virginia and then ye put all them stories together and ye understand the history of a whole country like the United States. But she told us that the little stories git lost cause some people cain't read or write down what thar lives was about and the onliest thing left is what is called oral history, the tellin' of one story, then another, and a person writin' hit down and puttin' hit in a book, like ye're doin' with Aunt Orlene. Are ye goin' to make a book about Aunt Orlene when ye finish writin' down what she says and what iffen she don't git to the end? What will ye do then?"

"Gracious sakes, child. Fer certain yer mind seems to be workin' over time and gittin' ye all riled up here at the end of the day. First of all, I

{ *October 16, 1939* }

ain't writin' no book. I'm jest puttin' some of her thoughts on paper and I'll pass 'em on to whoever wants to read hit and iffen one person wants to copy some of hit down, that'll be well and good. Second thing is this: When Aunt Orlene passes on, whatever she ain't told, whether hit be of a private nature or due to the fact that time run on, well, we cain't do nothin' about what's left undone. Still thar are plenty of folks around who know a story or two about how she borned them or others in the family, their children or grandchildren, nephews, nieces, cousins, neighbors, and sech. The namin' of each and ever' one goes on and on. The deeds of Aunt Orlene is goin' to be hangin' around these parts fer a long, long time. Why, even yerself, Wavy Quesinberry, ye'll have a say in the matter of Orlene Hawks Puckett. Ye kin tell how ye was with her in her last days and what she had to say about her life up here on the mountain. She was the one who brung you and yer mama, Iduna, into this world. Keep all these memories alive, Wavy, fer whoever comes along and is willin' to listen. Now, as I done told ye, run on home and pester yer mama fer awhile. I'm plumb wore out with listenin' to Aunt Orlene's ramblin's, not to mention tryin' to answer the questions that keep on poppin' into that head of yers."

October 17, 1939

"H IT'S NEAR TO NOONDAY and we ain't heerd a peek outa Aunt Orlene this mornin'. I kin hear her breathin' but hit's slow and raspy soundin'. Do ye think she's goin' to wake up or jest go on sleepin' like that till she's passed on? She ain't moved one bit since I walked in the door and that was jest as the sun was comin' up. I told Mama I wanted to be with Aunt Orlene as much as possible in her last days. Since hit's Saturday and I didn't have to go to the schoolhouse, she let me come without so much as doin' my chores."

"She's moaned onct or twict and she seemed to be talkin' to herself early of the mornin', but I couldn't make no sense of what she was sayin'. She's mumblin' about somethin' goin' on at the foot of the mountain, but the words is run together so's ye cain't make heads or tails of hit. My mama done the same thing when she was dyin'. We would try to listen and answer back, but thar warn't no use. I reckon hit's the way most of us come to our end. We got somethin' to say, but no way to git hit out and hardly a body to listen, much less understand what we've got on our mind.

"But Aunt Orlene won't be neglected. People's been comin' by askin' about how she's doin' and bringin' food, offerin' to help stay with her so's I kin take in some extry rest. Thar ain't nary a soul about that don't have a tie to her, whether through marriage or sons and daughters, nieces or nephews, cousins, fer nigh to near five generations. She's touched many a life the same as that Pastor Childress she was tellin' us about yesterday. Hit's mighty possible seein' her layin' on that bed that his story might be the last one to be heerd from her own lips and we's the last to hear her tell hit. Let's have us a bite to eat 'fore noon, so's we'll be able to give her the attention she needs when she wakes up."

"Do ye believe she'll be wakin' up today, Aunt Tavia, and that she'll be able to speak to us and hear us iffen we answer her back?"

"That's somethin' only the good Lord knows, Wavy, but we'd best be prepared iffen hit turns out to be so."

I kin hear the two of 'em talkin' and my mind says that I'm talkin' along with 'em but I cain't hear my voice sayin' one word. I smell the smoke from the fire and the coffee that sets warmin' on the stove, but I

{ *October 17, 1939* }

don't feel no hunger in my stomach nor pain in these ole bones, though my legs, from my feet up to my ankles and knees on up to the insides of my thighs, has done provided one ache after another due to all the walkin' and ridin' Roadie and bein' carried from one farm to another by them rickety old farm wagons bouncin' up and down the cowpaths that was took to be roads.

I'm tryin' hard to push myself up off the bed and git my legs under me so's I kin stand up, but I don't feel nothin' workin'. I'd be ready to believe that I've up and died but I ain't see'd Jesus yet, and instead of a heavenly choir, all I'm hearin' is Tavia and Wavy yappin' away, wonderin' this and that about the state of my bein'. Iffen I could join in, I'd confess to the fact that I'm a wonderin' along with 'em. I'm wonderin' iffen I'll set in front of that warm fire agin or tell Tavia and Wavy about the night I come down to The Holler to borne two babies, two little girls at the same time, the onliest twins I was privileged to witness in my life time.

"Ever' child is a miracle, a blessin' from God. Ever' child…"

"She's tryin' to tell us somethin'. I think she's wakin' up. She's talkin' that's fer sure. Maybe iffen we listen real hard, we kin figure out what she's sayin'."

"I kin hear ye talkin'. Kin ye hear me? Iffen ye kin, I'm right thirsty. A cup of cold water would maybe clear my head and soothe my throat and these parched lips o' mine. Don't want nothin' to eat. I ain't hungry but I'm right cold. Kin ye and Wavy pick me up and take me to my chair by the fire? Don't seem like my legs is wantin' to work this mornin'."

"What about yer nightshirt and yer bed? Are they dry? We kin pick ye up to set on the pot and change ye into fresh under garments 'fore we put ye in the chair. Ye don't weigh much more'n one of them red birds a flittin' around outside the winder."

"Thank ye, Tavia, but I ain't sure I got the strength to do more'n have a few sips of water. Hit's hard fer me to take in that I mighten ne'er walk down this mountain agin. I kin hear that red bird a chirpin' about but I don't reckon I could see 'em or even step outside to look about. My eyesight has left me fer sure. I've been tryin' to open my eyes all of this mornin' but I cain't see yer faces and hit pains me to tell ye sech. Hit seems thar's a veil been pulled o'er my face and took my vision from me. I knowed hit was fadin' away fer a time now but I didn't have the heart to say hit to ye cause then I knowed hit would be the truth fer sure."

"We'll take care of ye, Aunt Orlene. We could tell ye wasn't seein' right good, but we didn't let on. As fer me, ye ain't missin' much not seein' this face, but Wavy here, she's about as purty as they come. Ever'one knows ye ain't no blood kin, but people's always remarkin' that Wavy reminds 'em of ye with yer blue eyes and that white-yellerish hair."

"I hope the child has more hair than I do," I laughed. "Cain't be but a few raggedy strings left to tie up on top of my head. Prob'bly why my head feels so icy cold most of the time. I'm ne'er as bald as the top of the Buffalo."

"Ain't no time fer vanity, Aunt Orlene, least ways fer the two of us. Wavy here kin save up what's left of our'n fer her own use as she needs hit. Fer now we'll make ye as comfortable as we kin and have ye settled in front of the fire in no time. Wavy and me wasn't sure ye'd be up and around today."

"Well, I may be up but I ain't sure about the around part. Depends on how ye look at hit, I'm supposin'.

"Aunt Orlene, ye was speakin' as ye was a stirrin' around. Maybe ye was talkin' in yer sleep but hit sounded like hit had somethin' to do with babies. 'Ever' child is…'"

"A miracle. I was thinkin' hit in my head and hit jest tumbled right out. Some babies come easy jest like puttin' butter on a biscuit. Some takes a long hard time and puts the mama and the whole family through torment, wonderin' if the child will be alive or have some damage to hit. Some come out yellin' and mad at the world and ye know they's goin' to give anybody and ever'body down the road a hard time, but still when ye hold that newborn child fer the first time, ye cain't help believin' that God is givin' the world a gift, another chance to to do somethin' good, to bring light and a bit of hope into the world.

"They was times when I didn't know what to do or how to help a poor woman that was strugglin' so hard fer both herself and her baby. Husbands and children and other kinfolk would be standin' by beggin' me to do somethin' whilst they was prayin' to the Lord to intervene and 'save this mother and her child.' The first time the baby come out with the chord wrapped around his neck and he warn't breathin' I thought I would faint right thar and then, but some force I could not name took my hands and told them what to do. When the cord come loose and the baby turned from blue to pink and started mewin' like a newborn kitten, relief come like a flood over my body and my soul. People was praisin' me and pattin' me on the back whilst I was tryin' to tell 'em that hit was all the work of the Lord. I had no idee what I'd done or how the child come to live. What was workin' through me was nothin' less than a gift and we owed Him the praise and all the glory.

"After the last of my own babies died, I thought my broken heart would never mend, but would ye believe that when I was called to go tend to Laurie Bowman despite my lack of faith and without ever bein' a granny woman 'fore that night, seein' that baby come out of his mama and holdin' him in my hands give me the feelin' that in some way, that baby *was* my own child. And that's how hit was fer ever' one of 'em that come afterwards. They was my babies in a way that I cain't explain, even to this day. The Lord took mine away but He give back over and over agin so's I could hand 'em over to them that would take care of 'em and raise 'em.

"I made my peace with the Lord many a year ago when hit come to me pure and simple that He kin take ever' trial and tribulation that comes our way and turn hit into good. That's what I was thinkin' layin' in my bed. I could hear the two of ye talkin' and thoughts was goin' through my head that I was fer certain not goin' to git up this mornin' or any mornin' hereafter. I couldn't feel my arms nor my legs and my lips warn't wantin' to move even though I had a terrible thirst. So this is how hit ends, I was sayin' to myself. I cain't do nothin' fer myself. I cain't move nor talk and even iffen I could, who would understand a word I'm sayin'. Then hit come to me. One by one, I was seein' them tiny faces and hearin' a mama call out a name till I warn't thinkin' of my own endin', but of all the beginnin's I've witnessed, ever' one of 'em a miracle.

"I must have said them words plain enough to be understood and then I was wakin' up and I was feelin' that I wanted to git up and set 'fore that warm fire one more time so's I could tell another story or two to you two. Hit don't appear that the Lord is ready fer me jest yet so I ain't goin' to complain no more, leastways till the next time."

"Are ye up to tellin' any more stories about the babies that ye done borned? Aunt Tavia told me that ye borned both my mama and me. Do you recollect any of the particulars about how my mama come into the world, since I reckon that was sech a long time ago?"

"Must've been near to thirty-five years ago. How old are ye now, Wavy? Near to fifteen, I reckon and yer mama was somewhar's atween seventeen, maybe eighteen or nineteen, when ye was borned. I was in my early sixties, I reckon. I'm thinkin' I walked to yer mama's place 'cause hit warn't more'n three or four miles at the mostest. 'Fore Roadie come along, Coy would let me ride his horse, Roy, iffen hit was far. I kin recall goin' twenty miles or more on that horse or the mule if thar was a need. Anyways, one of yer uncles come to the cabin right early that mornin' and by the time we made hit to the house, yer mama was well on her way into the world. Warn't hardly nothin' fer me to do but to reach down and grab her 'fore she hit the floor. What stands out in my mind was what took place after I handed her over to her mama. Yer grandpapa asked her what she was goin' to name the child and yer grandmama, who was driftin' off to sleep, said somethin' to the effect that she didn't know but hit come out real soft and slurred, sounded like 'I don't know' but run together and whispery. So yer grandmama leaned down and asked her agin, 'What's the baby's name to be?'"

"She tried hard but the words was jest as unclear as the first time they come out. The papa looked about and told them that had gathered about, I think she's sayin' Iduna, a name that was not known in them parts that I recollect, but hit stuck and leastways as I kin tell, yer grandmama ne'er disputed the name or how hit come to be.

"When yer grandma was restin' with her baby, yer mama, I headed on back to the cabin, but as I come up the hill thar was a young boy standin' near the cabin waitin' fer me. Said I was needed down in The Holler fer a neighbor's wife. I filled up my bag with fresh supplies and headed on down, even though I had to walk the distance cause thar warn't time to make hit to the Hawks' to borrow Roy. Took most of the afternoon to git thar, and the girl, who was no more'n fifteen or sixteen, was plumb scared through the whole birthin'. But the baby, a little boy, come right easy jest as had yer grandmama so I thanked the Lord that He hadn't made the day's work harder than hit might have turned out.

"When I made hit back to the cabin late that evenin', John was settin' outside, smokin' his pipe. 'Don't ye think ye need to be getting' inside and preparin' our supper,' he called out to me.

"My feet was hurtin', my back about broke in two, and the sun had been mighty hot that day. Seemed like I'd already put in a good day's work so his demandin' words brung out the contrariness in me. I walked on in, put down my bag, and headed to the table whar I crumbled up a piece of cornbread from mornin' time and then poured some buttermilk from my mama's blue and while pitcher o'er hit.

"Then I set myself down.'What are ye doin' in thar?' I heerd him holler out. 'I'm havin' my supper,' I called back, 'what'll ye be havin'?' Seemed to me the man could take of hisself, seein' that I was out and about all them years and away from the cabin many a day and night. Was he starvin' when I warn't thar to cook fer him? I reckon not. Men kin do fer theirselves iffen they want to but they'll set back and be waited on as long as we're willin' to do hit. That evenin', the day I borne yer mama and that baby down in The Holler, I wasn't willin' to tend to nobody but myself. John finally had to come to terms that he was married to a workin' woman.

"As to yer own arrival in this world, Wavy, though I ain't tellin' hit to make ye ashamed of yer mama, but that mornin' when one of the Quesinberry's, the family yer mama married into, come to take me to yer papa's place, he said right straight out, 'Iduna's carryin' on somethin' terrible, Aunt Orlene, and her mama says hit's harmful to both her and the baby. Ye need to come right now and git the woman settled down.' Of course, yer mama was jest a child when ye was born as was most of the women when they had their first babies.

"Some twenty years or so had done passed since yer mama was borned. I was in my eighties by that time and I warn't doin' so good healthwise that mornin' so I told the young man that I hadn't had no breakfast, not even a cup of coffee and I didn't reckon I had the strength to be bornin' a baby, no matter whose hit was, that day. Land's sakes, when he showed up, I was still a wearin' my night shirt. By that time, another of the Quesinberry's had come by and them two had a pow-wow right by the door and the first one took off on his horse:

"Whar's he goin'?" I wanted to know.

"Well, since ye ain't able to come to Iduna' aid, he's ridin' on over to Volunteer Gap. People are sayin' thar's a new granny woman livin' thar and he's gone to ask fer her help. Iduna's goin' to raise a whole new ruckus when she finds out some stranger's comin' to birth her first child, which would be your great-niece or great-nephew, if I calculated right."

"Maybe iffen I had me a fresh cup of hot coffee hit would perk me up a bit," I offered. So he put the pot on the stove and helped pull my old black dress over my nightshirt whilst I showed him whar my medicine bag was a settin' and told him what needed to go in hit. By the time I finished my coffee, I was feelin' like a new woman at least fer a minute or two so's he took me out and set me up in the wagon and off we headed to yer papa's farm.

Sure enough, when we was nearin' yer mama and papa's house, we could hear the worstest yellin' and carryin' on, sounded like a couple of wild animals fightin' in the woods. He set me down and helped me make my way inside whar the family was doin' all they could to git yer mama to calm down, but she was moanin' and groanin' so loud, the menfolk jest cleared out.

"Iduna," I said onct I was in the door, "ye hush up right this minute. Ye're goin' to scar this child fer life with yer weepin', wailin', and gnashin' of teeth," and I pointed my finger right in her face. I didn't know what all them words meant, but they was from the Bible and sounded good enough to put the fear of the Lord in her, I was hopin'.

Would ye believe that within a matter of minutes Iduna was as gentle as a lamb and ye was makin' yer way into the light of day, jest as calm and peaceful as a fine spring day. Ye had a dimple on yer cheek and a coverin' of blondish curls right on the top of yer head.

"I'm goin' to call her Wavy," yer mama said. "Ain't she a purty child?" When we cleaned ye up and handed ye to her, she looked at me right proud. "Thank ye, Aunt Orlene, fer comin' to bring me sech a special present, yer own great-niece, Wavy Quesinberry."

"Was I yer first great-niece, Aunt Orlene?"

"Land's sakes, I done lost track of which ones and how many a long time ago, but I kin tell ye this, Wavy. Ever' one of ye was special to me in a way I'll ne'er forgit and don't ye forgit hit neither."

"The sun'll be settin' purty soon, Aunt Orlene. We done passed this whole afternoon bornin' Wavy and her mama, Iduna. I ain't meanin' no disrespect, Wavy, but Aunt Orlene's tellin' of how she come by that name makes right good sense. We ain't heerd of nobody by that name 'fore or after yer mama come along, Wavy. We'd best be gittin' ye to yer bed, Aunt Orlene, so's Wavy kin help me afore she heads fer home. I'm fer certain ye'll be havin' a good night's rest after all this talkin'."

"Hit seems to me, Tavia, that relivin' that day when I catched them two babies, one up on the mountain and the other in The Holler down below, has brung back mighty powerful remembrances. Ye ain't goin' to understand, but in some ways, the tellin' of them times does seem harder work than bein' the granny woman that helped git 'em borned."

October 18, 1939

THE SMELL OF COFFEE WAKES me, but I cain't seem to recall whar I am nor nothin' else as fer as that's concerned. My mind is as blurry as these old eyes of mine. Even iffen I knowed whar my glasses was and could put 'em on, I'm fer certain they wouldn't make me see one thing a bit better'n I kin right this minute. Hit seems like the fog done moved into whatever space I'm a takin' up and wiped away all my surroundin's.

I kin hear voices somewhars off in the distance, but none of 'em is familiar. Two or three of 'em sound like menfolk and ever' onct in a while a woman's voice chimes in. Still the voices seem muffled as with sheep's wool or the down from Mama's soft pillers.

Hit comes to me real slow-like that I'm tryin' to lift my hand and touch my lips as a signal that I need a drink of cold spring water. I want to tell whoever's doin' the talkin' that I kin hear 'em, but they need to speak up and say the words clearer so's I kin understand what the fuss is about. Thar must be a fire a goin' but I'm as cold as iffen I'd been out in a blizzard and hit comes to me that maybe that's why I cain't see nothin' and I cain't move. I've been caught in a mighty winter storm comin' back from catchin' one of my babies and I've lost my way and done fell into a drift. The snow has pulled hitself o'er me like one of Mama's quilts and soon I'll be goin' to sleep. Iffen a body finds me 'fore I've been froze to death, well and good. Iffen hit don't happen, hit's the Lord's will. Aside from that, I've heerd old-timers tell that sech is a peaceful way to die. I ain't sure that I put too much stock in what they say is a blessin' since they's still alive, so how does a body know?

Same as when the preacher talks about the joys of heaven and the terribleness of hell. What makes the man so sure he knows how hit's goin' to be? I give up sech worries a long time ago. I take my comfort from the words that Jesus said to that thief hangin' thar on the cross next to Him right after the criminal on the other side mocked Jesus. The thief give that man his comeuppance and Jesus told him right then, "This day ye will be with me in paradise." No hell fire and damnation sermons, no "come down the aisle and repent of yer sins," no "maybe I'll forgive ye, maybe I won't." He made hit plain and clear that paradise was waitin' fer him the minute he took his last breath. And I'm takin' His word fer hit here and now while I'm waitin' fer the breath to leave me.

In the meantime I'm hopin' this commotion will settle hitself down and give me some peace and quiet. I'm also prayin' this ole body of mine will move jest a bit so's one of them loud voices will turn towards me and see that I'm in need of a cup of water and clean bedsheets. I keep workin' at bringin' some spit to my mouth so's I kin git a word out to make 'em pay attention, but hit seems like I might as well be dead as far as they's concerned. Could be that I am dead, this is my wake, and I'm lookin' down on my own funeral. I cain't ne'er convince myself of sech a truth 'cause iffen heaven is the peaceable kingdom, this ain't hit, not with all the cryin' and carryin' on that's disturbin' my peace.

"John, is hit ye, John? Are ye home from the war?"

"Listen. Be quiet, all of ye. Sounds like Aunt Orlene's wakin' up."

"Or maybe she's jest talkin' in her sleep, havin' a dream."

"She's called fer her mama off and on the last two or three evenin's after we settled her in the bed fer the night."

"John, have ye seen the baby? Ain't she purty? That little boy that come a week ago? He looks like ye, John. What are we goin' to do, John? What are we goin' to do about all the things they's sayin' about our babies?"

"She's relivin' the past all right. That's what they do whilst they're a waiting' to go on home to heaven. I've heerd the same many a time. When my grandpapa was a dyin', he was talkin' to my grandmama who died not long after I was born. My step-mama was settin' thar a listenin'. I asked her if hit bothered her none and she replied that hit didn't, iffen hit was bringin' him comfort durin' his dyin' hours."

"Wavy said she was talkin' to her mama last evenin' after we put her to bed. And now she's talkin' to John about them babies that died. 'Twas the saddest thing that could happen to a woman in them days, losin' ever' one of the children that was borned to ye. The thing of hit was Aunt Orlene took her own sorrors and turned 'em into other people's blessings—fer her kinfolk and fer John's and the rest of her neighbors, even them that lived miles away from her cabin."

"John, kin ye bring me a cup o' water? I'm right thirsty after walkin' down to The Holler and back."

"She's puttin' her hand to her mouth. She mighten be talkin' to John but I reckon hit's fer one of us to give her some water. She's startin' that moanin' that we was hearin' early of the mornin'. She appears mighty agitated, shakin' that finger of hers towards the side of the bed."

"Make sure them scissors is in the bag along with them drops to put in the baby's eyes. That come down from the state of Virginia, one of the laws that's on the books. John, kin ye bring Roadie up to the door and help me up to his back. Now, don't go complainin', John. I'm puttin' food on yer table with my tradin'. I give 'em a baby and they give me a bushel a taters or a side a bacon. Hit works out fer the both of us. Tell 'em hit's so, Mama."

"Aunt Orlene, are ye awake? Here's the water ye been askin' fer. Coy here will hold yer head up a bit and we'll give ye a sip at a time."

"What's Coy a' doin' here?"

"Why hit's his homeplace ye're a livin' in, mine and Coy's. He's been helpin' us take care of ye, cuttin' the wood fer the fire and bringin' in fresh milk and cream fer bakin' yer biscuits and churnin' fresh butter. He's been here all along even though Wavy and me's been here with ye in the house the mostest. And yer kinfolk has been comin' by and bringin' food and settin' here while ye're restin' or tellin' yer stories."

"My eyes. They's so bad I reckon I didn't take note that they was others here. Am I dyin' now? I hear whisperin' and movin' about but I cain't see even the quilt on my bed. Are they come to see me die?"

"I reckon thar ain't a soul in this part of the world that wants to see ye die, Aunt Orlene. They's a stoppin' by to see how ye are and iffen thar's anything they could be doin' to help ye in yer hour of need."

"Is John here? Did he come up from our house in The Holler, and did Mama come with him? She sent word that she was comin' from the farm to help me tend to the new baby."

"I think he's here somewhars. Yer mama ain't here as of now but yer brother Richard passed hit up from Rocksburg that she's on her way."

"And the baby? Is he still livin'? I ain't nursed him this mornin'."

"He's a livin'. Ye was sleepin' so hard we put some sugar water on a soft cloth and let 'em suck on hit. Hit satisfied 'em and when ye're stronger we'll put 'em to yer breast."

"Then I'll take me a little rest and when I wake up I'll take care of my baby. Does he look like John?"

"The Pucketts says as much, but them's on yer side of the family will testify that he's the owner of a better disposition! Take yer rest now. We'll be right here iffen ye be needin' anything."

"Aunt Tavia, she ain't in her right mind. Talkin' 'bout John and that baby boy o'hers, hit jest plain gives me the chills. Will hit be this way, her a driftin' in and out of her past, till she comes to the end? I don't think I kin bear bein' here, seein' her bony fingers a pointin' at me and squintin' her eyes like she's willin' herself to tell who I am and who else is here watchin' and waitin' fer the end. Is hit in her mind that she's a dyin'? When she's talkin' about Uncle John, is she seein' him fer real, like he's comin' fer her from the other side, or is she seein' him in her mind, the way he was when he was alive and they was livin' in the cabin?"

"My gracious, child. Ye never give up, do ye? I cain't answer a one of yer questions, Wavy, 'cause Aunt Orlene is the onliest one who knows what's she's a seein' and whether hit's part of the past or what's waitin' on the other side. Whether she knows she's dyin', only the good Lord knows but He is merciful, Wavy. Hit ain't in me to believe that He abandons us in our hour of need or allows us to suffer more'n we kin bear. The mind keeps a workin' while we're a dyin' jest the same as hit does whilst we's a sleepin'. We might well have heerd the last words of Orlene Puckett. Still, she might join us fer a spell or two 'fore hit's her time to go. That's mostly the way hit is with old folks iffen they ain't taken by acts of their fellow man or by a terrible sickness that swoops down and carries 'em away. Them that have lived past the years allotted to us has their own way of dyin', somethin' we ain't ne'er goin' to understand till we come to that place, the good Lord willin'. I reckon we oughter git some rest fer ourselves. That feisty old woman ain't goin' to give up the ghost without a fight, so we'd best be conservin' our own strength fer the final battle."

"John! Ye ain't goin' to start beatin' on me agin, are ye? Hit ain't my fault the young'un come afore his time. Thar warn't no way ye could tell fer a fact that hit was a boy or a girl. Hit ain't my fault, John. Somethin' must be wrong with my female parts, so's beatin' up on me ain't goin' to do nothin' but 'cause more harm. I'm beggin' ye, John! Don't!"

"Wake up! Wake up, Aunt Orlene. John ain't here and he ain't a beatin' on ye. Wake up now. Ye're in a warm bed in the cabin and nobody's goin' to be bringin' ye any harm. Kin ye hear me? Hit's yer niece Tavia Hawks, Coy's wife, and ye're safe and sound. Hush up, hush up, now. No need fer cryin'. Don't git yerself all riled up. Ye was jest havin' a bad dream, warn't she, Wavy?"

"That's right, Aunt Orlene, ye was havin' a mighty powerful dream but hit was not real, not one bit of hit."

"That's what ye know, girl. John Puckett was like a two-headed dog, one side was kind and good hearted, all sweetness and light, whilst the

{ *October 18, 1939* }

other was pure meanness, quick as a lightnin' bolt to bite any hand that would feed hit. What made the difference was whiskey, our fine mountain moonshine. Iffen he stayed away from hit, things went along right peaceful and calm, but onct he put a cup to his lips, I knowed to stay outa his way."

"Is she awake and in her right head or is she jest dreamin'?"

"What are ye talkin' about, girl? I'm a tellin' ye about yer uncle John and his ornery ways. Oh, he mellered out a bit onct he got up in years but hit didn't take long fer them lovey, dovey early years to turn sour. First come the war. Turned out he didn't have the stomach fer hit and had turned to drinkin' away the bad times way 'fore he run away from hit and headed home. Fer a while he was calm and hard workin', lookin' after me and Julie Ann, but after she died the follerin' March, he was ne'er the same. He took to drinkin' onct agin and went at hit real hard, so's hit hardly seemed that he was e'er in his rightful mind or way of doin' things.

"Then come the evenin' when he was drinkin' more'n he was eatin' as fer as takin' his supper. When I called him on hit, he hit me and knocked me to my knees. Then run off and left me alone whilst the war was still a ragin'. He finally come home the next spring. I found him up on the hillside plowin' fer a garden. He acted like nothin' had e'er happened to make trouble atween us and started tryin' onct more to have our family. But one child after another died or was borned dead or come a floodin' out of my body till we was both wore out from the hardships visited upon us, not to mention bein' tore up inside from all the grievin' that was tearin' us apart.

"The war come to a end, but not my and John's tribulations. Ever' time we lost another baby, the more he took to his drink. Then hit seemed he turned aginst me, maybe due to the fact that his brothers was givin' him a hard time about the barren wife he was saddled up with. One bad thing led to another, the gossipin' and the speculatin' amongst them that was family and friends, not to mention any foes slinkin' around in corners, though's I ne'er heerd that a body had ought aginst either me or John. At first, hit was whisperin's and hintin' at this or that, till hit was out in the open, erupting' like one of them volcanoes in wild places, spewin' ashes'n meanness o'er everthing that get in hits way.

"Ye done heerd that part of the story, how the rumors was heatin' up and boilin' over that me and John was takin' the lives of our own children. Hit ruined John, ruined him fer the rest of his life. He turned in towards his self and away from me, till he jest kept his distance fer a long time after the last boy was buried at the foot of the mountain.

"We come up the mountain to live his dream of buildin' a home fer us. He stayed away from the whiskey fer a while, at least until another baby died, then three more and all hell broke loose. Ain't a Christian way to say sech, but them years was as closet to hell fire and damnation as I e'er want to be. Many a time I run to hide under the cabin, prayin' he'd pass on out and fergit whar I was and why he was wantin' to hurt me. He'd come to and call my name, 'Orlene, Orlene, honey, come on out. I ain't goin' to hurt ye.' I'd come back in and we'd pretend that nothin' had happened. Sometimes hit seemed to me that the silence was more deafenin' than the storms with the winds a moanin' and the thunderin' boomin' all about.

"When John knowed thar warn't goin' to be no more babies, hit took the heart out of him jest as hit is fer me talkin' about the troubles that come to separate us."

"Mighten ye want a sip o' water? Aunt Orlene, ye been at yer story tellin' a fair while now and ye needs be restin'."

"Seems like water is all I'm a cravin' these days. My appetite's gone fer sure, but a body that's dyin' don't have no use fer good food, I reckon. Hit'd be a waste of yer good cookin', Tavia."

"Gone on with ye, Aunt Orlene. Thar's a pan of hot biscuits on the stove. Let me butter ye up one and spoon some honey on top of hit."

"I mighten take ye up on yer offer 'fore I'm put to bed, but me and John ain't come to the end as of yet and I've a mind to tell the end of hit 'fore I take my rest, whether fer the last time or not, I cain't say.

"As I said the first years up here was hard. John was drinkin', I was near to the end of my childbearin' days. Both of us was not yet to the point of givin' up, even after the four babies was buried up the hill acrost from the cabin. John kept on with the farmin'. We kept busy jest as mostest of us done on the mountain, tryin' to provide fer our needs. The next thing I knowed I was in the granny woman business. John went along with hit. Give him somethin' to do, mainly seein' that I had this gift and givin' me advice about this and that and braggin' to his kinfolk about my good deeds and so on, in spite of complainin' and carryin' on about sech things as the cost of a mule and bein' gone all them nights and not takin' care of the cookin' and the milkin' and whatever dislikes come to his mind at the moment."

"Did ye love him, Aunt Orlene, did ye love Uncle John? I'm wonderin' how ye would love a man that would drink so much he would hit ye and say mean things to ye."

"Lovin' a man don't keep us from seein' his faults nor wishin' fer him to be different, Wavy, but in them days a man and a woman stood up in front of a preacher and said vows to be man and wife till death separated 'em, even iffen one or both of 'em was in no way religious. That's how hit was. A man and a woman mighten be separate in their ways and in their minds, but they stayed together at least on the outside till one of 'em was gone."

"How did Uncle John die? Was he old?"

"Not hardly, though fer his time he was old. War does that to men, makes 'em old 'fore their time. John was seventy-three when he died of consumption in nineteen hundred and thirteen. I did my best to nurse him through his sickness, but hit took him fast. Years after, I filled out some papers, put my X on hit, fer a pension fer widers of the war. They told me, 'Well, ma'am, our records show that yer husband was a deserter. That means ye're not eligible fer a pension.'

"I answered that mighten be true, but told 'em afore John took off, he had to stand guard duty durin' a long bout of mighty cold, rainy weather and hit damaged his lungs right bad. He had terrible coughin' spells fer the rest of his life and had a hard time puttin' in a day's work 'cause he was always havin' to stop and git his breath. I said, 'I reckon I'm as entitled to a wider's benefits as any other woman who lost her husband durin' or after that war. Them that come home suffered from hit fer the rest of their lives, along with them that had to care fer 'em and live alongside of 'em.' After I had my say, one of the men looked at the other and told 'em to sign the paper. 'As fer as I'm concerned, the woman's earned her pension. She argued her case as good as any lawyer and if we turn her down, she'll prob'ly show up tomorrow and we'll have to hear hit all over agin.' I had me a good laugh o'er the whole business."

"And ye got a big smile on yer face right this minute from the recallin'. I reckon ye've done enough talkin' fer now."

"Afore I go to sleep, since thar ain't no guarantee that I'll be wakin' up on the morrow, thar's one thing I want to say to Wavy and to ye, Tavia, iffen ye want to hear hit. Ever' onct in a while, a body asks me how hit was with me and John. Was he sech a bad person? How could I bear bein' married to a man who beat his wife when he had too much whiskey to drink? On and on as to how things from the outside looked to be a mighty uncomf'table marriage. I always wanted to be truthful without bringin' harm to John nor his family. No, many a time I didn't like John's ways or his talk. When he brung the anger out of me, fer the most part I backed off and held my tongue. I hadn't been brung up to argue and fight. I figured I was supposed to take what come and not complain. That's what my papa larned me. Don't complain; hit ain't goin' to change nothin'. That was our lot as women. That's what the Bible said, the preachers told us.

"But one day, hit come to me real plain. Most of us don't know ourselves all that good, so hit comes down to the Lord knowin' what is and what is not. I cain't judge nobody but myself 'cause I ain't been in that man or that woman's place. Guard yer own truth and keep hit as pure and as honest as ye kin. And give yer neighbors the benefit of the doubt. Iffen I don't come to in the mornin', I'm thinkin' them last words would look mighty purty on my tombstone. And speaking of tombstones, thar's one thing I've been mullin' o'er in my mind concernin' me and John. When I'm put to rest next to John Puckett, I ain't got a doubt in my mind that the two of us'll git along a whole sight better'n we did when we was livin' together fer all them years. I figure we got most of eternity to work out whatever the differences was that brung us so much misery and pain."

October 19, 1939

"SHE'S LOOKIN' MIGHTY peaceful this mornin', ain't she, Aunt Tavia. Look at her face. Jest as soft and clear as a newborn baby's. And her wrinkles seems smoothed out, like someone come along and erased ever' one of 'em. Aunt Orlene always referred to herself as plain, but layin' thar right now she appears the purtiest I kin e'er recall. She's so quiet, I kin hardly hear her breathin', but watch her hands. They's movin' back and forth like she's workin' at makin' somethin', maybe one of them aprons she puts so much stock in. Do you think she'll come to sometime durin' this day and have somethin'else come up from her memory that she wants to tell us afore she dies?"

"Don't know, child. They's signs that her body is shuttin' down. Her bowels ain't moved fer a few days and she's about stopped makin' water. She's sleepin' longer and longer and her breathin' is slowin' down. Onct in awhile she calls out fer John or her mama, and durin' the night, I thought I heerd her talkin' to Julie Ann. Afore the sun come up this mornin', she was tellin' Richard, that was one of her brothers, somethin' about why she didn't want to go back to the schoolhouse. She's relivin' her life, not in the order of one year after another, but as she recognizes a face and puts a memory to hit. I watched hit happen with my own mama and papa and with my grandmama, though I was too young at the time to understand what I was hearin' in them last days."

"This is the set-and-wait time fer the family, Wavy. They ain't no predictin' when the end will come, maybe hit'll be within the hour or won't come till a week from now. Tendin' to the physical needs, sech as the feedin', the washin', and changin' diddies and bedclothes seems to be a terrible burden at the time. Hit takes all yer patience, yer strength, and yer courage to do what has to be done, but the hardest part is the waitin' cause hit drains ever'thing outer ye. Part a ye wants hit to be over. Part scolds the other part fer entertainin' sech a notion since we cain't put a picture in our minds of a world without the person we have loved fer so long goin' away and leavin' us behind.

"So's, we keep on puttin' food in our mouths and sharin' the news of our neighbors, maybe even havin' a laugh or two, sech as ye're hearin' right now from yer uncle Coy and the other menfolk gathered round out in the yard thar. After a time, one of 'em might pick up a fiddle or a banjer or one of them Irish whistles and begin playin' a tune or two. Might be a sad song, more'n likely a hymn, and afore long, people will be gatherin' around hummin' along, singin' the words. They'll come early and stay late, waitin', waitin' fer the end, hopin' hit won't come but knowin' hit will. No matter how many hours or days hit takes and how much preparin' goes on in their minds, when death finally makes his appearance, hit's always somethin' we ain't expectin', leastways not at this very minute, and we ain't ever goin' to be ready to let go."

"But we ain't even heerd yet the stories of all them babies that Aunt Orlene done borned."

"And ye ain't ne'er goin' to hear all of 'em either, child, leastways not from Aunt Orlene. They's just too many to be told, even iffen she had another lifetime to live, which she ain't in this world. Whatever stories are to be told, others will have to do the tellin', the families and the children theirselves. They's some out thar that don't even know that they's connected to Orlene Puckett in sech a way, but I reckon they be few and far between. Our boys was borned by Aunt Orlene and I'll make sure they don't ever fergit her even though they's jest young'uns and don't rightly understand the meanin' of her relationship to them."

"Mama said she'll be on her way after she's give Papa his noon meal. She says she's stayin' till Aunt Orlene's done made her way to heaven. And she's bringin' along a basket of food she's been preparin'. Says folks will be showin' up from all over these parts 'cause the word's done gone out that Orlene Puckett ain't long fer this world."

"Most of the week, women been stoppin' by along with the children that was borned by Aunt Orlene, bringin' food and lookin' in on her, askin' if thar's anything they kin be doin' to help. They was tellin' the little ones how she brung 'em by the house in a big basket and left 'em at the door. The older children laughed and giggled whilst they was a listenin' to sech tales but then a mama would flash 'em that look that threatened a switchin' and they quieted down like they be gatherin' fer church on a Sunday mornin'. In the evenin' time, some of the menfolk come by to see how things was a goin'. Mr. Pruitt brung them two little girls of his'n up from his farm near Groundhog Mountain to pay their respects.

"He said, 'Seems contrary to the way hit ought'n to be to wait till a human bein' is dead to pay our respects. Whether she kin hear us or not, I told the girls to go in and tell Aunt Orlene that they was grateful, as was their mama and papa, that she come along to help 'em to be borned in this world. Maybe hit's beyond their understandin' fer now, but one of these days hit'll make a powerful memory fer 'em to draw on when they have their own children and grandchildren.'

"That's how hit's been, the Bowmans, the Marshalls—"

"Which one of them Marshalls are ye talkin' about?"

"Aunt Orlene! Are ye awake? We cain't hardly hear what ye're sayin'. Yer voice ain't no more'n a whisper."

"The names ye was callin' out? Was any of 'em my relations or John's? Was there someone I knowed they called John? Hit sounds like a name that has a special meanin' fer me but cain't fer the life of me recollect why hit strikes me hard."

"John was yer husband, Aunt Orlene. He ain't here right now."

"Gone off to fight them Yankees, has he? Better be gittin' on back to see that purty little girl of his'n. Is she sleepin' in that fine cradle he made fer her?"

"She's sleepin', Aunt Orlene. She looks right peaceful. Ye need to be gittin' rest fer yer own self so's ye'll be able to take care of her and John when he comes on home."

"No, I ain't restin' no more this day. Thar's too many chores to be done. My mouth's dry as a bale o' hay. I'm goin' to walk on down to the spring fer a cup of that cold, sweet spring water whilst I'm waitin' fer John. I need my strength 'fore I head down the mountain to catch that Childress baby."

"Ye don't need to be walkin' to the spring, Aunt Orlene. We brung some up early of the mornin' in case ye'd be askin' fer hit. Wavy's holdin' a cup fer ye and she'll touch hit to yer lips till ye have yer fill."

"Then I'll pick up my bag, have John to bring Roadie to the stoop and we'll head on down the mountain. I need to be on my way. Lum's babies, skinny as they is, don't waste no time gittin' here. Always in a hurry, jest like they's business they have to be tendin' to. I hear voices, some that I know fer sure but I cain't see nary a thing. Has my glasses done slipped off my face? I reckon one of them pesky boys done run off with 'em. They's always playin' some mischief on me. Called me out one night to go to catch a baby whar some newcomers had jest moved in.

"When I turned up late in the night, a young feller and a pretty girl come to the door. 'I come to help borne yer child,' I told 'em. 'Why, ma'am, me and my bride jest come up from the church early in the week. That'd be mighty fast work, I'm a thinkin'.'

"I left thinkin' that I'd beat them young'uns iffen they'd e'er showed their faces at my door agin."

"I cain't find yer glasses, Aunt Orlene. Jest shut yer eyes and rest a bit whilst I look fer 'em. Is thar anything else Tavia or me kin do fer ye? They's hot chicken broth on the stove. Would ye take two or three spoonfuls iffen I brung a bit to ye? Ye ain't nary had a thing to eat fer the past day or two. Ye need to build up yer strength fer goin' down the mountain to catch the Childress baby."

"Ain't that baby come yet? Iffen the snow gits much deeper, I ain't goin' to make hit down in time. Has John got my bag ready?"

"Thar ain't no hurry. Hit ain't started in snowin' as of the last I looked out the cabin winder. Ye rest up this evenin' and iffen hit's clear come mornin', one of us will go with ye."

"Has he been up here to see me?"

"Who are ye thinkin' about, Aunt Orlene?"

"That nephew a mine, Stewart Puckett, who moved so far acrost the country. I reckon he's rich, ain't he? He drove one of them automobiles up here and took me in hit to borne one of the Martin children."

"He ain't been here today but he sent word that he's comin', maybe tomorrow."

"Let me go on back to sleep then and when he gits here, he kin take me whar I been sent fer in that contraption of his'n. Roadie was slow goin' but he didn't make nary as much noise comin' and goin'."

"I'm pullin' yer covers up and Wavy's puttin' more wood on the fire so's ye'll stay warm. Kin ye hear me, Aunt Orlene?"

"She ain't answerin' ye now. Her eyes is closed but her hands is still figetin' with the quilt. She's tryin' to pull the threads apart, seems like."

"That ain't the way to do hit, Orlene. Pull them threads tight so the pieces won't come apart, jest like I'm doin'. Ye see them tiny stitches I'm makin'? Take yer time and be patient. Practice makes perfect, ye know. Ye'll make a fine seamstress one of these days. Ain't no doubt about hit. No doubt about hit."

"She's relivin' the times with her mama. She mighten even be seein' her. All we kin do now is watch and wait, give her what she needs, make sure she's comf'table and keep on prayin'. I kin hear my own grandmama settin' aside my grandpapa's bed while he was a dyin'. 'We're prayin' him to heaven,' she said over and over durin' his last days. I suppose that's what's left fer us to do fer Aunt Orlene. We need to start on our own prayin' her to heaven.

"I'll be puttin' some more logs on the fire. I reckon one of us best be stayin' awake so's to be with her iffen she lasts through the night. Coy and some of the menfolk can take their turns, but ye need yer sleep, child. Yer mama will be here soon and Libby and Hattie done gone up to the loft 'cause they come prepared to stay till the end and through the funeral preparations. They ain't much time left fer Aunt Orlene, I'm afeard, but she wouldn't want us feelin' sorry fer ourselves. No, she ain't been one to complain, even for the loss of all her children. When the man come to pay fer her land, she told me that she was determined not to be sad or to grieve o'er her earthly possessions.

"She said, 'I've lived a good long time, longer'n most, and life fer the most part, has been good to me. Hit'd been a blessin' iffen that old stork had left me a child to raise that would've stayed by my side through old age, but I reckon hit warn't the will of the Lord. He's sent me a heap o' babies through the years to place in another woman's arms and I'm mighty grateful fer his wisdom and his guidance. Don't let people recollect Orlene Puckett fer the miseries of her life. Let 'em recall her fer the way the Lord put her to use to help others.'

"I think we all done enough talkin' fer this day. She looks right peaceful, don't she? Her hands has stopped movin' and her breathin' is easy. Each of us kin say a prayer that she don't suffer or linger beyond what her body, or our'n, can stand. His will be done. That's the finest prayer that can be prayed 'cause the Lord told us so hisself. Then we can pray that He'll give us the strength to go with her the rest of the way."

October 20, 1939

"SHE AIN'T MOVED ONE BIT since last evenin'. Is she still breathin', Hattie?"

"I've been settin' aside of her since the sun come up this mornin' and thar ain't been no change as fer as I kin tell. Her breathin' has slowed down right much and hit's so soft I keep leanin' o'er the bed to put my ear to her face to make sure hit ain't stopped, but she's still with us. Ever' onct in awhile she moans and her eyes come wide open like she's seein' some one she knows. She tries to say a word or two, but I cain't make out what hit is."

"I reckon she's makin' her way through her life and seein' them that was part of hit and has gone on, the way she was relatin' to John and her mama last evenin' when Wavy and me was settin' here tryin' to carry on a conversation with her as iffen hit made sense to us."

"Do ye think she'll be able to talk to us or say who's here with her today?"

"Prob'ly not, child. The signs say she's in a deep sleep and hit won't be long till she jest slips away from us and makes her way to heaven. We'll know when the time comes."

"I recall when Uncle John died. Aunt Orlene cried and carried on so, people said ye could hear her near to a mile away."

"Maybe so, Iduna, but Coy Martin told hit about that after John had been gone fer a bit, Aunt Orlene took to tellin' hit about that John Puckett had always enjoyed hisself a good fire. Then she up and laughed, 'I hope he's enjoyin' a good one now.' Course that had to do with the talk about John mistreatin' her over the years. Some folks believed the tales, some asserted that John Puckett was fer the most part a good man, exceptin' when he took to drinkin'."

"But she worked hard at makin' the best of what she had. I've heerd all my life that she could work as hard as any man. Foy Hawks tells jest about any person that will listen about the time he walked down the mountain with her and she was carryin' a twenty-five pound bag of flour. Says he was five years old and Aunt Orlene was near to eighty or eighty-five by his calculations. He said to her that she was the strongest person he knowed, and she laughed and told him that was nothin' to brag about, since he was too young to know all that many people.

"I've always heerd that she ne'er took money fer any of them babies that she borned."

"That's the truth, Wavy, since mountain people was poor. Most of 'em didn't have money to speak of. They made a livin' with farmin' and tradin' or barterin' one thing fer another. Mostly Aunt Orlene was give produce that come from a garden or orchards. Mighten be honey, jelly, or piece of fatback or pound of fresh butter. Aunt Betty Puckett, who's gone on to her own rest, used to tell me that Aunt Orlene did a mighty fine job of providin' fer John and herself after she went into the midwifin' business, since he had a hard time makin' a go of bein' a farmer hisself.

"One day I was walkin' down to The Holler when a little girl come running up to us:

"Are ye Aunt Orlene?" she asked, lookin' right pleased with herself.

"Yes, child, I am," she declared.

"Well, my papa told me how ye come to our house carryin' me in a basket and that I was so purty and so special, he walked up the mountain when the sow had her litter and give ye the bestest of the whole bunch. My mama said ye was a real special lady and I've been a waitin' to meet ye and ask if Papa was tellin' the truth."

"Hit's the truth and ye are a right purty child. Yer mama and papa has a right to be proud and I declare to ye that I was mighty proud when yer papa brung me that fine little pig."

"Did ye eat 'im?" she asked. "Papa says that's what ye was supposed to do with him, but I'm hopin' ye kept him fer a pet cause I didn't tell Papa when he took him, but he was my favorite."

Aunt Orlene didn't hardly know what to say to that. She didn't want to tell the truth and hurt the child's feelin's, but she was mighty strict in follerin' the commandments. She looked at me and I shook my head. I could tell her mind was workin' hard at preservin' the truth while avoidin' a lie.

"Hit seems to me that he needed fattenin' up a bit and we overdid hit till he was so big we couldn't keep him in his pen. He broke out of hit two or three times and tore down the fence in the yard. He was too big to be a pet, so…"

"Hit's alright, Aunt Orlene. I know about pigs turnin' into hogs and how mean they can be. I hope the sausage and hams was good.

Hit was nice to meet ye. I like yer costume."

Hit ain't a costume, she started to say, but stopped. She didn't want to make the child think she was correctin' her. "Hit was a pleasure to meet ye, agin, Miss. I like my costume, too. Seems to suit me jest fine."

"Did ye ever hear about the time Mr. Allen come up the mountain on his horse to git Aunt Orlene fer his wife? He brung another one fer Aunt Orlene to ride and on the way down the horse stumbled and she come tumblin' off the horse. Hit was a hard fall but she didn't seem hurt real bad, so he got her back on the horse and they made hit down to the house in time to catch his new baby. When she finally come back up the mountain, she told the story to friends and neighbors who kept bemoanin' the foolishness of her attemptin' to ride a horse at her age, which was speculated to be in the late seventies. Ever' time she told hit, however, she give credit to the Lord fer takin' care of her, even though Mr. Allen always put in a word that he was the one who came to her aid, got the horse back on hits feet with her safely in the saddle, and made sure she had not broke her arm or leg. He was always braggin' about how he come to her rescue, but she ne'er failed to give the praise to the Lord for keepin' her safe through all her comin'' and goin's. After a time, Mr. Allen stopped tellin' his version of the story as Aunt Orlene ne'er failed to git in the last word."

"As ye say, ever'one has a Aunt Orlene story that most people know by heart. The one that beats all happened one night when I was stayin' at the cabin with Aunt Orlene and the Bowman man. I cain't fer the life of me recall his Christian name. He showed up with a horse to take her down the mountain to attend to his wife. I recall that thar was a full moon and Aunt Orlene was gittin' things ready to go in her bag but she was havin' a hard time 'cause her eyesight was failin'. She come out on the stoop and Mr. Bowman was holdin' her horse, but Aunt Orlene wasn't payin' attention and somehow in the commotion of gittin' her up on the horse, she ended up settin' on hit backwards. Well, Mr. Bowman and me started laughin' and couldn't stop. She asked what was the matter with us and seemed mighty perturbed that we was holdin' up the gittin' her to her destination. I couldn't say one word I was laughin' so hard, but Mr. Bowman explained that she was not in the right position to be ridin' that horse so we was goin' to have to help her down and git her turned in the right way.

"But no, sirree, she wasn't goin' to have hit. Told how old she was and that she had no business ridin' a horse no way and that hit took her forever and a day and that he was jest goin' to have to lead her down the mountain with her turned the wrong way, but she would hold on and pray all the way down the mountain. I watched 'em head out, still a laughin', but Aunt Orlene made hit down the mountain in one piece. She took care of Mrs. Bowman and borned that baby late that evenin', and Mr. Bowman brought her back up the mountain three days later, ridin' the horse facin' in the right direction. Course I'd already put out the story, but Aunt Orlene couldn't resist tellin' hit over and over. She would end the adventure by sayin' with a sly grin, 'Sometimes hit's a good thing to see whar ye been.' And people loved hearin' her tell that part. They'd start laughin' right at the beginnin' when she told 'em how Mr. Bowman showed up with the full moon risin' 'cause they knowed the rest of the story and couldn't wait to git to the end."

"Seems like ever' person has a story about Aunt Orlene that comes to mind when they's settin' around talkin' about how hit was to grow up in these mountains. She's played a mighty big part in the lives of the Pucketts and the Hawks and jest about any other family ye could name. One day when I was six or seven, follerin' her acrost the field to a neighbor's, I said somethin' unkind about her that I had overheard from one of mama's friends. 'Iduna,' she said, 'No more of sech talk. Here's a good rule fer ye to recall: We don't talk about each other up in these parts due to the fact that all the families up here are related to one another by blood or by marriage. Don't matter how long the thread might wind or how thin hit might be, family is family. They's many a one that's been split apart by meanness or jest plain thoughtlessness. There ain't a person on this earth who gits through life without family, but iffen they's been tossed out on the brush heap like a broken down old chair, they ain't goin' to be there when ye need 'em the most.' Them words have stuck to me like glue fer my whole life."

"Aunt Orlene was always braggin' about her mama and how smart she was. Matilda Puckett had gone to her own reward long afore I come along, but one thing is sure in my mind: Orlene Puckett was a woman of wisdom and good judgment. No person could fault her as far as I ever knowed. When her time comes, the man who preaches her funeral is goin' to have a hard time of hit, 'cause there ain't no end to the kindnesses he's goin' to be hearin' about, right up to the minute that he steps behind that pulpit."

"This day's passin' mighty fast. Don't seem like she's goin' to come to, does hit, Hattie?"

"I've been a watchin' fer signs that she might come around, but she's as still as kin be. Her breathin' seems to be more raggedy than hit was early of the mornin'."

"Mama, is thar anything we kin be doin' fer her? She looks real peaceful, but how do we know she ain't hurtin' or bein' uncomf'table in some way? Do ye think she was a listenin' when whilst ye were tellin' about the old times? Does she still know our names and kin she separate our voices one from the other? Hit don't seem right to set here and talk about her as iffen she ain't even here. We ain't tryin' to include her in the conversation like she's one of us. Hit hurts me bad to watch her shrivel up right here in front of our eyes till she ain't nothin' but skin and bones and what makes up the human part is done left her."

"I'm sorry, Wavy, that the waitin' is so wearisome fer ye. We forgit, I reckon, how young ye are and that this is yer first relation that ye've watch go through the dyin'. Why don't ye go over to the table and fix ye a bite to eat, that's what we've been doin', eatin' when hit comes to our minds. Thar's a mighty good spread on the table, on the stove and in the oven. Plates is stacked on top of the safe. Git ye somethin' to eat and ye'll feel better."

"Do ye reckon we could git Aunt Orlene to take some nourishment? Some soup or mashed taters might go down easy."

"Honey, Aunt Orlene's eatin' days is over, as hit is with the rest of her body functions. Don't mean to be hard or cold about hit, Wavy, jest the way life is. When hit's comin' to the end, our organs stop workin'. She'll stop breathin' and her heart will quit. We know hit, but hit'll still be a shock. Womenfolk will cry and men will stand around, tryin' to figure out what to do. They'll comfort their wives and daughters and pat each other on their backs. Maybe slip outside and have a swig or two. Each person will grieve the best he or she knows how."

"I reckon she'll be gone this time tomorrow. Best we feed ourselves and git rested up fer what's to be done when she takes her leave. She brung her burial clothes with her when she come and I cain't recollect whar I done put 'em."

"Her burial clothes? She has 'em all ready? When ye find 'em, kin we take a look at what she'll be wearin'? That a way hit won't be such a shock to us when she's laid out. I ne'er heerd of a body pickin' out clothes fer buryin'. Seems real strange to me."

"Wavy, hit ain't strange at all. Old folks like to be prepared so's others don't have to make all the decisions. Womenfolk pick out the dresses they want to be wearin' when they's layin' in their coffins and they pick out the menfolk's as well cause men usually have jest one suit and one good shirt to begin with and don't want to be bothered with sech details. When ye're finished with yer supper, ye kin help me find whar I put Aunt Orlene's things. Hit'll take our minds off the sorrow that we'll be facin' soon enough, I reckon. Then we'll take a look at 'em and see whether they need pressin' or mendin'. Iffen my memory don't fail me, thar's a story that goes along with how she come to make sech a fuss over something that don't amount to a hill o' beans, not to mention the fact that a bit of barterin' went along with hit."

"I want to see her clothes 'fore I head up to the loft. Do ye reckon she made the dress herself since she was knowed to be sech a fine seamstress? Mama told me her stitches was so fine a person could hardly see 'em with looking through a magnifyin' glass."

"Aunt Orlene kept them things in her pie safe back at the cabin. Seems to me I put 'em on the bottom shelf o' my safe right behind the kitchen table. I don't want to have to go searchin' fer 'em tomorrow when they'll be other things that need tendin' to. Well, here's the dress. Black, jest like the one she wore most ever'day of her life, 'cept this'n ain't ne'er been wore. And look at the hose. Nylon. Not a woman in these parts, as far as I knowed, ever had a pair of store-bought nylon hose.

"I wonder whar an' how she come by 'em?"

I could tell you, but hit might take all day I reckon. That young woman wanted to trade me those nylons fer some hand-knitted ones. I told her hit weren't nothin' to me. I weren't going to be seein' 'em anyways."

"Has her coffin been made yet. And the preacher lined up fer the funeral?"

"Coy and Mr. Bowman cut down a big ole walnut tree from the cabin site right 'fore the land was sold. They sawed the boards back in the spring and started puttin' hit together two weeks ago. Hit's nigh to bein' complete. Ms. Bowman's been crochetin' a linin' fer her to rest on. Aunt Orlene told me she wanted that plain quilt of her mama's to be placed o'er her. 'To keep me warm in that cold, cold ground,' she laughed, 'whilst the Lord's decidin' whether He's goin' to admit me to the promised land.'

"The woman was forever makin' fun of herself, even to the point of dyin'. 'Mighten as well laugh,' she would say, 'beats cryin'. I done enough of that in my lifetime.' And she'd laugh agin and go on with whate'er she was doin'. Speakin' of which, we'd best go one with gittin' some sleep. I'll stay up with her fer a while and each of ye kin take a turn. She's breathin' real easy and don't seem to be no pain nor distress. Say yer prayers that she'll make the crossin' without a struggle of the body or sufferin' of her soul."

I wanted 'em to know that my mind hadn't closed down and my ears was still listenin'. I wanted to tell 'em that I knowed I'd be alright when I come to the end. I hoped they could hear me and I was makin' my words clear. I'll be alright. I'll be alright.

"Did she say somethin'? What's she's tryin' to tell us, Wavy? Listen real hard."

Don't worry. I'll be alright. It was more of a whisper than a real sound.

"I think she said, 'I'll be alright.' She don't want us worryin' no more."

October 21, 1939

"SHE AIN'T MOVED ONE INCH durin' the night. Her breathin' has a raspy sound, what they call a death rattle. I'd say time's nigh to run out fer Aulene Hawks, the name her mama give her, or Orlena, though most folks dropped the 'a' and jest called her Orlene Puckett."

"What'll happen when she dies, Mama?"

"Us womenfolk will wash her body and her hair, what she's got left of hit, we'll dress her in them clothes she put aside. One of the menfolk will make sure her eyes is shut by puttin' silver coins on 'em. They'll bring in the coffin they done made from that ole tree that was cut down, lined with Ms. Bowman's crochetin' she's been workin' on. Friends and family and I reckon people from all around will come to show their respects. Kinfolk will set up all night with her after she's ready fer buryin' come the the next day."

"The family's done decided to hold the funeral here at the house. We's hopin' fer good weather so's hit kin be out in the yard and not all crowded up in the house. Aunt Orlene was one fer bein' outdoors and she had a reverence for God's creation. I kin hear her voice almost a singin', whether she was settin' off fer a birthin' or walkin' to the spring fer a a bucket of water, 'My, ain't this a glorious day?' And us children who was uset to follerin' her about would answer like we was in school, 'Yes, ma'am, Aunt Orlene, hit sure is a glorious day!' She would laugh and grab a child's hand and off we would go as iffen we was takin' on some grand adventure. I will wager ye thar's many a grown-up around who was at her heels as she was makin' her way from one birthin' to the next and hit's a memory that will stick with 'em as long as they live."

"Have ye heerd, Tavia, who is preachin' the funeral?"

"Coy has sent word to Pastor Noonkester and Elder Quesinberry to be ready fer the call. He said the family agreed that those that wanted to say somethin' on her behalf would be called on to speak. He wanted me to ask the ones that's been settin' up with her to make a list of some of her favorite hymns, ones that most people knows and finds comfort in singin'."

"She told me onct that they sung 'When I Am Gone' at most ever' funeral she could recall from Julie Ann's on to John's. She said, 'Seems like hit become the final hymn fer most of my family that I can recall. Hit might as well be the one that carries me o'er the River Jordan. Leastways, people should know the words. They's sung 'em enough.'"

"Hit makes me sad to think that Aunt Orlene will be leavin' us and we won't be seein' her no more. Her cabin's gone and soon she'll be gone along with hit, jest like they was ne'er a part of our lives and our way of livin'. When a person we love dies, does the memory of how they looked when they was livin' stay clear in our minds? Or does hit jest fade away like we cain't recall how that apple tree looked to us when hit was bloomin' last spring? Hit scares me to think that one day I'll wake up and I cain't recall how ye looked the day ye was settin' in that chair whilst we was waitin' fer Aunt Orlene to die. Or how Papa looked this mornin' when he come in the door and asked fer a cup of hot coffee. I don't want to fergit the faces of family and friends but I know I will and I cain't bear to think about hit."

"Wavy, honey, ye're gittin' yerself all worked up o'er things we cain't do nothin' about. When we stop seein' them faces in our minds, hit's the memories that'll keep 'em dear to us. We need faith that the Lord will guard our memories and keep 'em true."

"There's a sayin' that the school marm had us to write one mornin' that comes from a poem that was wrote a long time ago. Hit come t'mind whilst Mama and the rest o' ye was talkin' about Aunt Orlene. I cain't recollect the whole poem but hit ends up like this, 'though lost to sight, to memory dear.' When her face has done faded from my remembrance, I'll jest hold on tight to the stories I've larned from mama and her kinfolk and my own as well and keep 'em dear to my own heart so I kin pass 'em on to them that will listen. They'll ne'er be lost as long as one of her children has breath."

"That's a mighty fine speech, Wavy. I reckon no preacher man could hardly do better. Them words from the poem is worth recallin' and passin' on in regards to Orlene Puckett. I don't reckon thar's been a thought wrote down that suits her better."

Though lost to sight, to memory dear. I wonder who will keep my memory dear after I've done took my last breath, the final hymn has been sung and they've put me in the ground. I've heerd all I kin stand about Orlene Puckett's doin's, words, and deeds. Some of 'em they got right, some they didn't, but hit don't matter a hill o' beans when ye walk up the mountain on a cold, clear night and look up at the stars, shinin' like tiny snowflakes, more'n a body could count in a lifetime. Makes ye feel small, smaller than a flea on Old Shep's back. What did Orlene Puckett have to do with the world and hits business? We's here fer a second in time. Ye blink and time's up. People take on like hit's somethin' to write up in the history books, but they's got hit all wrong. Ne'er read a history book, but I knowed the stories about famous people, presidents and generals, and writers and such. They made their marks but sooner or later, forces of man or nature will erase ever' one.

I could prob'ly tell 'em another thing or two, call out a name and make 'em think I'm still here amongst 'em but I ain't goin' to. I've had my say. Whether hit's worth recallin' or not, they's goin' to have to make up their own minds. I've lived through some terrible times. Thar ain't no denyin' the pain and misery of losin' ever' child that ye carried in yer body or diggin' in the ground fer roots and nuts to feed yerself while a war was bein' waged right up to yer doorstep or havin' a husband who loved liquor more'n his own wife and neighbors who gossiped and spread rumors that brung dishonor to yer name.

But the Lord gives one day at a time to balance hit out so that we kin reap the good along with the bad and keep on goin', whether hit's follerin' yer husband to the top of the mountain or ridin' a mule down to The Holler to borne a stranger's child. I've ne'er been without work to do or somethin' new to larn, even iffen I couldn't read nor write. I wisht I could've wrote my own story and that one person mighten have took the time to read hit, maybe fer comfort or a laugh or two. But I ain't goin' to complain since, as my papa used to say, hit would not change one thing. Another war would come along. A man would make a machine that runs on four wheels by some contraption called a engine. John would still die of consumption cause they warn't no cure fer hit. The gover'ment would take my land fer whatever money they decided to give me, my cabin would come down, and I'd still be a dyin' at my niece's house instead of in my own.

Lay in on their hearts, Lord, when I'm gone that them left behind needs to move on with their own lives 'cause they ain't goin' to live forever. I kin testify that life is all around us 'cause I see hit plain. Thar's life in the clouds passin' above us, life in the sweet songs of the birds, life in the seeds that fly out from the milkweed and the dandelions. Why, thar's life even in them hard ole rocks that cover the land causin' mules to stumble and plows to bend. Hardly a soul on this earth is payin' attention to what matters the most, how ye treat yer friends and neighbors and listenin' to the voice of God that's inside each of us. Leastways, I've come to believe and I'm holdin' on to that promise till I take my last breath. Seems like I kin hear that hymn Mama loved to sing most ever'day whilst she was workin' at the house or in her garden. Always sounded sad to me, but now that I've come to the end of my days I'm hearin' the words like they was makin' a joyful noise. "Jest a wearyin' fer ye, Jesus, Lord, beloved and true, wishin' fer ye, wonderin' when ye'll be comin' back agin, under all I say and do, jest a wearyin' fer ye." I'm done wearied out, Lord. Ye don't have to make me wait no longer.

"Hit's gittin' to be late in the day, Mama. Papa and the others is askin' kin they come in and have a bite to eat while they's settin' around waitin'. One or two of 'em brung a fiddle and a guitar and they've been down on the hill playin' and singin' some of the hymns they recall from bein' in church when they was jest boys. They was singin' 'When the Roll Is Called Up Yonder' but Uncle Coy told 'em they was makin' too much of a racket fer a body that wanted to die in a quiet, peaceful manner. Foy Hawks up and questioned how did he know that Aunt Orlene wouldn't want a rip-roarin' sendoff? The rest of 'em took off laughin'. Uncle Coy lightened up a bit, sayin' that Aunt Orlene enjoyed a good time same as the next person and told the men to play the Virginia reel. 'Hit mighten bring the old gal offen that bed yet,' he called to 'em, 'even iffen she proclaims to be a Baptist!'"

So that's what hit comes down to. No respect fer one of their elders layin' here workin' hard fer ever' breath that's squeezed out of my old lungs. But the music sounds mighty fine and iffen thar was one ounce of strength left in this ole body, I'd be out thar dancin' and singin' along with the best of 'em. Better'n layin' here whar ye kin hear a pin drop after the womenfolk done talked theirselves into a pile a gloom. I kin hear what sounds like cryin' from Hattie and Iduna, as iffen they's nothing useful they could be doin' like tryin' to bring some warmth to my feet and my hands which is feelin' all froze up like our pond in the winter. Another blanket would hold off the draftiness swirlin' about me. Iffen they'd offer me a swig o'whiskey sweetened with a spoonful of honey, I don't reckon I'd refuse. Hit seems they's shifted their thinkin' from the comforts of me to their own, due to the fact that as far as they kin tell, I'm dead to the world, even iffen my raspy breathin' is fillin' up the whole space.

Ever since I kin recall, I've heerd folks say as to how them that's dyin'

{ *October 21, 1939* }

always lives their whole lives in a flash whilst the last breath's leavin' their bodies. All this time here at Tavia's I've been relivin' mine in my dreams both wakin' and sleepin' and the tellin' of my trials and troubles fer them that wanted to hear. How long I've been in this place I cain't seem to recall. How long hit's been since I got up with my own strength and walked out that door, I have no idee whether hit's been months, days, or jest a hour ago. Time's a blur to my mind same as sight to my eyes. I kin hear the sound of voice,s but the words don't seem to have a meanin' I kin git my thinkin' around.

What does hit come to, Lord, this business of livin'? I uset to look up at them tall pine trees with them long knotty branches lookin' fer all the world like they was liftin' their arms to ye in prayer and think to myself, now why would God let a tree live longer'n a human bein'? Didn't seem right to me when I was a young'un. Now I ain't so sure. When yer body's wore out and nothin' ain't workin' the way hit's suppose to, I reckon the time's come to let go and move on. My mama's voice keeps on repeatin' them words she loved so much, 'This world is not my home, I'm jest a passin' through, if heaven's not my home, oh Lord what will I do?'

I'm hopin' heaven is my home and ye'll be thar waitin' fer me when I git rid of this tired ole, broken down body of mine so as to give me a brand new one fit fer walkin' them streets of gold to my heart's content. I'm countin' on ye linin' 'em with purty pine trees that's got fox grapes climbin' all over 'em. And, iffen ye don't mind, throw in a few blackberry and huckleberry bushes so's I kin whip up a batch or two of my preserves as a thank you fer the angels that's been lookin' after me since ye give me to my mama and papa.

Why, look. Here they come now. My goodness. I cain't recall that the two of 'em e'er looked so young and so strong. And smilin', like they's seein' somethin' real special. Mama always was a wearin' a smile on her face, even when she was givin' us children a big dose of them words 'ye better never be doin' sech agin, do ye hear me?' that put the fear of the Lord in us. But Papa was a solemn man, not given to showin' pleasure or enjoyment. I cain't recall seein' my papa with a smile that covered his whole face.

"Look. Aunt Orlene's eyes is a flutterin'. She's tryin' to lift her hand. Take hold of hit, Wavy, and let her know that she ain't alone. We're right here with her."

"Her mouth's movin' but I cain't hear nothin'. Go to the door, Iduna, and call the others to come in iffen they want to say their goodbyes. I don't think she'll be with us much longer. Her breathin' is comin' mighty slow. Tell Coy to bring me that little mirrer over thar on the dresser."

"What will she be needin' a mirrer fer?"

"She ain't goin' to need hit. One of us will hold hit up to her face when hit appears she's done stopped breathin' to make sure no breath is left in her body. That's what has to be done afore we git her ready fer the buryin'."

"John?"

"He ain't here, right now, Aunt Orlene. He'll be here directly. Help me git the piller up under her head a mite more and her quilt straightened up, Wavy."

"I don't think she's callin' fer John, Aunt Tavia. I think she's seein' him. Her eyes is open and she's smilin'."

John. Is hit ye, John? And who's that purty little girl ye're holdin' in yer arms? And all them other children follerin' behind? They's laughin' and runnin' along, lookin' like stairsteps, jest like they was headed fer school or a church meetin', out havin' a good time. Some of 'em looks like the Puckett family, some like us Hawkses. A few of 'em has the features of both families, but I kin tell fer sure that each one of 'em is one of my babies, full grown and perfect in body and mind. And Mama and Papa are standin' back thar, watchin' this grand reunion. They's all here, ain't they? I was afeard that I'd a forgot some of the names, but they's comin' back to me now. I suppose a body's memory is full restored when ye git to heaven, jest the same as yer body gits a whole new suit of clothes the likes as was ne'er see'd in our life on earth.

"They've come to welcome ye home, Orlene. We've been waitin' fer a long time fer ye to git here, but the Lord kept tellin' us to be patient, that He knowed from the beginnin' that ye was a strong and willin' soul and He had put ye in the place whar ye could use yer mind and yer talents fer the good of others. 'I'm not lettin' her off easy,' He told me after I got here, 'cause that ain't the way she sees the world. As fer ye, John Puckett, ye made hit jest by the skin of yer teeth and yer good wife's prayers, not to mention the prayers of others who could look down and see somethin' worth savin' in a man who was nearly done in by the battles he endured both in body and in mind. Time don't mean nothin' in eternity, so Orlene'll be along afore ye know hit.'

"Course He didn't say all that exactly in them words, but our souls do the communicatin' and somehow or other we all end up on the same page, no matter whar we come from or how we come to be here. But we have more important business right now. Yer children have been waitin' to meet their mama ever since they left ye. They know their papa and we've made our peace. That's somethin' ye don't have to deal with. They know how much ye loved them before they was born and after they went away. Now we kin know one another as souls made complete and whole through God's grace. Once upon a time on earth, each identity was tied to the names of John and Orlene Puckett. Now we're part of God's larger family, those who have made their journeys over earth's mountains and valleys and moved on to a distant, but fairer, land. Their names and their faces may have been erased by the soil and the sea, but God knows us each one and calls us by name.

"Step up, children, one by one and say a word of greetin' to yer mama. Don't need to tell her yer name or when ye was born. She knows, even iffen the mountain stones has done forgot. Yer names was always in her heart and she brung 'em with her. That's yer mama's reward and part of yer own, I reckon."

The Lord never lets up, does He? The mystery of death is as terrible as the mystery of birth. Is my dream part of my dyin'? Or is my dyin' the beginnin' of the dream of heaven? The voices have gone silent. The only sound I can hear is the tickin' of the clock. I am too weak to ask if I am in heaven. Only Tavia's mirrer will tell.

Becoming Aunt Orlene

(an author's note)

THOSE OF US WHO LOVE POETRY have discovered more than once the proverbial pot of gold that so many others have overlooked. The poet can summarize in one line the acquired wisdom of life experiences while the rest of us constantly search for what we would not recognize even if we found it. This was brought to mind recently while rereading Robert Frost's famous lines of "The Road Not Taken." For me, however, the metaphor hinges on the road I have taken during the past seven years by assuming another persona, that of Orlene Hawks Puckett, a legendary Virginia midwife who lived from 1839 to 1939 in the area that borders Carroll and Patrick counties near the Blue Ridge Parkway.

In the summer of 2003, I began to perform the life of "Aunt Orlene" in a one-woman play that has taken me to three different states and an estimated total audience of 4,000 people. The most meaningful performances take place at the Puckett Cabin during the summer through the sponsorship of the National Park Service and the Friends of the Blue Ridge Parkway. During this time, I've met and talked with members of the Hawks and Puckett families as well as with men and women brought into this world by this remarkable woman. They have told me their stories and presented me with pictures of them as children and young adults standing in front of the cabin with Aunt Orlene. Notes, newspaper clippings, and e-mail by those who have come to hear the story of her trials and tribulations have provided added benefits that now fill a scrapbook to keep alive my own memories of my life as Orlene Puckett.

However, this transformation into the historical Aunt Orlene did not occur overnight or by happenstance. Bringing a person to life from words written on paper is a daunting task, demanding long hours of study and concentration. The business of becoming the person I am today has been a long, difficult process and the labor involved never ends. Perhaps our "becoming" will never be complete until the moment we take our last breath. Even then, chances are we will be left wishing, wanting, and regretting. Given all that, why would a person choose to become someone else of an unfamiliar time and place? It's a fair question, one I'm frequently asked as I travel about portraying her.

A trip on the Blue Ridge Parkway Mother's Day weekend of 2001 proved to be the beginning. As we set out, there was no way of knowing that way would soon "lead on to a way," or that a turning back would eventually lead to my own less traveled road.

To make up for my children's absence on that Sunday, my husband planned a special retreat for us at an inn off the parkway, a long-term favorite destination for our family since our first camping trip in 1969 to Doughton Park. For over forty years we have traveled every mile from Front Royal to Cherokee. After giving up our camping gear, we started exploring various sections as my husband began to dream of owning a log cabin near the parkway. When our daughter married a young man who owned a little house off Orchard Gap, we spent some time with them getting to know this area of the Virginia mountains. This was the land, with its rolling farms, cattle, horses, and sheep, that unfailingly beckoned to us.

That weekend, we dropped in on a local realtor, sharing our dream of owning a home nearby and asking if there were any bargains in the area. We were promptly whisked into his vehicle for a tour of possibilities. The first one we visited, he informed us, was the "best buy" on the parkway. No wonder! A small, dilapidated box of a house in need of much TLC stood on an acre plot less than a half-mile from the parkway. The yard was filled with weeds, the paint was peeling, and the windows were in various stages of falling apart. This was an aging house fast going downhill. The inside looked no better. Yellowed linoleum lay on all the floors, old bathroom fixtures stood desolately in the one bath that also served as the laundry. One room was painted bright turquoise with a Mickey Mouse border running atop the four walls. I didn't have to look at my husband. I knew his reaction even before I turned to see him shaking his head from side to side.

When the realtor told us the price, I was astounded. "We can afford this," I almost shouted. "With a little paint and…" Before I could finish, Bob had taken my arm, gently leading me out the door. "We've done this once before with the house in Lexington," he reminded me. "I'm too old to tackle another fixer-upper."

The rest of the day we looked at bigger and more expensive homes, none of which captured our imagination or desire to pursue financing.

The next day after visiting a local winery for lunch, Bob suggested we drive back to the first house, walk around, and take a second peek in the windows. The door was unlocked so in we went and carried on a "what if?" conversation, but the result was the same as the previous day. Bob wasn't interested. We headed back home.

The next weekend found us making one last trip to put together a list of what would be absolutely necessary to make the house livable. I emphasized the difference paint and new floor coverings would make, along with new appliances, fixtures, a paint job with shutters, and so on. "Yeah, but what will all that cost?" Bob wondered. I pulled a figure out of my hat, along with how we would go about financing the whole deal. Bob listened, but still he was in a mostly negative mood as we headed up the mountain to meet the realtor at the house. Once more we did a thorough walk-through, asking the realtor whether he knew people who could paint, install carpeting, put in new windows; the list grew longer and longer. Bob was making his list and checking it twice so that by the time the realtor left, we were headed back down the mountain. This time my husband was emphatic. "There's no way we can pull this off. I don't see the potential you're talking about. The bottom line is I'm not interested." That was that.

Except for me, it wasn't. By now my temper was rising to the surface. It was my time to put my foot down. I informed Bob that as far as I was concerned, this was our last hope. At our age, we hadn't the time or the money to be picky. If he wanted his dream of a home near the Blue Ridge Parkway to come true, he'd better make an offer on this one; otherwise, I would not, and I pronounced each word with great precision, come back to look for property in this area again. He obviously believed me. The next morning, he called to make an offer, which was accepted, gratefully, I am sure, by the owner that afternoon.

By the middle of June we had closed on the house, made arrangements for new windows and carpeting, had a painting blitz weekend attended by children and grandchildren, and selected fixtures for the bathroom and appliances for the kitchen. Then we left for a previously planned vacation. Two weeks later, we were back to put on finishing touches of ceiling lights and fans, electrical switches and door handles. By the middle of August, we had moved furniture into place, in spite of a series of mountain storms that threatened to soak the new sofas and mattresses. In no time at all, we were settled in and spending most of our weekends in our happily transformed mountain cottage.

What does all this have to do with becoming Aunt Orlene? The answer is simple. Less than one mile from where we found our little fix-me-upper stood the reconstructed home of Orlene Puckett, a tribute to the woman who delivered over 1,000 babies in this area without, according to legend, losing a mother or baby, even though she had previously lost twenty-four babies of her own. The cabin was a familiar spot from our numerous camping and sightseeing treks with our children and friends. Now the cabin was my neighbor, and each time we took note of it on our way to adventures on the parkway, I felt myself drawn to the story behind it. I began to take frequent walks to the cabin and often found myself trying to imagine the midwife's life there. One afternoon as we headed out for lunch, I announced, approaching the Puckett Cabin, "I'm coming here to be Aunt Orlene, because someone needs to tell her story." And the rest, as they say, is history. It is also, I believe, a special kind of Providence, as subsequent events reveal.

In early winter, we arrived at the house to find a leak in the corner of our bedroom. Calling our closest neighbor, we asked if he knew someone who could fix the problem. He gave us a name and number of a local handyman who arrived early Sunday morning and performed a makeshift repair, also informing us that the roof would probably need replacing within the next two years. Mr. Logan, quite a loquacious man, and my husband began to converse as he collected his tools. Somehow in the discussion, I brought up the topic of the Puckett Cabin. We were told that he lived across from the cabin and that Aunt Orlene was buried in the cemetery on his property near a small Primitive Baptist Church that bore the Puckett name. I told him of my interest in researching Orlene's life and perhaps writing a play about her.

"Oh," he replied, "maybe you'd like to take a look at the Puckett family history. They have their reunion up there at the church and one of them gave me a copy last year. You can borrow it and keep it as long as you need it. I'll drop it off the next time I come this way." In less than two months after announcing my intention to "become" Orlene Puckett, the genealogy of John Puckett, her husband, found its way into my hands.

That was not, however, Herman Logan's only contribution to my new endeavor. When he arrived to deliver the packet, he added another piece of information that further convinced me of my calling. "If you want to get some first-hand knowledge about Aunt Orlene, you need to go talk to Wavy Worrell over on Little Bit Road. She's Orlene's great grand-niece and she was borned, as they call it up here, by Aunt Orlene

{ Becoming Aunt Orlene }

herself. She has a good many memories of her aunt and she'll be glad to talk to you. She has a son who lives with her, but he's out and about, and Miss Wavy looks forward to having visitors. ...She'll tell you a lot of good stories, maybe some that you can use in the play you're writing."

Soon I made the call that led me to several long interviews with Wavy Worrell and her son Wade, who was also full of stories about the locals, including the Pucketts and all their kin. A picture of John Puckett in his Civil War uniform hung over the sofa in the living room and greeted visitors as they walked in the door. Miss Wavy, who was in her late seventies and in poor health, always sat to the right of the door. The first time I went to her home, I discovered an old woman with a very young face framed by long, blonde Shirley Temple curls. I did not think her hair had been colored. She had several missing teeth, but Miss Wavy continually smiled and laughed as she shared favorite anecdotes about beloved Aunt Orlene and all the kinfolk that were related to her.

I was soon lost as she traced one relative back and back into history, adding marriages and babies, who in turn married and had babies, for more generations than I could name. Miss Wavy had been fifteen when Aunt Orlene died and she claimed that she had clear memories of her. On one occasion, she left her chair and invited me into her bedroom where she began to open drawers in various chests to show me pictures, handiwork, and pieces of clothing associated with her mother and grandmother, both borned by Aunt Orlene, along with aunts and uncles, brothers, sisters, and cousins, all ancestors of many of the people who live in this area.

I visited Miss Wavy several times that winter, including one cold, overcast day when Wade informed me that we should be heading back to Lexington. I asked if he expected it to snow. "Did you hear any noise when you was coming up here?" he asked.

"No, I don't think so. I really wasn't paying attention, although it's pretty cold out there," I offered.

"Well, that's a sure sign snow is coming, so if I was you, I'd cut short this visit and head on home." Back at the house, we packed up and left. The next morning, we heard on the news that there had been a heavy snow in Carroll County. While gathering the morsels of Aunt Orlene's life, I was gleaning knowledge of mountain living.

I was also making the acquaintance of my neighbors along Doe Run Road. One just happened to be a woman who, along with a sister, had been borned by Aunt Orlene. The icing on the cake was the fact that she was married to a Puckett, a descendent of one of John's brothers. Our early conversations centered on the families in the area related to both Orlene Hawks and John Puckett, many of whom were brought into this world by the famous midwife. Stories flowed freely whenever her name was mentioned, and by the following summer, I was certain I had enough background information to begin writing Aunt Orlene's monologue.

What writing skills I possessed came from my training as an English teacher who had also taught drama and speech. I had been active in community theatre as both actor and director and had published a book of poetry. This project was the culmination of a dream: to develop the character of a strong, memorable woman and bring her to life through my play. My visits with Wavy Worrell had provided me with the model for my portrayal of Orlene Puckett. I pictured her as competent, dedicated, a woman of heartfelt convictions, not easily overcome by the vicissitudes of life. One day I had said to Miss Wavy, "From what you tell me, I see Aunt Orlene as a woman of faith, with a great sense of humor; a woman who loved life and felt a calling to be of service to others. Is that how you remember her?"

"That was Aunt Orlene, all right. Everybody loved her. She was never sent for that she didn't go out, no matter the weather or time of day, to get wherever a baby was being borned." Then she added, though I'd heard it before, "She borned me, and my mama and my grandma, you know."

"Yes, I know, and just about everybody else in these parts!" She nodded and we had a good laugh before I said my goodbyes and headed out the door.

By the spring of 2003, I had finished the monologue and decided to contact Frank Levering, who owned a nearby orchard and ran an outdoor theatre during the summer, featuring the work of local actors and playwrights. My phone call produced an invitation to meet with him to talk about the play with the possibility of putting me on the upcoming summer schedule. I had put together a costume based on what family members had told me of their memories of Aunt Orlene, so on the day of my audition, I pulled on my long black dress with a black-checked gingham apron, donned my big black bonnet and high top shoes, and made up my face with multiple lines and shadings for the sunken eyes and sallow skin of a ninety-nine-year-old woman before driving down the mountain to meet with Frank at his home.

{ *Becoming Aunt Orlene* }

When I walked up the path to his rustic house leaning on my crooked rhododendron cane, I greeted him as the aged Orlene Puckett, leaning heavily on her cane and speaking a word of greeting in the mountain twang I had practiced during the writing of the monologue. "Good day to ye, young man. I'm Orlene Puckett and I've a come to tell ye my story." There was a moment of silence as Frank took in the apparition standing before him, but he replied in kind, "It's good to meet you, Aunt Orlene." I had become Orlene Puckett. Later Frank told me that I was the first actor who had ever shown up for a first meeting in character and seeing me coming toward him had brought back memories of his own grandmother who had lived in the house where we met.

I shared with Frank my purpose for writing the play and the process behind it. He asked for a copy of the script. Within a week, Frank called to tell me that this would be a perfect piece for his Cherry Orchard Theatre and we set the dates for three performances in July. The next step was to memorize thirty-five pages of Aunt Orlene's story over the next two and a half months! Regardless of the difficulty of the task ahead, I felt confidence in my purpose. I was transforming myself into the legendary Orlene Puckett. Her pioneer spirit was alive and well in the writer who had been born the same year that Orlene had died.

In spite of two weeks of rehearsals on the stage at the Cherry Orchard Theatre, Aunt Orlene's first appearance took place in the apple packing barn in the orchard. It had rained hard all afternoon. Family and friends from church had made the trip up the mountain to support my debut. By the time people arrived, and there were over fifty that night, the rain had stopped. Though I was nervous, Orlene Puckett's persona soon took over and the response from the audience was overwhelming. Two following performances brought good crowds, including many members of the Hawks and Puckett families, resulting in an invitation for Aunt Orlene to come back for two weekends the following summer.

One evening when I arrived, Frank greeted me with startling news. "There are about eighty Pucketts here tonight who have come all the way from West Bend, North Carolina, to see you." Butterflies made right for my innards. "I just hope they didn't bring any tomatoes." They didn't. At the end of the second weekend, two National Park Service rangers came to see the play. I was invited to bring Aunt Orlene to the cabin for an October Sunday performance. Though it was drizzling when Aunt Orlene sat down in the old rocking chair under the big tree by the cabin, about fifty people had turned out to brave the weather. By the time Aunt Orlene uttered her last words, the sun was shining. My dream had come true. Orlene Puckett had come back to tell her story.

The past seven years have not passed, but rather have encircled me in their arms. Aunt Orlene has traveled far beyond the realm of Groundhog Mountain and its surrounding counties. She's appeared in theatres, churches, retirement homes, mountain festivals, schools, in backyards, and at the Puckett reunion. She walks slowly out of the woods or down the aisle of a church leaning heavily on her rhododendron cane, holding tightly to her medicine bag, a relic of the Civil War. The plaintive ballad, "Talk about Suffering," accompanies her as she makes her way through the audience to an old rocking chair, covered with a worn quilt. Sometimes a hand reaches out to steady her or a person stands up and helps her maneuver a step or two leading to her chair. She hears the whispers of "She really is an old woman, isn't she?" or "How is that old woman going to stand up there and tell us anything?" The mood of the audience is both somber and expectant as she takes off the old black bonnet hiding her face to reveal the heavy lines of time and sorrow.

Then she speaks, humorously referring to the large crowd, a strange looking dog, or the threat of bad weather. At the cabin, whether the morning has often arrived with rain or the threat of storms, the sun has always appeared, causing Aunt Orlene to comment, "Ain't this a glorious day? The Lord surely does love Aunt Orlene, 'cause it ain't rained us out in all the time that I've been a-comin' here." Then she commences to tell her story, moving about the area under the trees, talking to the people about her growing up years on the farm, her first day of school and why she never returned, her marriage to John Puckett and his going off to fight in the War. She remembers the loss of her first baby to diphtheria. She tells of John's drinking, his desertion from the army, and the beatings that led her to hide under the cabin. There is the struggle to move up the mountain, the loss of twenty-three more babies, and the call from her mama's voice to "go out and help these mountain ladies get their babies borned." She speaks of going out into the cold and the snowstorms at all hours of the day and night, first on foot, later riding her old mule, then finally riding in wagons to go from farm to farm, until the delivery of her last child in 1938 when she was ninety-eight.

Her stories provoke nods of agreement, laughter, and tears. Purses rustle as tissues emerge to dab at damp eyes, not all of them the eyes of women. During some of her observations and admonitions, a voice occasionally speaks up to answer her as if the two of them were having their own conversation. Children gaze up at her, trying to figure out who this old woman is with her stories of a past that they do not know. An hour and a half is over and gone in what seems an instant, they tell her after she has finished and taken her bows. As if Aunt Orlene would ever take a bow or even know what one meant.

After her story, people gather to speak to her, telling of their connections to the Virginia legend. A young man who is a Puckett relates to her that he is the great-grandson of the first baby she delivered over on Groundhog Mountain. An older man, a Hawks, hands her a sheet of paper showing that he is a descendent of one of her brothers. A young woman introduces her father, who was one of John's grand nephews, also delivered by Aunt Orlene. They bring pictures and write down their names and addresses for future references. Another woman tells Orlene that her father told her that he paid for her delivery with a pig. Eventually that becomes one of the anecdotes in Orlene's story.

Foy Hawks, a relative who has attended Orlene's appearance on several occasions, speaks of the time he walked down the mountain with her when he was a child. She was on her way to a trading post where she bought a twenty-five pound bag of meal, which he watched her carry back up the mountain. According to Foy, Aunt Orlene was eighty-five when she accomplished that feat. I have been the recipient of so many special revelations and tales over the years that I can truly identify with Aunt Orlene as she remarks at one point, "Oh, if only I could've wrote it all down when it was a-happenin' so I could recall all the names and places and times. The stories I could tell, if I could jest remember 'em." Then she laughs, thinking of the foolishness of trying to bring back ninety-nine years of living.

But what Aunt Orlene does remember is validated by those who come to listen. Several summers ago, a ninety-five-year-old member of one of the famous rock churches that we attend while we are here, came up to thank me for reliving the history of the Civil War that he had heard from his father. "You see, my father was a Confederate soldier and everything that Aunt Orlene told, the soldiers coming through, the hiding of food, the taking of the livestock, all the hard things that families had to endure, those were the things he talked about when I was growing up. You made me remember and I want you to know how much I appreciate what you're doing."

I didn't question his veracity but the math did not seem to add up. How he could be the son of someone who had lived during the 1860's? I was sure he must have been referring to his grandfather; however, when he returned to the cabin this past summer, he reminded me of his father's involvement in the war. This time he explained that his father had been sixty-six when he was born, so I was able to comprehend that this dear old friend was only one generation removed from those who had fought and lived through the Civil War. These bits and pieces of information have confirmed that the insights that have come from interviews and research are proving to ring true.

As for the effect Aunt Orlene has had on her creator, I have to admit that at times I slip into her mannerisms and speech so easily that I surprise myself. My husband finds the practice of my engaging him in conversation as Orlene a trifle irritating as it often catches him by surprise. Riding down the parkway, I proclaim, "Ain't that jest the purtiest thing you done seen?" as I spy butterflies floating over the heads of Queen Anne's lace. He looks at me and nods, not answering. But that is not the end of it, for once I assume her person, I can go on and on and often have a hard time returning to the real me, whoever that might be.

Like Orlene Puckett, I am a great traveler, walking up and down the hills that surround me, to chat with neighbors or take treats to horses in nearby pastures. Though not out to deliver babies, my intent may be to birth a poem or two, pick sweet peas, or gather bags of fox grapes to make jelly. I am usually accompanied by my adopted dog, Princess, who has found in me a friend and roaming companion, and always by my trusty walking stick, for beating back briars, or warning away suspected snakes. A local character stops, looks at my stick, then informs me, "We ain't that mean up here."

One such encounter last summer led me into the house of a neighbor, one of Aunt Olene's distant relatives. He asked me if I would like to see the bed in which she had birthed his younger brother, the last child Orlene delivered. I, having the curiosity of a cat, took the bait. Near the back door, I was shown the lantern that Orlene carried as she made her forays into starless mountain nights. Inside a huge portrait of John and Orlene, probably in their mid-forties, stared at me from above the kitchen table.

The wife was not at home. I was alone inside a strange house with a man, deemed "strange" by neighbors, I hardly knew. He was, however, eager to produce every ounce of Orlene memorabilia that lay within his domain, telling the anecdotes that went with them, confiding that he shouldn't be telling me this, and that he wasn't much for talking to strangers! Time passed. Eventually he led me to the basement were he showed me a round box that contained a bag of Aunt Orlene's snuff, teasing me with "I'll bet you don't know what this is." Next, he withdrew a tiny rectangular box.

"You don't have her glasses, do you?" He cackled with delight, removing a tiny pair of gold rimmed glasses and dangling them in front of me.

"How much you give me fer 'em?" he asked. While I pondered a fair price, he laughed, withdrew them, and said, "I'm saving 'em fer my daughter."

Making my excuse to go, I was treated to a look at a couple of logs from the original Puckett cabin. Glancing at my watch, I became aware that I had been away two hours with a stranger and without my husband knowing where I was. But what is time or circumstance when a person is on the quest of finding herself?

So way has truly led on to way from that one day my husband and I turned back to give that run-down old house another chance. For both of us, taking another path has made the difference. He realized a long-held dream of owning a home near the beauty of the Blue Ridge Parkway and I found my way to becoming Aunt Orlene.

About the Author

AFTER TEACHING ENGLISH IN several North Carolina high schools for over thirty years, Phyllis Stump has found a new career as a playwright and actor as she brings her one-woman show, *They Call Me Aunt Orlene*, the story of a Virginia midwife, to schools, retirement homes, museums, theatres, and the Blue Ridge Parkway. She is also the author of two books of poetry, *The Heart Knows*, which won the Oscar M. Young Award from the North Carolina Poetry Council in 1980, and *Walking the Gunnysack Trail: A Mountain Journey in Poetry*, published in 2006.

Phyllis has been a finalist in the Reynolds Price Short Story Contest, sponsored by Salem College, and a third place winner in a recent Sherwood Anderson Short Story Contest, held in Marion, Virginia. She has also won several other awards for both poetry and non-fiction. For her master's thesis in liberal arts at Wake Forest University, she completed a novel, *Pictures from the Past Imperfect*, which she hopes will find a publisher one day, along with three other partially completed novels residing on her hard drive. The inspiration to write—whether poetry, fiction, or nonfiction—is the motivation that keeps her constantly on the move, searching for the "something new, something unique" that most of humankind tend to overlook.

She and her husband divide their time between their two homes in Lexington, North Carolina, and Hillsville, Virginia. They have three children, six grandchildren, and a multitude of hobbies including nature study, travel, reading, gardening, and crafts. They've also been involved in mission trips to China, Brazil, and Belize with an emphasis on working with children. At the age of 68, Phyllis took up a lifelong dream of horseback riding; however, in 2009 she experienced a life-changing event—a massive stroke in her left brain. With the help of doctors, family, her husband and children, she has fully recovered and is resuming her horseback riding lessons!